DEATH *of a* BATTY GENIUS

A STORMY DAY NOVEL

BOOK #3

ANGELA PEPPER

PROLOGUE

How does a dead body continue to walk around without anyone noticing?

While I frantically asked myself that question, the person holding the gun took aim. The gun was not aimed at me, but at another person's chest.

The holder of the gun snarled, "If only I could kill you twice."

My whole body tensed with dread. Another person was going to die, unless someone did something. Like a good detective-in-training, I accepted the responsibility to be that someone.

I jumped to my feet, exclaiming, "You've got it all wrong!"

All the focus turned on me. Unfortunately, the tip of the gun also turned on me.

My father's words echoed through my mind: *Stormy, never make a plan, because plans go wrong.*

Well, I had a news flash for the sometimes-helpful version of Finnegan Day residing in my head. I didn't have a plan. Not a detailed one, anyway. But I did have a process.

I'd been investigating the unusual death ever since the body showed up. At first, nothing added up. But now I had new evidence, and a picture was forming in my head. A very strange picture.

I asked myself again: *How does a dead body continue to walk around without anyone noticing?*

There had to be an explanation.

What would help me think faster?

The hand holding the gun aimed at me was shaking with rage.

Yes, being shot would help me think faster.

If it didn't kill me first.

CHAPTER 1

A GOOD DETECTIVE knows the best way to deal with unwanted confrontation is to spot the storm coming and step out of its path.

That night at the restaurant, I didn't notice the trouble brewing because my attention was on the handsome man seated across from me. Had I not been preoccupied, I might have heard the other diners talking about the strange events happening around town that evening.

Instead, my focus was on my date, Logan Sanderson. A client from his law firm had gifted us with a bottle of pricey champagne, and Logan was about to propose a toast.

I leaned in, my heart racing. By the look in his sky-blue eyes, he'd realized he was madly, deeply, passionately in love with yours truly, Stormy Day.

Cue the marching band, and release the party streamers! Begin the tasting of the wedding cake samples!

My relationship with the suave-yet-woodsy Logan Sanderson had been purely professional so far. He was my tenant, renting one side of the duplex I owned, and he was also my sometimes-boss, hiring me for investigative work on behalf of his legal clients.

We'd become friendly over the last three months, but neither had made a move… until now.

The bubbling champagne awaited. Our future awaited. Even the rest of my lemon mousse awaited.

But before Logan could make his toast, one man came along to ruin everything, like a big ol' cow plop in the middle of a country picnic.

The man stood near the entryway to Accio Bistro, at the hostess station. He straightened up with recognition when he met my gaze.

Logan asked, "Stormy, who's that guy, and why's he staring at us?"

I apologized and explained that he was not just *some guy*, but my former fiancé.

"That's Christopher Fairchild?" Logan blinked with disbelief. "That's *the* Christopher Fairchild, of Fairchild Capital? But he's wearing a blazer with jeans and sneakers."

"Not just any sneakers. He only wears Vans." I nervously fluffed the back of my hair, making my short wavy locks puff out like a duck's butt.

"Why's he here?"

"I can't even begin to imagine, but let me apologize to you in advance for whatever rude thing he's going to say when he invites himself to our table. I bet he starts with my haircut."

"If he does, he'll be sorry." Logan locked his blue eyes on mine. Thick, dark lashes accentuated the brightness of excitement in his eyes, and he was smiling—genuinely smiling.

"Logan, get a hold of yourself. You've got your going-to-court face on. Trust me, you don't want to tangle with Christopher. You never win, and it's like wrestling a pig in mud—you get dirty, and the pig likes it."

His going-to-court smile only broadened. "What do I need to know about him? Top three facts."

I counted off on my fingers. "One, he's from a wealthy family. Two, he's very charming when he wants something. And three, he *always* wants something."

"Anything else?"

"He's afraid of spiders."

"Good to know."

Logan pushed his chair back and stood. "You must be Christopher," he said warmly.

I kept my back to Christopher, because I didn't want to face him yet. Last I'd heard, he'd moved from Portland up to Seattle, Washington, which wasn't exactly on another planet, but it was a good half day's drive away from quaint little Misty Falls, Oregon.

I was turning to ask Christopher why he was there when the world went sideways. My chair and I toppled over, pushed by Christopher as he lunged past me violently.

His fist flew through the air, grazing Logan's cheek. I landed on the restaurant's weathered hardwood, where I heard the sound of someone being punched, then the messier sound of someone dropping to the floor.

I got to my feet within seconds. Christopher lay balled up on the floor groaning. Logan loomed over him, rubbing his knuckles and looking downright dangerous, like a lumberjack in tailored bespoke wool.

I should have made a joke to lighten the mood—something about the restaurant having enough delicious lemon mousse for everyone, and how there was no need for fisticuffs. The word *fisticuffs* alone can often defuse tension.

But a rush of adrenaline put me into mama bear mode. Christopher was barely taller than me. With his slim frame and his white-soled sneakers, he looked like a defenseless kid curled up on the restaurant floor. I hunched over him protectively, while I verbally tore into Logan with some terminology that would make a statue blush.

When I paused to inhale, Logan said, "Stormy, I'm well aware of the criteria for self-defense, and he threw the first punch."

I responded by telling him where to shove his *criteria for self-defense*. That's when I heard a gasping sound, from the people all around us, who'd been trying to enjoy their nice dinners a moment earlier.

Someone said, "That's her, right? That's Stormy Day."

A woman responded, "Quite the temper, indeed."

Ignoring them, I cradled Christopher's head on my thighs as he groaned. Logan stood behind me, saying something about getting ice, but his voice was muted to me, along with the chattering speculation of the other diners.

"Stormy-Lou?" Christopher moaned. "Is that really you?"

"Don't call me that," I said. "Why are you here? Why'd you punch my friend Logan?"

He didn't answer, just stared into the distance, his hazel eyes unfocused.

I sniffed the air over his mouth. His uncharacteristic aggression plus his confused state pointed to intoxication, yet he didn't smell of alcohol. Drugs didn't fit either, because Christopher didn't take any, other than large doses of caffeine. He'd tried magic mushrooms one time, on a dare, and hated the experience. So, why was he behaving so strangely, and soaked with sweat?

"Christopher?"

He scrunched his eyes shut, as though everything was too much for him.

I repeated, "Why'd you punch Logan?"

His voice cracking and gravelly, he said, "I had to protect you from him. I know *what he is.*"

"What he is? He's a lawyer. You usually like lawyers, for going over contracts and threatening to sue people."

"That's not all he is."

"Are you high?"

Christopher opened his eyes and tried to focus on me. "That man is Forest Folk. I have special vision now, and I can see his true animal nature. He's a Sasquatch cannibal. Stormy-Lou, you've got to listen to me. You're his next victim."

I had to smirk. My concern shifted to amusement. "Listen, Christopher, not everyone is a fan of Logan and his beard, but I assure you, he's quite human."

"You're in danger."

"Haven't you heard? These days, I'm always in danger. What drugs did you take? Are you on any new prescription medication?"

"No drugs. But I had a smoothie, and it tasted funny."

"Can you get up? We should go talk about your conspiracy theories somewhere else. Somewhere less like a restaurant and more like that place with the stomach pump."

His eyes widened, revealing bloodshot webs around his hazel irises. "Hospital? No. You can't make me." He shuddered in horror and squeezed his eyes shut again. His jaw was red along one side, from Logan's knuckles.

Logan returned with a cloth napkin full of ice and tapped my shoulder. I looked up to find all the wait-staff from the restaurant, plus a few big fellas from the kitchen, standing in a ring around us.

"He'll be okay," Logan said. "I barely touched him."

"I heard the sound of you hitting him. It was a movie punch. *Pow*."

"So, I'm the bad guy?" Logan asked.

"Of course not. I just…"

"The word you're looking for is *sorry*. As in, *Logan, I'm sorry I called you those terrible things*."

"Sure." I snatched the ice from him, sending a spray of water at the waiters gathered around us. One of the young guys flinched and cowered as though shot. Another one announced he was calling the police.

Logan and I exchanged a look. Whatever differences we had over my feisty communication style, we didn't want to be there when the cops arrived. Both of us were on the bad side of the local captain.

Working as a team, we started hauling Christopher out of the restaurant—me on the legs and Logan hoisting him by the armpits. This would have worked well on a person who'd passed out. Unfortunately, Christopher was very much conscious, yet very much in an *altered* state of consciousness. He believed Logan was a member of the legendary local Forest Folk, and was only gripping him under the armpits to better rip off his arms like crab claws and eat them.

Screaming about not wanting parts of himself dipped in butter, Christopher wriggled free and ran back through the restaurant. He dodged left and right, evading capture by the waiters, slowing only to grab warm bread rolls from people's tables. When he couldn't hold any more rolls, he made a break for the exit.

Logan and I chased after him, out into the dark and snowy parking lot, where he disappeared into the night.

Great.

Christopher had created a rift between me and Logan, given the locals a truckload of new dirt on me, and now I'd be spending the rest of Saturday night finding him. Plus my lemon mousse was sitting on the table inside the restaurant, untouched.

Logan touched my elbow to get my attention. Softly, he said, "I'm sorry I hit your friend."

"He had it coming. I'm… really sorry I called you all those things."

"I've never been near a goat, much less…"

"Bygones?"

"Bygones." He nodded. "Now we need to find your friend. He's scared of me, so I'll stand back and keep an eye on the perimeter of the parking lot, especially the side along the main road, and you go check between the rows of cars. I'll holler if I see anything."

"That's a solid plan. I can tell you've done this often." He looked confused, so I asked, "As a forest-dwelling cannibal, do you always play catch-and-release with your human prey?"

"Only when they run." He leaned over me and growled, "Spoiler alert: They always run."

I shied away, pretending to be terrified, then began my patrol, looking for my crazed former fiancé. I rubbed my arms as I checked between the rows of vehicles. We'd left the restaurant in a hurry, so I wasn't wearing my winter coat. The parking lot had a row of trees on one side as a wind break, but it didn't stop the breeze coming from the other direction.

"Christopher," I called through chattering teeth. "Come out, come out, wherever you are."

The silence that followed chilled me even deeper than the night air. I walked faster, searching as fast as I could in my dress and heels.

As the minutes passed, the gravity of the situation set in, and I began to panic. Christopher had been sopping wet with sweat, and wearing only a lightweight blazer. If we didn't find him soon, he could be in danger.

And, on top of everything, I couldn't shake the sensation I was being watched, from high above.

Suddenly, something moved at the edge of my vision. At the same instant, my right foot hit a patch of ice, and I started to fall.

CHAPTER 2

IN MISTY FALLS, there's a colorful expression for falling down. Just saying it takes away some of the sting.

When I slipped on the ice, I went *tail over teakettle, dumping crumpets everywhere.*

Flat on my back, the wind knocked out of me, I could do no more than stare up at the night sky, noting the feathery halo of multiple rings around the moon. Bad weather was coming.

I rolled my head to the side and found a benefit to my predicament—a bug's eye view of the parking lot. I easily spotted Christopher's retro-style Vans sneakers, three cars over.

I got to my feet and snuck up behind Christopher. He was squatting and nibbling on a purloined bread roll, holding it with two hands, in the manner of a squirrel.

"Hey, there," I said softly. "Aren't you cold?"

He looked up and began to shiver, as though he hadn't realized it was chilly until my question.

I dusted some twigs off his blazer and got him standing just as Logan trotted up, looking worried after seeing my fall.

Christopher flinched, about to bolt again, so I grabbed his hand and locked my fingers between his.

Over on the main road, a police cruiser with lights flashing drove by, followed by an ambulance, and another cruiser. To my relief, they kept going, off to another call, and not coming to arrest Christopher for causing a disturbance and petty theft of baked goods.

Logan, keeping his distance, led us over to his SUV truck. He opened the rear door for us, then jumped in up front to get the engine and heater running. "I'll be back after I run back in to pay the bill," he said. "We don't need to get charged by the police for a dine-and-dash."

"Thanks for the fun dinner," I said.

After Logan was gone, Christopher relaxed, curling up with his body on the seat and his head on my lap.

Despite my annoyance at his chaotic interruption of my life, I found myself smoothing his wavy, light brown hair, and rubbing his back.

In addition to his beloved white-soled Vans sneakers, he wore gray jeans and a blazer over one of his favorite button-down shirts. The shirts weren't custom-made, but they did come from a boutique company that secured its first round of financing by crowdsourcing on the internet, before partnering with Fairchild Capital. The shirt's fabric looked like a weave, but stretched like a knit, and was made of a wrinkle-resistant material that wicked away moisture. Christopher was dry already.

"These shirts really are durable," I said, unsure if he could hear me. "I can see why you like them. I kept a sample of one of the women's models, but I can never figure out what looks right with what."

He didn't stir. The interior of the vehicle was silent, except for the sound of the heaters on full blast. Christopher's eyes were closed, but not clenched, and I sensed he was listening to me.

I continued, "Lately I've been buying entire outfits off store mannequins. How decadent is that?"

He answered, "You and those ugly cut-off denim shorts. And the army boots. You need to take off your dirty army boots if you want to sit on the bed."

"What army boots?" I was wearing heels that matched my dress. But many years ago, I had worn a beloved pair of Doc Martens boots all through Europe, including the night Christopher and I first met.

"Take off the boots and you can sit on my bed," he said.

He was hallucinating, remembering the evening we met. I gently asked him to tell me where we were.

He snorted. "We're in the hotel, silly. The Lancaster Hotel."

"And what are we doing?"

"Not much. My cousin's in the bath with your two friends, and I got ditched with you." Softer, he added, "But I don't mind. Underneath all that dark makeup, I think you're pretty."

"Christopher, if we're really in the Lancaster Hotel in Paris right now, can you tell me my name?"

"You said it's Stacy, but I think you're lying. You're not really a Stacy."

I silently mouthed a *wow* to myself. Whatever drug he'd taken, it was giving him uncanny powers of recall.

He adjusted his position and wrapped one arm around my legs possessively. "Sleep here at the hotel tonight. It's getting late, not safe for you to travel back to whatever bed-bug-infested hostel you're slumming at. Stay with me, and we'll order room service in the morning."

"Room service," I mused. Buttery, flaky croissants. Fresh strawberries. Bowl-sized lattes. All served on gleaming silver trays in the luxury suite.

Backpacking across Europe had taken a turn for the glamorous when I met Christopher and his cousin at a rock concert in Paris. The band playing was from Japan and played American Rockabilly music. I was traveling with two other young women, and the five of us danced all night. We left together, with Christopher's cousin promising us secret access to the catacombs under the city.

We never did find the entrance to the catacombs, but—conveniently enough—we did end up near enough to the guys' hotel to make a "pit stop."

My thirty-three-year-old self would see right through their plot, but I was young and eager then, with all the wide-eyed wonder of a small-town girl with more enthusiasm than money.

So, while Christopher's cousin did some very French things with my two travel companions on the other side of the washroom door, Christopher and I watched dubbed American movies from the eighties. He even let me sit on the bed—after I'd removed the offending army boots.

When the sun came up, we awoke fully clothed, spooning on top of the covers. I said good morning, he declared that I was more beautiful than all of Paris in the sunshine, and we kissed for the first time.

"No," Christopher groaned from my lap, tugging me out of the sunny memory and back into the dark truck.

"No," he moaned again.

"Shh. You're just having a bad trip." I smoothed his fine hair, which had gotten damp and curly at the temples. "You took mushrooms again, didn't you? After you swore you wouldn't."

The driver's side door opened, and Logan slid in with a pocket of cold air. He looked back at Christopher, who still had his head in my lap.

"Keep him just like that," Logan said. "If he throws up, it'll be on your lap and not my leather seats."

"He's feeling calmer now," I said crisply. "Thanks for asking."

Logan handed back my jacket as well as his, both of which I draped over Christopher.

"Where to?" Logan asked. "We should blow this popsicle stand before Captain Milano shows up to handcuff me to a freight train leaving town." He put the engine in gear. "Did your friend happen to tell you where he's staying?"

I patted Christopher's pockets, then dug inside and located his keys, phone, wallet, and a gas station receipt, but no sign of a hotel pass card or motel key.

With a formal air, I announced, "Mr. Fairchild will be staying at our place."

Logan chuckled.

"Are you laughing at me, Mr. Sanderson?"

"Not at all. It's just... I like it when you say 'our place.' I don't know why."

I let out an amused huff. "It's because that duplex is a fantastic investment property in an up-and-coming neighborhood."

He glanced back over his shoulder, blue eyes twinkling. "That must be why." He turned around, stepped on the gas, and pointed us toward home.

During the drive, Christopher relaxed even more, rocked by the gentle motion. Whatever he'd taken, I hoped he'd learned his lesson.

We pulled into the wide driveway, next to my car, then Logan came around to get Christopher. He picked him up easily and cradled him in his arms—which was what we should have done at the restaurant. Seeing this really drove home how big and strong Logan was, especially compared to my former partner.

Logan crunched through the snow, carrying Christopher diagonally across the lawn, past my side of the duplex and on toward his own door.

I asked where he was going, and Logan explained, "I've got a spare bedroom, and you don't. Your friend can sleep it off on my side."

"He'll probably irritate you as soon as he wakes up."

"I'll consider myself forewarned. Forewarned is forearmed." He hoisted Christopher to get a better grip. "Would you open the door for me? My keys are in my front pocket."

"Sure thing, boss." I reached into the pocket of Logan's trousers. The funny thing was, I'd not had a second thought about rooting around in Christopher's jeans, but touching Logan's hip-front pocket area gave me the giggles.

It was all I could do to keep a straight face while we got inside. We held Christopher between us as though he were a limp marionette so we could walk him down the hall and into the spare room's pull-out bed.

Logan went looking for a thermometer while I coaxed Christopher to sip a glass of water. His temperature was normal, so after a quick consult with Doctor Internet, we decided to let him sleep off his bad trip under Logan's supervision.

"He's going to be obnoxious when he wakes up," I said.

"Forewarned," Logan replied.

"He'll probably demand room service and a monogrammed bath robe."

"Get out of here before I change my mind."

I thanked him for everything, then left and ran along the shoveled walkway to my side, where I flung open the door. I was already laughing in anticipation of telling Jessica about my crazy night.

"Jessica?"

The lights were all on, but nobody answered.

I found my gray cat on my bed, but my redheaded roommate and best friend wasn't in her usual nest of blankets on the couch, nor was she in her bedroom, the bathroom, or even in the basement laundry room. I sat on her bed and called her phone with mine. I followed the ringtone to the empty kitchen. Jessica's phone, which rarely left her side, sat on the kitchen countertop.

The phone did its vibration dance next to the blender and two empty glasses, dirty with the residue of a thick drink.

Two glasses. A smoothie.

My energy surged as I connected the dots.

I ran to my bedroom, changed out of my dress and into jeans and a sweater, pulled on some sturdy boots and a heavy jacket, then ran out the front door, calling Jessica's name.

She didn't answer. At least her car was still parked there. If she was on foot, that was a good thing. I knew where to find her.

I didn't even stop to tell Logan where I was going. I just headed straight for the ravine that lay past the park.

I clenched my fists, punching the air as I alternated between walking and running. Why hadn't I thought about Jessica earlier and called to check on her?

Christopher must have gotten the name of the restaurant from someone. He'd mentioned a smoothie, and now it was clear she could have been drugged in the same way.

I should have asked him more about the smoothie, and who else he'd given one to. Being thorough is the domain of the private investigator. But anyone can do research. It takes a good detective to look at a situation, then use logic and reasoning to work forward, backward, onward, and inward.

If my father, who'd been mentoring me on my way to get my private investigator's license, could see me jogging toward the ravine right now, panting desperately, he'd have advice.

He'd say something like, *Stormy, let's take the Batmobile. I don't care if the Queen of England and all her corgis have gone missing. I'm not running anywhere. Hip surgery, remember? I'll let you drive while I eat this pulled pork sandwich and get sauce and coleslaw all over your car interior. Don't make that face. A real detective eats in her car. And since you drink so much coffee, you should start saving up empty mayonnaise jars. Did I ever tell you about Detective 'Sun Tea' McAdams?*

I shook my head to clear the voice of my father. He was probably at home with his feet up, watching a true crime show. If I needed his help I would call. But I was at the ravine already, and I could handle the situation.

The light from the nearby street lamps was just bright enough for me to follow some fresh boot tracks. The tracks, which I hoped belonged to Jessica, marched through a thin crust of snow, along the ravine.

In the spring, Misty Creek would run through the ravine, bisecting the town and providing a watery highway for the annual Misty Falls Charity Ducky Race. Now, in late February, the ravine held only snow.

I followed the boot tracks right to where I'd predicted they would go, an old treehouse Jessica had discovered while exploring the neighborhood. For the last week, when she wasn't at work or curled up on the couch, she'd been at the treehouse.

By the warm glow of light coming from the treehouse, she was there again, or so I hoped.

CHAPTER 3

THE FREE-SPIRITED IMAGINATION of a child is a guiding hand that makes all their inventions beautiful.

If not for the creativity of its construction, the old treehouse would have been ugly. The crooked hut, made from a patchwork of materials, hung between four trees. The structure was in its final days, one strong gust of wind from becoming fuel for a bonfire. But it had been made by youthful dreamers, and so it was still beautiful, even in its decay.

I climbed the rickety ladder and popped my head up through the trap door opening, expecting to find Jessica inside, in a state to match Christopher's.

Instead, I found a pair of startled men.

Grown men.

On the plus side, they were fully clothed, which— if you happen to discover a pair of grown men in a treehouse—is how you'd prefer them to be.

"Sorry, guys," I said. "I saw the glow of your lantern, and thought I'd find my friend up here."

In a baritone voice, the man on the left said with a smile, "Now you've found *two* friends." He looked to be in his early forties, with big round cheeks that gave him a diamond-shaped face, and he wore his black hair in short curls. With his deep, rich voice, he introduced himself. "I'm Dion, and this is Franco. Come on up. We don't bite."

"Speak for yourself," said the other man, Franco. He had a nasal voice that made his joking comment sound like a taunt. Franco was the opposite of his friend, pale, with gaunt cheeks and a narrow face. He had straight dark hair in need of a haircut, falling over one eye and giving him the look of a wild, hungry horse.

Dion waved for me to join them. "Get up here before that old ladder breaks. What brings you to the Batty Genius Clubhouse on this fine February evening?"

The flat surface of the treehouse was more stable than the trembling ladder, so I took a seat with my legs dangling down through the trap door.

Franco looked me over, sniffed, then said to his friend, "She's not the redhead who's been hanging out up here. Her hair's too short."

"My hair's not *too short*. It's just right." I glanced around the bare interior, which didn't take long, as it was barely five feet by five. "I'd ask what two grown men are doing in a treehouse on a dark night, but I have more pressing business. Have either of you seen my friend Jessica? She comes here sometimes. She's thirty-three, about my height and size. She's got long red hair, which she does tend to leave everywhere."

The guys looked at each other, trading expressions like two people who've been friends their whole lives.

Franco said to his buddy, "I only got here a few minutes before you, man, and I didn't see anyone."

Dion shrugged, then said to me, "We haven't seen her, sorry." He got an impish grin. "Then again, I wasn't looking out for your redhead friend because I was too excited about my secret meeting with my lover, Franco."

Franco cuffed him on the back of the head. "You idiot. Don't joke about that. Customers can never tell if you're serious, plus it's rude to people who actually are gay."

"Which we are," Dion deadpanned.

Franco cuffed him again. "Idiot."

Dion rubbed the back of his head. "Actually, we're just up here to take some pictures of the gang's old treehouse for a reunion."

"Sure, you are," I said with a smile as I shifted my weight to exit the treehouse. The old wood groaned under my movements. "Have fun, guys. I'm off."

Dion called down after me, "Tell your friend she's welcome to use our treehouse any time, even though she's a girl with girl cooties."

I replied, "It's not *your* treehouse. This structure is on town property, and you shouldn't volunteer to take responsibility. It's probably a hazard."

"Probably? More like definitely."

I heard another whack, then Franco giving Dion grief for embarrassing both of them.

I was stepping off the ladder when a business card fluttered down past me.

"We're not just treehouse squatters," Dion called down from the trapdoor. "We run a legitimate business, and there's a voucher for a free drink on the back of that card."

The card was for the town's English-style pub, the Fox and Hound. Both men were listed on the card as the owners, and the back side really did have a voucher for a free drink.

I thanked him and tucked the card into my pocket.

A wave of anxiety washed over me. I'd barely been in the treehouse a few minutes, but time was wasting, and I still had to find Jessica.

* * *

There were no signs of her in the ravine or the park. I jogged back toward home, calling Jessica's name.

I rounded a corner and nearly bowled over a woman walking her fluffy Pekingese. She put her gloved hand on my arm and asked, "What breed is your Jessica?"

"She's a person."

The tiny woman, who appeared to be in her eighties, smiled, her whole face wrinkling with joy. "Aren't they all, dear? Miss Molly won't eat dinner until she's got her little bib on. People say that Pekingese are willful dogs, but who wants to spend their days with a pushover? Not me. My dear Harold, bless his heart, might have preferred someone with fewer ideas of her own, but I'll tell you one thing: I kept that man on his toes, right up until the day he departed, and then I got Miss Molly, and life goes on. Where were we? Yes, you were about to tell me the breed of your Jessica. If she's not a purebred, that's okay, because there are plenty of mutts and strays who need homes, too."

"Actually, Jessica is a human person. I'm worried she might be wandering around the neighborhood, lost and confused, from… food poisoning."

"Food poisoning?" The woman wasn't buying my story, but she didn't seem any less concerned. "Miss Molly and I have been on our walk for the last forty-six minutes—I plan to see my hundredth birthday, so I keep up my fitness routine, and tomorrow is aqua aerobics—but I haven't seen your human person tonight. Should we call the police? I hear they've got a young whippersnapper on the force now, a cute one who could be on one of those calendars the ladies have up at the hair salon. The girls always apologize when I come in for my perm, but I tell them that just because my courting days are over, that doesn't mean I don't enjoy a peek."

I laughed. "You must be talking about Officer Dimples. I mean Officer Dempsey. I will give the police a call right away. Thanks for the idea, ma'am."

"Olivia Catfish." She offered a gloved hand and gave me a surprisingly strong handshake. I leaned down to give her Pekingese, Miss Molly, a pat goodbye, then set off toward the house again. I took Olivia Catfish's good advice and pulled out my phone to put a call through to the police department's non-emergency line.

A gruff voice came through the small speaker. "Misty Falls police department. Captain Milano speaking."

"Tony Baloney," I replied with fake enthusiasm. "So nice to hear your voice. Shouldn't there be a receptionist answering this line?"

"Yes, usually. Stormy? Why are you calling the main line and not my direct number?"

"Because you've gotten all cranky lately, and every time I talk to you, we're one step closer to one of us getting smacked."

"And whose fault is that?" He sighed. "Don't answer, I don't need the aggravation. Why are you calling, and how many ambulances should I dispatch?"

"None, unless—"

"What's going on with you? I just got back from the restaurant where you had dinner and put on a show. Is it true you started a brawl? I talked the owner out of pressing charges."

"Pressing charges? On me?"

Icily, he said, "No charges, and you're welcome. Hang on." His voice was muffled while he spoke to someone else. He came back with, "We can talk about you and your restaurant hijinks tomorrow. I'm busy now."

"Tony," I said, but the call had already been terminated.

I was back at the house again. I hurried inside and did a hopeful search for Jessica, but she still wasn't there.

Jessica was an adult, so the police might not take her disappearance as seriously as I did, but I wasn't giving up on getting help.

I would hit redial on my phone, but first I needed to know more about what I was calling in to report. I examined the evidence on the counter. The empty smoothie glasses smelled pleasant, like malt and cherries. According to the instructions on the empty bag, it held a powdered mix for two servings, equal to a full meal for each person. The dry residue in the bag reminded me of boxed cake mix.

The packaging itself was premium quality, an opaque white zipper-seal bag, full-color print on both sides, with a background of illustrated jungle foliage and a colorful group of four exotic tree frogs. The artwork looked expensive, drawn by someone with talent, yet slightly off balance. I knew from my research into packaging design that objects were more visually pleasing when found in odd numbers, such as three or five. Four tree frogs were an unconventional choice, but I couldn't let myself get hung up on such a minor detail.

The company logo, BIGGS, was one I recognized. I'd read about Biggs Foods in the local paper, because the owner, Benjamin Biggs, was from Misty Falls. He'd graduated from high school a decade before me, so we hadn't crossed social paths, but I'd felt a kinship with the man, and had enjoyed the article in the Misty Falls Mirror, the way all residents do when one of our own does something interesting in the world.

"Benjamin Biggs," I mused. "You were one of the town's rising stars, and now you've gone and poisoned us with your *Rainforest Delight*."

CHAPTER 4

WHEN YOU WANT HELP, you need to ask. If they don't hear you, ask again. Louder.

The second time I called the Misty Falls Police Department, they hung up on me.

I called a third time.

An irritated female voice came through. "Wiggles."

"Officer Peggy Wiggles? It's me, Stormy Day."

"Tell me something I don't know."

I sucked in air between my teeth. Peggy Wiggles, the department's new fifty-something rookie, had been warming up to me lately, but right now she sounded as though she wanted to test their new taser equipment on my buttocks.

Jeffrey, my mischievous and gray feline roommate, jumped onto the table and playfully swatted my hand for attention. Petting his soft fur gave me an idea.

"Officer Wiggles, how's your cat these days? His name's Peekaboo, right? Now, is he more ginger or more marmalade?"

"Ginger," she said without hesitation. "He's good. He put on a little weight over winter, because he thinks snow is the devil, but spring's coming." She took a slow, audible breath. "What can I do for you tonight? Are you in trouble again?"

"No, it's my roommate. This is going to sound crazy, but I think she got drugged or poisoned by a powdered smoothie drink. The brand is—"

"Rainforest Delight," she interrupted. "With a bunch of googly-eyed tree frogs on the packaging."

"Oh, no. I mean yes. This is bad, Peggy. How bad is it?"

"About a dozen individual disturbances across town. We've traced the supply back to a gas station that must have gotten the recall notice on the merchandise and had the genius idea to put the stuff on sale rather than send it back." She made a tsk-tsk sound. "The contaminant hasn't been identified, but the good news is, it hasn't been lethal. You said your roommate had the smoothie? Keep an eye on her and let her sleep it off. The doctors are saying no need to take her to the hospital, unless the symptoms get worse. Any sign of paralysis or coma, bring her in."

"What if she's gone missing?"

"Then you need to find her before she does something crazy and hurts herself."

I swallowed the lump of worry in my throat.

Voice cracking, I said, "Can you help me? I've been looking for Jessica, and I can't find her. She's on foot, without her phone, and I'm worried. I already checked the ravine, where she likes to walk, and I was so sure she'd be there, but she wasn't."

"Do you know the protocol for an urban search?"

"A little bit. I can look it up. Good idea. Thanks, Peggy. I'll let you know when I find her. Good luck with—"

"Stormy, I'm as good as on my way. You're at your house?"

"Yes, but…" I tried telling her that I could handle it, and I didn't want to take away police resources when they had so many other calls, but Peggy politely told me to let her do her job. She asked for a physical description of Jessica, plus her full name, so she could let the other officers know and put in a notice with the hospital, "just in case."

While I waited for her to arrive, I grabbed my notebook and started thinking on paper while refreshing my memory of the police procedure for an urban search. My father had been on a number of calls over the years, typically for people with memory-related diseases who'd wandered away from home.

Jessica didn't fit the age profile, but just like those people, she might have gotten confused about the date and been trying to get back home to her old apartment. I would check there next.

I grabbed her phone to review her recent calls or messages. Luckily for me, we didn't have that many secrets from each other, and when I'd told her about using the word *bacon* as my password, she'd made it her password as well.

She hadn't made or received any phone calls between the time I'd left the house and called her myself, so that was a dead end. I used her address book to get her mother's phone number, then called and broke the news as gently as I could. Mrs. Kelly talked to her daughter every day, sometimes multiple times, and was understandably upset.

"Not again," she sobbed. "I can't have someone disappear like this."

"Jessica's a tough cookie," I said. "And smart. Don't you worry. Even if she's not quite herself, she's still got more sense than most. And we're going to find her. Do you have any ideas about places she'd walk to?"

"She mentioned a treehouse, near the ravine." Mrs. Kelly started sounding more hopeful. "She must be there!"

"Good idea," I said, hating myself for the white lie. I promised I would keep Mrs. Kelly up to date, and she offered to make some calls and work on a list of other places to search.

After I ended the call, I double-checked the text messages on Jessica's phone. There was a draft message sitting in the outbox that hadn't been sent.

The text was addressed to me: *Don't freak out, but your ex is here at the house. He just showed up, no warning. I thought it was you at the door, so I answered it with no pants! Just a shirt and boxer shorts! What a dork! Now Christopher wants to surprise you by showing up at the restaurant. That would be a bad idea, right? He's very*

She hadn't finished or sent the message, which meant she'd been interrupted, possibly by the smoothie kicking in.

"And then what?" I asked out loud. "He's very what? Persistent? Aggravating?"

Jeffrey tried to help me with my pen and paper, but discovered he didn't have opposable thumbs and therefore couldn't write, so he dumped my notepad onto the floor instead.

"He shoots, he scores," I said dryly, then I gave him a kiss and went next door for some human help from Logan.

Logan had the local community station on his television, showing a live news update. The digital banner across the screen read *Rainforest Delight Outbreak in Misty Falls, Oregon.*

"Can you believe this?" Logan turned down the volume so we could talk. "My secretary called and told me I had to turn on the news. I was just about to come over and get you and Jessica."

"Good idea, but…"

The screen flashed to announce incoming information.

We both watched as the young woman reporter, the one who usually covered the weather forecast and pet adoption announcements, excitedly gave an update on the situation.

"*As of now, at nine o'clock, thirteen people are known to have ingested the contaminated Rainforest Delight smoothie mix. Oh my gosh, this is just… I can't even. What? Read the prompter? Okay… Police are asking for the public's assistance in locating a few of the people affected. We have a new citizen to add to the list of the lost or missing: Jessica Kelly. Age thirty-three, average height, long, red hair. What? Oh my gosh, it's Jessica who works at the Olive Grove. I know her!*"

The young woman stared at the camera, unable to speak for several seconds. Voices off-screen urged her to keep going. She opened a bottle of water, took a long drink, then continued, "*Jessica was last seen in the West Creek neighborhood, wearing a pink jacket. If you see someone fitting that description, please approach calmly and, oh my gosh I can hardly breathe. Daphne, pull yourself together! Um,*" *please notify the police at the hotline number on the screen. The number is area code five-four-one..."*

Logan turned to me. "Is this true?"

"Given the way that woman reports the weather, I'm shocked to say that yes, she's got all the details right. I was just coming over to tell you. I've already spoken to Jessica's mother, and I would call her friends, but now that Marcy's moved away, you and I are about it."

"We'll find her." He jumped up, then winced and touched his palm to his stomach. He no longer wore the bandages from his recent altercation with the pointy end of a sword, but the deep cut was still fresh.

I'd noticed him touching the scarred area whenever he was worried. It reminded me to be more careful in the future with my crazy ideas, because every action carried consequences. Safety had to come first. Whatever happened with my investigating career, I couldn't live with myself if I got one of my friends hurt. Again.

"Stormy? Don't fade away on me. We'll find her."

I nodded. "Officer Peggy Wiggles is already on the way over here. We'll follow police procedure and start canvasing a two-block radius." I glanced at the front window, watching for the police cruiser that would be arriving any minute.

Logan asked, "Jessica's not driving, is she?"

"Her car's still out front, and I think that silver car across the street is Christopher's, which means he took a taxi to the restaurant, or maybe he ran there, which would explain the sweating."

"He's sleeping now, but I'll go wake him and see if he can remember anything useful."

I put my hand on Logan's shoulder to stop him. "I'll go. You keep watch for Peggy."

"Or Jessica," he said. "With any luck, she'll find her way back home again."

My throat was too tight for me to answer, so I nodded again. I wanted to believe him.

While Logan kept an eye on the driveway and the news, I walked back to the second bedroom. Christopher was right where we'd left him, on the mattress of the pull-out sofa. His breathing was calm, and he seemed peaceful, despite being tangled up in his clothes. He'd gotten one arm out of his long shirtsleeve, and now the sleeve was wrapped around his neck.

"Wake up, Christopher, I need to talk to you. And not just about how your space-age shirt is trying to murder you." I started untangling the fabric and unbuttoning the front.

He stirred. "You want me," he said sleepily.

"I want you to keep breathing. Your shirt's all messed up." I continued unbuttoning the placket. "Christopher, where's Jessica? Was she here at the house when you left? Did she say she was going somewhere?"

His eyelashes fluttered, but he didn't open his eyes. "Who's Jessica? Did the Forest Folk eat her, too? We have to be very quiet. They're making the stew."

"Really? You're hallucinating about monsters again? What happened to the Lancaster Hotel in Paris?"

He smiled. "Paris."

I finished untangling his shirt and started pulling it off the remaining arm. He resisted, and then, as I was leaning over to get him free, he grabbed my waist and pulled me down on top of him.

I was so surprised, I let out a nervous laugh. His body was warm, even without a fever.

"This is perfect," he said. "The Lancaster Hotel. Just me and you."

The way he held me, I had a pretty good idea what kind of hallucination it was.

"Christopher, I need you to come back to America with me. Come back and tell me about when you visited my house and saw my roommate, Jessica."

He responded by nuzzling my neck.

"Focus," I said. "Back to America. You're at my house."

I tried to pull away, but he gripped me tightly.

That was when Logan, who could have been standing at the door for a while, cleared his throat.

"Logan!" I wrestled myself away from Christopher's embrace.

Logan said, "A police cruiser is pulling into the driveway."

"He was all tangled up in his shirt," I said quickly. "It's this fancy-man stretchy fabric, see?" I stretched out the shirt's sleeve to demonstrate.

Logan didn't sway. The room was dark, so he was backlit by the hallway light. I couldn't see the expression on his face, but he couldn't have been too impressed to see me snuggled up with my ex. He said he would go let Peggy in, and left the doorframe.

"Stupid shirt," I said. I balled up the fabric and tried to throw it on the ground, but part of it stuck to my palm. I lifted the fabric to my nose and sniffed it.

In addition to the scent of Christopher, there was something else. Pine.

The clues clicked together.

I ran out to the living room.

"Logan, I know where Jessica is."

CHAPTER 5

THE FLASHING LIGHTS of a police car are just as unnerving when you're inside the car, in the passenger seat.

Officer Peggy Wiggles drove us toward Accio Bistro, the restaurant I'd fled hours earlier.

Logan had stayed behind at the house to coordinate the local neighborhood canvas with the other officers.

Officer Wiggles asked me, "Any luck?"

I lowered my phone and dropped it in my lap.

"The line's still busy," I reported.

I'd been trying to reach the taxi driver who'd picked up Christopher at my house, to confirm that Jessica had gone with him to the restaurant, but I couldn't get through to the taxi dispatch.

"She's your friend," Peggy said. "If you have a hunch she's up a tree, that's where we'll find her."

"I wish I had more proof than a bit of twigs and pine sap on someone's shirt."

"How about a whole human? Will that be enough proof for you?"

"I just feel like I'm wasting everyone's time, and if I'm wrong, you'll hold it against me as proof that I have no business calling myself an investigator."

She cleared her throat and took a long look at me before returning her attention to the road.

"Stormy, we're five minutes out from Accio Bistro, which means we're five minutes from finding out if your hunch is correct. In your career, you'll have plenty of opportunities to be thrown under the bus by other people. Don't do it to yourself. Be confident in your strategies. Sell people on the possibility you might be right, that you might be the person with the answers. Everyone wants someone to believe in. If it turns out you're wrong, acknowledge that your idea was only one of several options, and move on. Most times, nobody will remember who was right and who was wrong, but they'll always remember your confidence."

"Thanks, Officer. I appreciate that."

"You can call me Peggy if nobody else is around."

"Thanks, Peggy."

She slowed down and steered into the restaurant's parking lot. She said, "Here we are, and it's been less than two minutes, not the five that I guessed. Does my being a bit wrong diminish anything I said?"

"No. Good point." I would have thanked her for being a great mentor, but I was too nervous about finding Jessica.

"Those are some tall trees," Peggy said.

I leaned forward to look up through the windshield as we rolled along the row of parked cars.

"Perfect for climbing," I said. "Jessica was always up in a tree when we were kids. It was the only way she could get peace and quiet away from her brothers."

"I'll put in a call to the fire department. We can use their ladder to get—Stormy! For crying out loud, wait for me to stop the car!"

I was already out and running. I'd changed clothes since I was last in the icy parking lot, and the grip on my winter boots made me sure-footed.

I ran straight for the white oak tree with the widest base. Its bottom branch hung low to the ground, inviting tree climbers to step right up. The oak was bracketed on three sides by bushy pine trees that etched my jacket with the same sap that had led me there.

"Jessica?" I peered up into the darkness, searching for a pink jacket somewhere between me and the moon.

She didn't answer, but something rustled, and gritty particles fell into my eyes. I blinked the grit away and started climbing the tree blind. Jessica *had to be* up there. She had to be the one moving around and sending dried tree material raining down on me, because if it wasn't her, it was a very large raccoon, and I didn't want to make friends with a raccoon.

I climbed, legs aching as I got higher and higher.

With my eyes still tearing up from the grit, I reached out for what looked like a knobby stick to use as a handhold. The stick moved away, leaving me grasping and lurching to keep my balance. With a groan, I hugged the trunk and waited for the dizziness to pass.

Something shifted above me, sending down more grit.

"Hello?" I said. "If you're a raccoon, please say something now. Make one of your scary raccoon noises, and I'll be out of this tree so fast it'll break the sound barrier."

Nothing answered, which I hoped was no-news of the good-news variety. I reached up and groped a shoe, connected to an ankle that was, thankfully, warm and human.

"Jessica, it's me." I squeezed her ankle.

She made a non-verbal sound that reminded me of Jeffrey's question-meow—the one he'd make after being awoken from a deep sleep.

I found a stable branch for my foot and got myself up to her level, then called down to Peggy on the ground, "We found her! She's right here, just like I said!"

Peggy called up, "You two boneheads aren't safe until you're on the ground. Get down here." She shone her powerful flashlight in my eyes.

I shielded my eyes from the light. "What's the rush? The view's great from up here, if you'd stop blinding us."

"Stay up there all night if you want. That big ol' raccoon two branches above you looks positively thrilled to be sharing her tree."

I looked up and spotted the shining eyes, illuminated by Peggy's bright flashlight.

"Uh-oh," I said under my breath. "Jessica, climb down with me."

I pulled on her jacket, but she hugged the trunk. The raccoon above us made curious chittering noises, then full-on complaint cries. The high-pitched distress calls scared Jessica into clamping onto the trunk tighter. That explained why she'd been stuck in the tree.

Flashing red lights flickered through the branches from below. Down on the distant ground, a firetruck parked alongside the tree. Deep voices—the firefighters coordinating with Peggy—filtered up to us on male laughter.

"Come on, Jessica. Shake a leg. Are you really going to let a bunch of *boys* rescue us from a tree? Like a couple of helpless kittens?"

The answer was yes.

The ladder extended up, and within minutes, I was being tossed over the shoulder of the biggest man I'd ever seen. Near the bottom, he handed me off as though I were a sack of potatoes and went up for Jessica.

The firefighters on the ground checked my eyes and reflexes before letting me join Peggy by the police car.

"I could have climbed down myself," I grumbled.

She raised her eyebrows. "Tell me you didn't have fun being tossed over that man's shoulder. Some women pay good money for that sort of treatment, every year at the Firefighters' Ball."

"It wasn't horrible."

"The boys volunteered to drop you off at home. I've got another call." She gave me a hint of a smile. "You two boneheads stay out of trouble."

Then she was gone, red taillights disappearing into the night.

I walked back over to the firetruck, elbowing my way through the crowd that had gathered. I kept my face down, avoiding eye contact.

I found Jessica clinging to the male firefighter who'd carried us down. She had her arms around him as though he were a tree—an understandable mistake, given his size. Twigs and dried leaves stuck out of her red braids, making her resemble a wild tree spirit.

"She's not usually like this." I kept apologizing as I pried her off his trunk of a chest. "She was a victim of the Rainforest Delight Outbreak."

The big oak tree of a man let out a deep laugh.

"Don't you worry, miss," he boomed at me. "Rescuing kittens from trees is the best part of the job. I'm Mitch."

He offered me his hand, which engulfed mine in a handshake.

"Mitch. It's nice to meet you, despite the circumstances. This tree sprite here is Jessica Kelly. She's my roommate."

One of the other firefighters came up to say the ladder had been secured and they were ready to roll out.

Mitch said, "Officer Wiggles says you live in West Creek? That's not far from our station. We'll drop you off."

I refused, saying we'd call a taxi, but he insisted, on account of how the local taxis all refueled at the same gas station—the one that sold Rainforest Delight. Many of the drivers had picked up the smoothie mix, thinking it was the perfect solution for meals on the job. And it might have been, if not for the powerful hallucinations.

* * *

Jessica still wasn't speaking, but she was calm and seemed to know who she was, if not *where* she was. The EMTs on the site cleared her to sleep it off at home rather than clog up the emergency room at the hospital.

We climbed into the fire truck for our ride home. The truck cab was full, so Jessica sat on the lap of Mitch, the oak tree fireman. They both looked very comfortable.

We pulled up at the house, where she jumped out without a word and ran toward Logan, who'd come out to the driveway to greet us.

I watched Mitch's face fall as he saw them hug.

"That's just Logan," I told Mitch. "He's not Jessica's boyfriend, in case you're wondering."

Mitch nodded, his smile returning. "Roger dodger, I read you loud and clear."

CHAPTER 6

THERE IS NO better smell to wake up to on a Sunday morning than the scent of cinnamon buns baking.

I sighed happily as I rolled out of bed. After all the action of Saturday night, I looked forward to a productive day at home, reading my textbooks for the Private Investigator Proficiency Exam. I was still far from having the fifteen-hundred hours of work experience required by the State of Oregon, but I wanted to be prepared.

I'd been consulting for Logan's law firm without a license, which was perfectly legal, but my access to government databases was limited. My reach was only that of the average citizen, unless I called in a favor with someone at the police department.

My most helpful contact was dimple-faced Kyle Dempsey. He'd get me information, but the fee was a drink with him. Meeting Kyle for an adult beverage would be enjoyable, had I not been his babysitter once upon a time. Flirting with a younger man is less fun if you can remember bribing him with juice boxes.

If I wanted unfettered access to information, getting my required hours then my license was the smartest way. With my books under my arm, I went to the kitchen to greet my in-house pastry chef.

Jessica was leaning over the stove, pulling out hot cinnamon buns.

"Coffee's on," she said.

"Marry me," I replied, because that's the only appropriate response when someone's made you cinnamon buns and coffee.

"Pick a date," she said with a laugh.

I poured coffee into my Get Your Bark On at Central Bark mug, then walked around the counter to sit at the table and gaze out the front window.

The duplex had a townhouse-style layout, with an open space from the kitchen to the living room. Jeffrey was prowling around, his smoky gray tail swishing as he chased the rainbows cast by the prism sun catchers in the front window. Other than us, the place was empty, which meant Christopher was still over on Logan's side. I just had to get rid of him, then I would hit the books.

Jessica left the buns to cool on a rack and joined me at the table, cradling her favorite mug—the one decorated with a quirky fox cartoon—in both hands.

She asked, "Was my mother here last night?"

"Yes. She stopped by to check on you, and she even met that nice firefighter who pulled you out of the tree. His name is Mitch, by the way. Remember him? Big guy, with curly dark hair, nice brown eyes, thick eyelashes, and all those muscles. Mitch gave us a ride back home, and your mother tried to feed him chicken soup. Do you remember her spoon-feeding it to you?"

"Sorta." Jessica scrunched her pale face, changing the pattern of the light freckles on her cheeks and nose.

"She loves you. And she's more than a little obsessed with chicken soup." I sipped my coffee. "What did you think of Mitch?"

She shrugged, then got up and grabbed us some not-quite-cooled cinnamon buns. She hadn't made icing for the batch, so I got the butter dish.

We ate, comparing notes about what had happened the night before. We still didn't know why Christopher had shown up in town, and both kept looking at the door, expecting him to walk in at any moment.

"These cinnamon buns are your best yet," I said. "We should make more, then drop by the firehall later today to thank Mitch and the guys."

"I'm never leaving the house again," she said with finality.

I sipped my coffee and tried to assess her mood. Even before the Rainforest Delight, Jessica had been in a funk for a while. Was it simply exhaustion from moving, or something more?

"Jessica, you can talk to me about anything. If I were you, I'd be pretty freaked out right now. And planning a lawsuit with Logan. Biggs Foods will probably go bankrupt immediately, but there could be settlement money."

"I just want to forget the whole night." She went quiet, focusing on frowning at the butter dish.

Someone knocked on the door. I expected Christopher, but found a weary-looking Officer Peggy Wiggles, who had the swaying stance of someone who'd been up all night.

She kicked the snow off her boots and stepped inside, but she politely declined our offer of breakfast.

Peggy said, "I'm heading home now. Just checking in, and I brought some things for Jeffrey." She held open the top of a paper shopping bag.

"There's half a pet store in that bag."

"You know how it is. Stop in to buy one little bag of catnip, leave with an armload."

"You'll find His Regal Grayness relaxing over there on the sofa. Please, go ahead and see if you can spoil him any more than he already is."

While Peggy plied Jeffrey with gifts, I told Jessica how the two had met at the police station back in December, when he solved The Case of the Mouse Who Nibbled the Snack Room Crackers.

"She's a cat person," Jessica said knowingly. "Enough said."

We both watched as Peggy introduced Jeffrey to a stuffed mouse attached to an elasticized string. He played catch-and-release, then trotted down the hallway with the stuffed mouse in his mouth, the string and plastic wand trailing behind him.

Peggy joined us in the kitchen. "Can I trouble you two for the packaging your smoothie mix came in? We're tracking down all the bags for the investigation."

Jessica retrieved the empty smoothie bag from our trash and handed it over. Peggy dropped the packaging into an official evidence bag and sealed it.

"What will happen next?" I asked. "And are you sure you won't take a cinnamon bun?"

"No, thanks. I should be going. As for the investigation, that's above my pay grade. This particular foodborne outbreak goes beyond this state, so now it's a federal matter, with the FDA getting involved." She let out a low whistle. "I would not want to be the one in charge of Biggs Foods."

"Me, neither," I said. "Somewhere out there are some very disappointed investors."

"Did you know the owner's from here? His aunt and uncle own the gas station that was selling the stuff. They got a whole case while he was here on a visit, so because they weren't on the regular supply list, they didn't get the recall notice. Turns out it was an honest mistake."

"The company owner's name is Benjamin, right? I remember reading about his story in the Mirror. Poor guy. It sucks to be a rising star and then crash and burn. It really sucks."

She put her hand on the doorknob, preparing to go. "I hope the locals don't hold it against the family. That little gas station has the best selection of root beer in town. I'd hate to see it disappear."

Peggy tried to open the door but couldn't, because Jeffrey was throwing himself at her feet. Jessica and I exchanged a look. The little brat was doing his impression of The Cat Who Never Gets Any Attention Except From Visitors.

"Where's your collar?" Peggy asked the cat. "Tell your humans you need a collar in case you get lost."

I assured her that I had a new collar on my shopping list, and he was without one now only because the old one had gotten too tight. She seemed satisfied with the explanation and left.

After we'd been alone for a few minutes, Jessica asked, "Did I say anything strange to my mother last night?"

"You were totally strange, but non-verbal. Why?"

"Don't tell anyone this, but when I was younger, I went through a phase where I suspected my mother had something to do with my father's disappearance."

I gave her a sidelong look, confused. "Do you mean by starting fights with him?"

"Never mind," she said. "Just crazy teenager stuff."

Now I was hooked, but before I could wrangle the details out of her, there was a light knock at the door, and then Christopher let himself in.

"Mr. Fairchild," I said. "I trust you slept well in our most luxurious suite? We call that room the Bachelor Experience. Did you notice the bed is also a sofa? It's the hottest new trend in boutique hotels."

Jessica giggled into her fox mug.

"The concierge told me the same thing," Christopher said.

"What else did the concierge say?"

Christopher helped himself to some coffee, then joined us at the table. "Just that the complimentary beverage service was over on this side. And he let me borrow this." He lifted his elbows to show how billowy Logan's dark blue dress shirt was on his frame. "It's a pirate shirt."

"Yes, that must be one of Logan's many *pirate shirts*," I said. "You seem chipper this morning."

"Chipper as a chipmunk."

He did have a chipmunk quality, with his fine, light brown hair sticking up all over. His cheeks were pale, but his hazel eyes were bright and alert.

He said to Jessica, "I'm so sorry about making you drink that smoothie. I don't know what I was thinking, purchasing a food product at a gas station, of all places, but the charm of the packaging tricked me. I've always liked tree frogs. What can I do for you, Jessica? How can I make this right?"

"Christopher, I'm not a situation that needs to be managed," she said. "Why are you here, anyway? Is Fairchild Capital doing business with the local factory that makes chopsticks? Or the potato chip factory? If I had the choice, I'd go for the potato chips, because I don't need a free lifetime supply of chopsticks. I'm more of a fork girl."

He laughed. "Jessica Kelly, *More of a Fork Girl.* We'll put that on your tombstone."

She slugged him on the arm, hard enough to nearly knock him out of the chair. Jessica grew up as the baby sister to twin boys, so she knew how to punch.

He rubbed his arm. "Let me make it up to you."

I narrowed my eyes at him. Here it came. The hidden agenda.

"You'll wash the dishes?" she asked.

"How would you like a three-day vacation at an exclusive resort, all expenses paid? One of the owners is a world-famous TV chef. You're going to love it. And after the stress I put you through last night, it's the least I can do to make things right."

"Ooh!" Jessica's cheeks flushed with excitement.

My eyes narrowed even more, threatening to close completely. She'd just told me she was never leaving the house again, but she was powerless to resist Christopher's sales technique.

I asked, "What's the catch?"

"No catch, and you're invited, too. In fact, I insist. Both of you deserve a getaway, my treat."

I shook my head. There was always a catch, but it was hard to ferret out when Christopher put on his charming deal-making persona.

"Is there a spa?" Jessica asked.

"A small one, but it's got state-of-the-art amenities. Have you ever been in a float tank? The sensory deprivation promotes relaxation. You float in saltwater while everything drifts away."

"Don't those tanks cause hallucinations?" she asked. "You said you wanted to make up for last night, not drive me to the loony bin."

He laughed. "You don't have to try the float tanks if you don't want to. There are also caves to explore, and hiking trails… or you could just hang out in the lodge with me and eat the great food."

"So, you're going, too," I said. "You swore there was no catch."

"A catch?" He grinned and held out his arms, the pirate-style sleeves billowing. "Some would say I'm a great catch!"

Jessica asked, "Where is this place? When are we going?"

"The lodge is up in the mountains, not far from here, and I'm planning to be there tonight. Is that enough notice for you?"

Jessica reached over and squeezed my hand. "Can we go? Can we? Please? Pretty please?"

"You know you don't need my permission."

She rolled her eyes. "I meant both of us. My boss already booked me off sick for the next week after he saw me on the news last night. And you don't really have a boss. So, can we? Both of us?"

"Let me think," I said.

While Christopher and Jessica talked excitedly about the resort and its features, I thought up excuses not to go. I didn't have many. I wasn't currently investigating anything for Logan, and as for my primary job as a gift shop owner, I could disappear to another planet, and my store would keep running tickety-boo, thanks to my capable full-time manager and new part-time employee.

As for studying my investigation books, I could do that anywhere.

I muttered about arranging for a cat-sitter and excused myself. I slipped on a coat, went outside, and crossed over to Logan's side.

He opened the door, saying, "It's not a pirate shirt. It's just a regular, button-down dress shirt."

"And it looks much better on you," I said.

"He can keep it. I don't think I can shake the visual of seeing him twirl around like a figure skater." He rubbed his beard and nodded for me to come inside. "What can I do for you? You've got that I-need-a-favor look on your face." He reached down and touched a horizontal line across his abdomen.

"My favor is that you *refuse* to look after Jeffrey's food and litter needs for three long days and nights."

"That's no problem. I can do it, or I can refuse. Would you mind telling me why?"

I explained about Christopher's proposition and how I thought the resort sounded amazing. "But I can't go, because I hate giving in to one of his schemes, and this has all the characteristics of one of his schemes."

To my surprise, Logan said, "You should go."

"He got to you, didn't he? How much did he pay you?"

Logan bristled. "He tried to tip me for the room, but I wouldn't take it. As for this trip to the lodge, I think you should go. I'll even pay you for three hours of consulting, plus you can bill me for the gas mileage."

"Consulting? For what?"

"The Flying Squirrel Lodge may have a quaint little name, but it's going to be a big deal. If they don't have someone local lined up yet for their legal needs, I'd like you to put in a good word for me."

"You need referrals that bad? Honestly, I'd rather wear a sandwich board and walk around downtown."

"No, you wouldn't. Just go on the trip. A break will be good for you and Jessica. Don't worry about your cat. We'll leave the interior doors open. It'll be one big house for him, and boys' night every night."

"But—"

Logan practically pushed me back out the front door. "Just go to the resort. Eat some of that TV chef's cooking on my behalf. And forget the three hours of investigating. I'll pay you for *eight*."

CHAPTER 7

WE DECIDED TO take my car up to the Flying Squirrel Lodge, since Christopher's silver coupe barely fit two people, let alone three plus luggage.

The drive would take us along winding mountain roads, and although Christopher estimated the journey at two hours, I prepared myself for three and packed plenty of bottled water.

Jessica transferred her cozy couch-nest into the back seat of my car, starting with her favorite patchwork quilt as a base and then layering flannel throws and electronic devices. She got herself settled in and was already reading on her tablet by the time I closed the trunk on my bags.

Christopher took the passenger seat, and as I backed the car out of the driveway, looking past him to check the road, he beamed a sunny, scheming smile at me. He was definitely up to something.

After a while, I finally had to ask, "What *are* you gloating about?"

"Gloating? I'm just smiling because this is fun and normal," he said. "A regular, normal, family-style road trip."

Jessica piped up from the back, "If we're a family, I'm playing the precocious pre-teen daughter."

Christopher kept smiling at me. I could feel his scheming even with my eyes on the road ahead.

Jessica continued, "Let's pretend I'm only eleven, but I'm a prodigy ballerina and genius computer hacker."

Christopher said, "Stormy-Lou, you can be the hot mom who does yoga and bakes perfect, gluten-free vegan cupcakes."

I rolled my eyes. "Don't call me Stormy-Lou, or I'll call you Chris."

He shrugged. "Go ahead. Sometimes I go by Chris now. I've changed a lot since you went on your sabbatical. I was always easygoing, of course, but now I'm super chill. Notice anything different about me?"

"You? Super chill?" I flicked on the signal light and whipped the wheel around, doing a U-turn on the bare road. "That's it. I'm turning this car around and we're going home. You're both obviously still high on drugs."

Jessica started to wail in protest, perfectly channeling her eleven-year-old self.

"Kidding," I said. "We're just making a pit stop for root beer."

Her pretend wailing stopped as I pulled into the B-Mart Stop and Shop.

Christopher gave me a confused look. "Returning to the scene of the crime? This is where I filled up last night and bought the Rainforest Delight."

"Popular place," I said.

A TV news van took up three parking spaces, on an angle. A dozen locals milled around, eager to offer sound bites on camera. The nervous weather girl, Daphne, was interviewing people. She appeared to be having both the best and worst day of her career.

"This looks like trouble," Christopher said.

I parked next to the pumps and shut off the engine. "We need fuel anyway, so how about I get the tank filled while you two go in and pick up some root beer. You can get junk food, too, but nothing greasy or drippy that'll make a mess in the car, and only two things each."

Jessica groaned, "Okay, Mom. Nachos with cheese and chili dogs it is."

"Sure, but you'll need to eat in the trunk or strapped to the roof like a carpet."

Christopher had that goofy smile again. "You make a good pretend mom."

"Get me a bag of those Old Dutch things I like." I made a hand gesture that only someone who'd been on a number of trips with me could have deciphered.

"Puffcorn," he said.

I nodded, my mouth already watering for the salty, kernel-free cornmeal delights.

While my road trip companions snuck past the film crew and entered the B-Mart's storefront, I got out and greeted the pump attendant, who looked about eighty and not very chatty. I handed him my key for the fuel cap and leaned against my car to wait. A modern Volkswagen Beetle, lime green, pulled up behind my car. The doors burst open, and three occupants jumped out as though they'd been on ejector seats. The female passenger, a woman with raven-black hair falling in perfect curls around a round face and full lips, caught my eye. She paused and gave me a self-conscious smile.

"Road trips," she said with an eye roll.

"Long journey?" I asked, just being friendly.

"I'll say," she replied. "Ten minutes so far with these two, and it's all I can do to keep from slappin' everybody."

I recognized her travel companions as the two gentlemen I'd met the night before in the treehouse.

"Dion and Franco," I said. "We meet again."

"Hello again," Dion said. "You must be stalking us."

"Yes. That's the only logical explanation for why I arrived at a gas station two minutes before you did."

The woman laughed and poked him in the stomach. "She got you, old man." She held out her hand, palm up. "Money?"

He frowned. "Della, ask your boyfriend. Franco's always got cash."

She poked him again. "You're closer." She kept poking until he relented and handed her some cash. She pecked him on the cheek then ran after Franco into the store.

"Kids these days," I commented.

"Della's not my daughter. She's my baby sister. Well, half sister."

"And your half sister's dating your friend?"

"My *best* friend." He frowned, his round cheeks succumbing to gravity.

I glanced over at the nearby news crew. The cameraman was shooting Daphne on her own, with B-Mart in the background. I turned my back so my face wouldn't be in the shot.

I could hear Daphne saying, "Oh my gosh, this is such a scandal! The owners of this gas station claim they had no knowledge of the contamination, but word on the street is that the elderly couple is at the heart of a chemical manufacturing scandal, and have ties to the underworld. Wait. Cut that. Start over. What does underworld mean? Is that a cult thing, like with devils?"

I snuck a look over at Dion. "Can you believe this three-ring circus?"

"Unfortunately, yes. This is exactly the sort of thing the whole town gets excited about." He kept his eyes on the slow-moving gas pump attendant. "Did you ever find that friend you were looking for?"

"She was up a tree. Thanks for asking." The attendant finished refueling and gave me a nod. "See you around," I said.

"Don't forget to use that free drink voucher."

I promised I would then slid back into my car before Daphne and her news crew could ask me for a word-on-the-street interview.

My friends emerged from the store at the same time as the other couple. By the look of Jessica's hand motions, she was describing to the other girl how she'd climbed a tree the night before. Della, who looked barely older than a teenager, threw back her head to laugh.

Christopher got back into the passenger seat and Jessica slid into the back.

Breathlessly, Jessica said, "Christopher, did you tell her yet? Did you?"

He answered tersely, "I've been in the car a millisecond."

Jessica grabbed the back of my seat and shook it. "We're all going up to the same resort! Della says they have a karaoke system in the recreation room. I'm going to pick out some songs right now, and then Della's going to sing a duet with me tonight. Awesome, right?"

"Is that girl a friend of yours?" I adjusted the rearview mirror and watched as the three of them fought over who was driving and who'd be sitting in which seat.

Jessica answered, "Not a good friend, but Della hosts the karaoke nights at the Fox and Hound, and she's so good. Stormy, you have to hear her sing. She's totally commanding when she's on the stage, and her voice is amazing. You have to hear her." She shook my seat again for emphasis.

The Beetle pulled up beside us, horn honking, all occupants waving frantically. Della was at the wheel, taking a picture with one hand and steering with the other. She hit the gas and zoomed out of the parking lot, still honking.

"Colorful bunch," I commented.

Christopher pressed a cold root beer into my hand. "Don't be cranky. We'll have so much fun it will feel like two days. Short ones. I bet by the end, you won't want to leave."

I stared after the green Beetle. "I thought your cousin's lodge wasn't open to the public yet."

"It's not," he said. "Those must be his wife's friends. Butch and Marie live in Seattle, but she's originally from Misty Falls. Her maiden name was Schwartz before she became a Fairchild. Do you remember going to school with her?"

"The name doesn't ring a bell, but if she's in her forties like Butch, we might not have crossed paths."

Jessica shook my seat again, like an excited kid. "Marie Fairchild! I know who that is. She had a cooking show, Marie's Cozy Kitchen. Such a shame she got canceled. Marie just needed one big moment to open up, to demonstrate some emotion, some personality, some…*anything*, but it never happened. I guess she was too shy to be on TV."

"Speaking of not being on TV…" I hit the gas pedal and got us out of the parking lot before Daphne and the local news crew could descend upon us.

* * *

The sun shone brightly overhead, making the weather feel more like spring than late February. The snow I'd predicted, based on the fairy rings around the moon, hadn't transpired after all. Rain was a possibility, if the weather shifted a few degrees warmer.

We passed a number of signs warning about mudslide hazards. The first part of the route took us over well-maintained roads. We transitioned onto narrower and rougher roads until we turned onto the last stretch, which was little more than a goat trail.

My car had all-season tires and good below-car clearance, but the trio riding in the lime green Volkswagen Beetle weren't as lucky. They fell behind and waved for us to pass them while negotiating bumpy sections warped by frost heaves.

I worried about them getting stranded, so we kept stopping to wait for them to catch up. I had a bad feeling there would be six of us crammed into my car by the time we reached the resort, but the Beetle managed to keep up. The three of us would cheer when we saw the round green car crest a rise behind us.

At long last, we came upon our destination. The resort jutted from the side of the mountain like a gargoyle. Rather than being made of the rustic logs I'd been expecting, the Flying Squirrel Lodge was all stone and glass, and more than a little intimidating.

"Swanky," I said. "But nothing like its name."

Jessica chimed in, "Nothing like a squirrel, flying or otherwise."

Christopher said, "Use your imagination. See how she sits, sunk into her haunches, as though she's about to push off and leap through the valley to that other mountain over yonder?"

"You're right!" Jessica exclaimed.

I shook my head. Christopher was a master salesman, but I'd built up some immunity. There was *no way* that glass and stone box resembled a squirrel.

The snowy parking lot didn't have any parking spaces delineated, so I pulled up alongside a construction trailer. I clicked the button to pop the trunk, and we all stepped out to stretch our legs.

The drive had taken longer than expected—a full three and a half hours—but now we'd arrived at the top of the world. The lodge wasn't on the very tip of the mountain, but we were still up high enough to look over a good chunk of eastern Oregon.

There are over fifty named mountain ranges in Oregon, and countless named peaks. We stood on Flying Squirrel peak, which wasn't even in the state's top hundred for height, but still impressive enough to make the three of us stand in silent awe, taking in the view.

I said to Christopher, "Your cousin Butch has outdone himself. I hope the Fairchilds are proud."

"If they get too proud, the family will need a new black sheep."

"You'll be the black sheep when they hear you've been hanging out with the likes of us."

I stretched, touched my toes, then glanced around for Jessica. She was kneeling and petting a cat who looked an awful lot like Jeffrey. And by *an awful lot*, I mean *exactly* like him, from the tip of his nose and shiny dark lips, to the swish of his tail. The cat walked over to me and bunted his head against my shin.

"Aren't you sweet?" I smiled down. "You could be Jeffrey's twin."

The cat bunted my shin again, then got so excited about rubbing my leg, he fell on his side, draping over my boot.

The Russian Blue cat was even more appreciative than my little guy had been a week earlier, when he'd gotten himself shut inside the bathroom cabinet for a whole afternoon and had to meow for me to rescue him.

In fact…

I whipped my head around. The trunk of my car was open, and the Blue Enchantment shopping bag I'd used for extra sweaters lay on its side, my packed clothes rumpled in a makeshift nest.

I stuck my hand in the shopping bag. Just as I suspected, the nest of sweaters was warm.

Jeffrey continued to lavish my shins with affection, feeling oh-so-grateful to be out of the trunk after a long, bumpy ride.

"You naughty stowaway," I said.

CHAPTER 8

WITH MR. JEFFREY "STOWAWAY" BLUE in my arms, we walked into the glamorous mountain resort.

The lobby pulsed with hard-hat-wearing workmen, but underneath the chaos and drop cloths were the bones of an impressive foyer. High overhead, a huge chandelier of multicolored blown glass caught the late afternoon sun's rays. The sculpture alone, with its candy-colored bulbs and swirls, was worth the drive up. My pulse raced in anticipation of experiencing the rest of the place— assuming the staff didn't send away people who showed up with their cats in tow.

We wove our way through the busy work site, to the pile of material most resembling a reception desk. Jessica and I waited there while Christopher went off in search of his cousin.

Jessica glanced around. "They're a *long* way from being open."

"I tried to warn you. Christopher's big stories are always ten times grander than the truth."

"We'll have fun anyway," she said with a smile. "You'll see."

"You wouldn't mind if I left you both here, would you? I'll come back to get you in three days, I swear."

"You're not going anywhere. You've been working too hard, between setting up the new computer system at your store, plus all the stakeout stuff you've been doing for Logan. You need this, Stormy. When was the last time you had a vacation?"

I batted my eyelashes. "Why, Jessica, my dear, every day in bucolic Misty Falls *is* a vacation."

"Bucolic? You make it sound like a dairy farm in England."

Elsewhere in the large lobby, one of the workmen started up a power tool. The noise made Jeffrey squirm in my arms.

"Oh, so now you have misgivings," I chided him. "Not when you climbed into the trunk of my car like some... *cat burglar* trying to escape maximum-security prison in a laundry hamper. What were you thinking?"

He blinked up at me innocently. If he could have talked, he would have blamed the whole thing on Officer Peggy Wiggles. She was the one who'd brought over the toys and the tantalizing catnip. When no one was watching he'd ripped open the bag and thrown a herb party to end all parties. High on the fresh supply, he must have found his way into the open trunk of my car when nobody was looking and decided to sleep it off.

On the bright side, he didn't seem worse for wear, and now I could enjoy a getaway without missing him—assuming they let us stay.

Ten minutes later, Christopher still hadn't returned, and the workmen continued to ignore us.

When we hunted down the construction foreman and asked him nicely about rooms and keys, he said, "Sorry, ladies. As you can see, the lodge isn't open for business yet. Do you always travel with your cat?"

Jessica looked the man straight in the eyes and said, "What cat? This is our son, Jeffrey. We're an unconventional family."

"I'll say," he said with a laugh.

After the foreman walked away, I asked Jessica to keep our *son* out of trouble while I called Logan to let him know not to worry.

Logan answered his phone on the first ring, and when I told him about the stowaway situation, he exclaimed, "He did *what*?"

I snickered. "You sound just like a dad. Don't be mad, though. It was all Peggy's fault, with her intoxicating catnip."

"The little stinker! And here I was, looking forward to some quality boys' time. Now I'm going to be lonely."

"That settles it. I'm coming home right now. I haven't seen a single person here who's on staff, and by the state of the lobby, I wouldn't be surprised if there isn't a bed or pillow in the joint."

"Don't you dare leave. I'm paying you for six hours of consulting."

"I thought you said eight."

"That was before you cat-napped my buddy. I miss him already." He chuckled. "But seriously, if I'm not needed for cat-sitting duty, I might take off for a few days."

"If you're looking for a vacation, I can't say enough wonderful things about the Flying Squirrel

Lodge. Why, it has a roof, and a floor. Who needs rooms or beds? The view is spectacular."

"Thanks, but I have something else in mind. There's somebody I have to see one last time, if that's okay with you."

"Are you asking me as your landlady? Because as your landlady, I have no problem with you leaving the duplex for a few days, provided you don't leave water running in your tub."

"I don't even have a tub. Don't you know your own house? My bathroom's the one with the tile shower."

"But you got the extra-large linen closet, which is much more useful."

"You can never have too much storage," he said.

I walked over to the lobby's enormous window to take in the view. Seeing all the trees and land between me and Misty Falls made me miss Logan, even though I'd only been gone for an afternoon.

Softly, I said, "I wish you were here."

There was a pause, and he answered gruffly, "I didn't get an invite." He cleared his throat. "Besides, I don't think Christopher would appreciate having me there."

"We're just friends."

"Like how you and I are just friends?"

The gravelly tone of his voice, plus his words, gave me a liquid feeling all through my body.

"No," I said, barely louder than a whisper. "Not like us."

"Good," he said. "Because I've been thinking that I'd like for us to be more than friends."

"Oh." I bit my lip to hold back a joke about knocking a bit off his rent.

The power at the lodge cut off, and the banging and power tools all stopped at once. A hush fell over the darkened lobby.

"Are you still there?" Logan asked. "No comment on what I mentioned?"

Just then, one of the workmen who'd been picking up paint cans near me bent over. In the quiet, the workman's body let it be known that he'd eaten beans for lunch. Many beans. The noise he emitted was distinctive, loud, and followed by cries of horror and celebration by his fellow workmen.

Logan said, "Excuse me?"

"Oh my gosh," I said, in a perfect imitation of Daphne the nervous weather girl reporter. "Oh my gosh, that wasn't me, Logan. I swear. The lobby's totally under construction and there are all these workmen here. It was one of them, and I think he did it on purpose."

Logan replied with a skeptical, "Mm hmm. Workmen, you say."

"I swear," I said. "And right now they're all eating from a big pot of baked beans, like cowboys in the Wild West."

"Is that so?"

The lights flicked back on again, and someone called my name. I'd been pacing, traveling all the way to the far end of the lobby. Back at the reception area, Christopher had returned with his cousin.

Hurriedly, I told Logan, "Sorry, I have to go check myself and my cat into a fancy mountain resort now."

"Go easy on the beans."

"Very funny, Mr. Sanderson."

"Have a great time," he said warmly. "Send me a message later, if you feel like it. I might not be in contact much, but I'll try to check in."

"Will do." We said goodbye and ended the call.

As I walked over to join my group, I held the phone to my chest and replayed the conversation in my head.

He'd definitely made a move. After months of being friends and living in the same duplex, it had taken me driving three-and-a-half hours away to finally get us together. Sort of.

When I saw Logan Sanderson again after this three-day vacation, everything would be different.

CHAPTER 9

CHRISTOPHER'S COUSIN, Butch Fairchild, took us on a whirlwind tour of the lodge.

I'd met Butch before, in Paris, on the same trip that I met Christopher. He was a decade older than Christopher, and had relished his role as the worldly, older cousin. He'd already been prematurely balding back then, but possessed a macho charisma that had girls approaching him, asking to touch his smooth-shaved head.

A few months after Christopher and I had started dating, he confided in me that Butch was technically a second cousin, from a branch of the family that didn't have much money, and so Christopher had paid for nearly everything on their trip. That arrangement hadn't sat well with Christopher; it felt too much like paying someone to be his friend, so he'd distanced himself from Butch after that.

They'd lost contact for several years, but by the look of their interactions on our lodge tour, with Butch pulling Christopher into a playful headlock every chance he got, the reunion was going well.

Butch looked different from the other Fairchilds I'd met over the years, with their fair hair and tennis-court-ready wardrobes. For starters, he was much taller and bigger than Christopher. With his smooth, shaved head, plus the many tattoos on his arms, Butch looked less like a tennis pro and more like a Navy Seal.

I had always liked Butch, because he had the good kind of tough guy personality—confident enough in himself that he could come across as powerful without acting like a jerk. His voice was deep yet soft, his manner gentle, and he smiled continuously. He was proud of the lodge, and passionate about the renovation.

We were all surprised to hear the stone and glass building wasn't completely new, but an extensive remodel and upgrade of what had once been a cabin.

"Not bad for an old hunting shack," Christopher said as we toured the in-house spa on the lower floor.

Butch winked at us. "It's no Lancaster Hotel, but I hear the food's okay."

"I'm really happy for you," I said. "It's been too long since I've seen you, and can you believe I only just found out you married a woman from Misty Falls?" I swatted Christopher. "This one forgot to tell me."

Butch winked again. "There's plenty this one doesn't know about. He hasn't even seen my newest tattoo."

Christopher pulled a face. "Is it even somewhere I'd want to look?"

Butch laughed. "All in good time. Let's pace ourselves, folks. We've got three whole days to fill with drunken debauchery."

Jessica and I exchanged a look. She had Jeffrey in her arms, and shifted her hand to cover his ears.

"No drunken debauchery in front of the cat," she told me. "He's young and impressionable."

"How about sober debauchery?"

She replied, "Can one even engage in sober debauchery?"

"I hear you need snowshoes for such a thing."

She nodded. "That makes sense."

* * *

After the spa tour, Butch showed us to our rooms, which were also on the lower floor. The lodge was a two-level, L-shaped building that hugged the south side of the mountain. With six nicely-appointed rooms on the lower floor and three spectacular suites on the upper floor, and a mix of beds and convertible sofas, it officially slept forty-two guests.

For the three-day trial run, there would be nine people, seven of whom we'd met already. The eighth person was Marie, Butch's wife, but we hadn't been given any clue as to the identity of the ninth.

"Gorgeous," Jessica said when Butch showed us the room we would be staying in. "Absolutely gorgeous."

Jessica and I were in a generous-sized room with two queen beds. Christopher's room was its mirror image, and connected to ours by an interior door.

Butch pulled some plastic wrap off the room's full-length mirror. "It's not finished yet, but you get the idea. Feel free to make notes of anything that's not to your liking. We want our guests to feel right at home in our little ol' mountainside hunting shack." He reached down to give Jeffrey a chin scratch. "Isn't that right, little buddy?"

I said, "Again, Butch, sorry about the cat situation."

He picked Jeffrey up and cradled him in his muscular, tattooed arms. "Uncle Butch doesn't mind one bit," he said to the cat. "You tell your mother that both of you are welcome here any time. Just remember you're on *my* side, and you have to back me up when my wife's old friends turn on me like a pack of hyenas."

Jeffrey's ears went back. He didn't know what hyenas were, but he didn't like the sound of them turning on anyone.

Jessica asked, "You don't get along with your wife's friends?"

Butch scoffed. "They call themselves the Batty Geniuses, but if you ask me, it's only the Batty part that's true. You'll see. Even Marie gets a little strange when she's under their influence." Still holding Jeffrey, he held open the room's door and nodded for us to follow. "Come on. I'll introduce you to the ol' ball and chain."

* * *

Back on the upper floor of the lodge, Butch led us through the dining room, where workmen were painting the walls a neutral taupe, and then into the kitchen, which was free of workmen and looked finished, ready for the grand opening in a few weeks.

Butch said, "As you can see, this is where the money went."

Christopher whistled in agreement. "You must be in deep with someone."

"Just to ourselves," Butch said. "We're self-financed, which means all the profits will be ours."

"In a few years, maybe. But what about operating capital to get you through startup? Money for wages alone will set you back—"

Butch clapped Christopher on the back. "Now, now. I didn't invite you here for a lecture. Besides, once people get a taste of Marie's food, the whole world will be dying to get a room up here. Isn't that right, Marie?"

At the mention of Butch's wife, we all looked around the steel and gray kitchen. Something moved near the sinks, and I realized with a start it was a person.

"Hello," she said with a meek wave.

Marie Fairchild wasn't the type of brassy, outspoken woman you'd expect as the wife of a macho guy like Butch. Everything about her was understated, from her plain brown hair, worn in a ponytail, to her thick eyeglasses, gray dress, and gray tights. The only bit of color was her rubber Crocs-brand shoes, bright candy-apple red, in the classic clog style. Her shoes matched the red dials on the stove. She blended with the kitchen seamlessly, which explained why we hadn't noticed her.

Christopher was the first of us to shake her hand. "So nice to finally meet you. I'm sorry I missed the wedding, but I trust you received the gift?"

Quietly, she answered, "Yes. Thank you."

Jessica and I introduced ourselves and the cat, who was still in Butch's tattooed arms.

"Tuna," Marie said, then disappeared into one of a pair of walk-in refrigerators. She emerged with a slab of raw tuna, and quickly got to work, searing the fillet in a skillet over gas flames.

"You don't have to go to any fuss," I said. "A can of something will do just fine, until I can run into the nearest town."

Butch answered for his wife, "The nearest town is the one you just came from. Don't worry about the fuss. Marie likes to spoil people, isn't that right?" He patted her on the shoulder. "This is just a warm-up for the crowds that'll be coming soon."

Christopher kept scanning the kitchen equipment. I could almost see the dollar signs in his eyes as he added up the renovation costs in his head.

He asked Butch, "How many months until you're out of the red ink on the day-to-day?"

Butch let out a deep laugh. "We're not going to worry about that until later, after we're open."

Christopher shot me a look. I nodded discreetly to let him know I'd caught the red flag as well. People who declare they're not going to worry *until later* should usually be doing the complete opposite.

"That seared tuna smells good," Jessica said. "Can I help you with anything, Marie?"

Marie mumbled about having everything under control.

Butch set down Jeffrey, who sat calmly on the floor, eyes wide and tail swishing as he watched Marie. Her proximity to the tuna made her the most interesting person in the room.

Christopher asked Butch about the ventilation system, and the two of them went off to look at vents.

Jessica stood at my side and whispered in my ear, "We are getting dinner tonight, right? Otherwise, Jeffrey might have to battle me for that pan-seared tuna."

"We won't die," I whispered back. "I've got some Junior Mints in my purse."

She elbowed me teasingly. "I haven't seen a single staff member, outside of the construction crew. In a place this size, there should be prep cooks in the kitchen all day. Dinner time's coming, and I don't see anybody trying to help Marie except for Jeffrey, and you and I both know that cat won't even peel a potato."

"He's not great with tools that require thumbs."

I looked around for signs of resort staff who might have been shy and staying out of sight, but found none. Jessica was right to be concerned. Three-and-a-half hours up the side of a mountain was well outside the delivery range for Golden Wok.

Marie delicately plated the tuna for Jeffrey and set it before him. He dove right in, which made her smile.

Jessica cleared her throat and pushed up the three-quarter sleeves of her shirt. "Marie, did your staff call in sick? Let me help with something. I work in catering, and I take direction well."

Marie gasped. "No, no. You're Butch's guest. I couldn't possibly let you help."

"Honestly, getting to work in a brand-new kitchen like this would be a privilege. And maybe I could put it on my resume."

Marie looked down at her red clogs. "I could use some help," she said weakly.

Jessica had already located an apron and pulled it on. She started washing her hands, right at home.

The Fairchild cousins had wandered off, so I gathered up Jeffrey plus his food, and excused myself to take him back to the room.

When I got to the room's door, the construction foreman was dropping off a plastic litter pan. "Now, that's just regular sand in there," he said. "It won't clump like the commercial litter, so I brought you an extra bag."

"Thanks! You've made us feel right at home." I pulled out some cash and handed him a tip.

The foreman seemed confused, but accepted the money and walked off.

Once we were inside the room, I explained to Jeffrey, "I didn't mean to insult the man. It's just force of habit from all my business travels to tip the bellhop."

Jeffrey jumped into the litter pan and started rearranging the sand so it was more to his liking.

"All the comforts of home," I mused to myself as I took a second look around the room.

A glass door led to the snow-blanketed patio. Beyond the perimeter were stone planters that would hold flowers in the summer, and beyond that was nothing but trees, a steep drop-off, and then the valley. Inside the room, the decoration matched the rustic setting, with walls the color of granite, and furnishings in every shade of bark, from the dark brown of pine branches to the silver-white of paper birch.

I relocated Jeffrey and his sand castles to the washroom, then plugged in my laptop while commenting, "Let's hope they paid the Wi-Fi bill before the start-up money ran out."

A minute later, I sighed. There was internet, but I needed a password.

"Just as well," I said, closing the laptop and reaching for my investigation manuals.

I'd just settled on the bed with a book when someone knocked on the door. I opened it, and found nothing but an empty hallway. I looked left and right. Nobody was there. I rubbed the goosebumps on my forearms. The patterned carpet running up and down the hall reminded me of that horror movie, *The Shining*. I closed the door quickly, before scary ghost twins could appear.

Someone knocked again, and that time I answered the interior door, the one connected to Christopher's room.

He had a map in one hand and a camping lantern in the other.

"Let's go check out the lava tubes," he said.

"You mean the caves? I don't know. Dinner's soon, and I was going to have a relaxing bath."

"You don't take relaxing baths."

"And you don't go spelunking. Where'd you get that map?"

"It's top secret, actually. Highly confidential. You've already seen too much." He folded the map and hid it behind his back.

I reached for it, curious, but he only yanked it farther from my grasp.

"Let me see that map. Is it for hidden cave networks?"

"What do you think?"

CHAPTER 10

THE FIRST RULE of being in a secret cave exploration society is you don't talk about being in a secret cave exploration society.

And you certainly don't share the maps with the general public.

I hadn't done much cave exploration, much less been in a secret society, but I'd always been fascinated by the idea. There were rumors of secret Oregon caverns and their entrances, but this information wasn't readily available, and for good reason. It took only a few disrespectful partygoers to ruin pristine underground sites with beer cans and graffiti.

But I wasn't planning to put any secret maps on the internet. I just wanted to see the yellowed paper Christopher had, because it was the closest thing to a treasure map that I expected to see in my lifetime.

"Please? Just a peek?"

Christopher kept backing away from me, laughing and tucking the folded map into his jeans pocket. "Come with me and you can do more than peek at my map."

Grumbling, I grabbed my boots and coat.

* * *

Christopher held the lantern low, at his hip, lighting the cavern without blinding us. Holding a candle or lantern ahead of your face looks great in movies, but blinds you in real life.

At the first fork, he led us to the left, to the smaller of two chimneys leading up. He hopped over some loose boulders and climbed up with ease.

Puffing as I hustled to keep up, I commented, "You're as spry as a mountain goat."

"Must be all the yoga."

I laughed. Christopher didn't do yoga, and made fun of people who did.

After twenty minutes of steady climbing, I asked, "How are your parents?"

"Getting older, with the exception of my mother's face."

"She finally got that second facelift she wanted?"

"And a new handbag! They made it with the leftover skin."

His joke made me laugh so hard, I stumbled on some gravel and nearly wiped out. Christopher caught me easily and held me with his free arm.

"A new handbag," I wheezed as I blinked away the tears of laughter. "Since when do you make jokes about your mother's plastic surgery?"

He grinned. "Credit should go to my father. He's been making that joke for months."

"Now I'm really confused. Since when does *your father* make jokes about your mother's plastic surgery?"

"People can change, you know."

"Sure, but they never do," I said.

His voice got soft. "People change if they have the motivation."

He was still holding me, our faces only inches apart. Our lips got closer and closer. I fluttered my lashes, closed my eyes, waited, and just as I felt his breath on my mouth, I reached down and yanked the map from his hand.

"Hah!" I cried, stumbling backward while waving the map in triumph. "I've got your super-secret map!"

He gave me a serious look. "Stormy-Lou, don't look at that. It's not for your eyes."

"Too late." I backed up a safe distance, then used my phone to take a photo of the map for later.

"I can explain," he said.

I studied the map for a moment, while my emotions rose up like storm clouds gathering.

"You liar," I said in disbelief. "This isn't some hand-drawn secret map. It's mass-printed on this yellow paper to look antique. There's a logo right here in the corner, from the Oregon Tourism Commission."

"There is a secret passageway, though."

I crumpled the map and tossed it at him. "You can shove your stupid map up your secret passageway."

"I'm not lying. There really is another system connected to this one, and I'm going to take you there."

I crossed my arms. "Why? What other surprises do you have in store? Are we going to stumble upon a bottle of champagne, candles, and a picnic blanket?"

He frowned. "Were you always this paranoid?"

I took a step back, bumping into the cavern wall. The narrow passageway was feeling smaller by the minute. The pressure made me feel like screaming, but I held back.

Through clenched teeth, I said, "I need to ask you a question. Why are we here?"

"To help my cousin."

"I'm going to give you one more chance to tell me the truth. Why are we here?"

He took a deep breath, then answered plainly, "To help my cousin. That's all."

"Fine," I spat. "Butch isn't here in the caves, though, so if you want to help your dear cousin so much, we should go back to the lodge."

"Go back already? But we've hardly seen any of the caves. Don't you want the full experience?"

"If you want the full experience of being in a cave, I think you should go *all the way*." I reached out and grabbed the lantern from his hand.

"You wouldn't," he said.

"Keep your ears on alert for monsters," I called over my shoulder as I walked away with the light. "Forest Folk aren't the only cryptids known to reside in these parts."

* * *

When I got back to the room, I found Jessica there in a towel, her pale skin still steaming from the shower.

She took one look at me and said, "You were off somewhere with Christopher." She squinted at my face. "You've got a weird look and your mouth is bare. You two were kissing! Your lip gloss has been all kissed away."

"Nice try, Detective Kelly, but I haven't been kissing anyone who isn't a cat. And I don't wear lip gloss anymore, because the gray fur that follows me wherever I go tends to stick to the lip gloss."

"Darn. So much for my powers of deductive reasoning."

"Actually, it wasn't deductive reasoning, but *inductive* reasoning, which is more bottom-up. You *wanted* to believe I was off kissing Christopher, so you looked for evidence to support it."

"You really don't wear lip gloss anymore?"

"Nope. And thanks to His Regal Grayness, I don't wear white pants anymore, either, but that's not much of a hardship."

"So, where were you just now?"

"Would you believe, spelunking?" I explained to her how Christopher had used the lure of a secret map to trick me into going to the caves with him, then how I'd called him out on his scheming, and finally how I'd left him alone in the darkness to be consumed by man-eating vampire bats.

Jessica said, "Give me a minute to put some clothes on and I'll go with you to rescue him from the caves."

"No need. He actually walked out behind me, hanging back just enough so he thought I couldn't hear him. Come on, Jess, do you really think I'd leave Christopher out there to give an upset stomach to all those innocent vampire bats?"

"You do seem pretty mad at him."

"I am. Or... I was. I don't know. He really gets under my skin."

Jessica got a jar of shell-pink nail polish from her bag and started shaking it. "Getting under your skin is not always a bad thing." She sat at the room's desk and spread out the complimentary stationery to protect the wood surface before painting her fingernails. "Stormy, if someone gets to you, that means, deep down, you care about them."

"Maybe." The softness in my voice surprised me. "Or maybe not. Sometimes a person gets to you because there's something very wrong with them."

"What's wrong with Christopher?"

I thought for a moment before it came to me. "The man actually *enjoys* arguing with me. Back in the cave, I swear his eyes lit up when I started to lose my temper. Like he was a vampire, sucking up all my negative emotions."

Jessica looked up from her nails, her blue eyes bright and curious. "Really? You've never said that about him before."

"I didn't really get it until just now, in the caves."

She nodded. "I'm no therapist, but I've dated a real assortment of guys. My non-professional opinion is that he's insecure, and"—she paused to give me a wincing, apologetic look—"you scare him with your strength and independence."

I practically snorted. "Isn't that what we women always tell each other when things don't work out with a guy?"

"Sure, but with you, it's actually true. You've achieved so much in your life. You already own a house and a retail business with employees, and now you're turning into a brilliant detective."

I glanced over at the stack of books, some of them still uncracked. "We'll see about that."

CHAPTER 11

JESSICA AND I were the first ones to arrive at the dining room. We got there in time to catch the *alpenglow*—a red band of light on the mountaintops to the east, formed as the sun set in the west.

Jessica tried to capture the view with her camera, but even when she used the panorama setting, the photo couldn't live up to the real thing.

We stood at the window, admiring both the outside view as well as the dining room, which looked stunning despite the construction materials. After a few minutes, Marie banged through the kitchen's swinging doors with a rolling trolley. She wore the same understated gray dress as before, but with plain black flats instead of the red clogs.

"We must be early," Jessica said apologetically.

Marie replied, over the sound of chattering glassware on the trolley, "Everyone else is late. Typical. Those boys are always late."

She bumped one wheel of the trolley over a workman's stray hammer, shaking her delicate freight. Jessica and I dove to steady the bottles of wine before they crashed to the floor.

"Thank you so much," Marie said, her voice cracking as though she was on the verge of a meltdown. "I'm such an idiot to think I could handle this by myself."

I patted her on the back. "Launching a new business is never easy. What you're feeling is normal. Everything will work out fine."

She blinked back tears. "That's what Butch says, too, but of course he can say that, because he has a wife who always takes care of everything. Who do I have?"

"Soon you'll have staff," I said. "And in the meantime, you have the two of us. I'm not as handy as Jessica, but I can probably wash a few dishes without setting the place on fire."

She sniffed, mumbled a thank-you, and disappeared back into the kitchen.

Jessica leaned across the trolley and whispered, "Can I tell you something scandalous?"

"Is it that Butch and Marie are having cash flow problems? That's not going to stay a secret for long. I think Christopher's here to get in on the first round of investing, at bargain rates."

Jessica wrinkled her nose. "This scandal isn't about boring money stuff. It's about Franco. I think Marie's so nervous because she has an enormous crush on him."

"Was he the stoner dude, or the skinny guy?"

"They both looked like stoners to me, but Franco's the scrawny one, Della's boyfriend." She tidied up the glasses on the trolley and started opening a bottle of Chardonnay. "When I was helping Marie with dinner prep, she kept going on and on about how Della was a spoiled brat who didn't deserve someone like Franco."

"Wow." I picked up a glass and held it out for her to fill. "Do Franco and Marie have some history? Did they date when they were younger?"

Jessica looked around carefully to ensure we were still alone, then whispered, "They used to *do stuff* in the treehouse, but it was top secret. She was his side girl, on and off, while he chased after more popular girls."

I wrinkled my nose in disgust.

Jessica asked, "Something wrong with that wine?"

"Not the wine. I just hate the idea of a guy who would string a girl along like that. I wonder if he'll be up to his old tricks during their reunion." I chuckled at the thought. "Marie's married now. Franco had better not try anything stupid, or he's liable to get himself thrown off the side of the mountain by Butch Fairchild."

"Who?" A man's voice boomed across the dining room. "Speak of the devil and he appears." It was Butch, who had entered in time to hear his name.

Jessica and I exchanged a worried look. I hoped that the tail end of the conversation was all he'd heard.

Butch joined us at the drinks trolley. "Now I've put a damper on the conversation." He rubbed one large hand over his smooth-shaved head, buffing it to a shine. "Ladies, please go back to whatever you were discussing, which was… what, exactly?"

I waved my hand casually. "Just those websites with all the reviews on businesses. There are some real cranks out there, who post things that aren't true. For example, someone named *Kartman879* is always complaining about the lackluster knife sharpening at my gift store. We don't even sell knives, much less sharpen them. I was just telling Jessica that if the lodge gets one of those cranks, you'll throw them off the side of the mountain."

Butch grinned. "I sure would. And I'd make sure they landed outside of the property line, so it didn't hike up my insurance."

He filled his glass and raised it to ours.

Jessica said, "Someone should make a toast. Stormy, your father always does the Irish toasts. I bet you know a few good ones."

Butch insisted, so I recited the first one that came to mind, as taught to me by my father.

"*May neighbors respect you, trouble neglect you, the angels protect you, and heaven accept you.*" We clinked our glasses as I added, in my best Irish brogue, "*And may you be in heaven a full half hour before the devil knows you're dead.*"

We finished the toast, then went to the dining room's windows to catch the last seconds of alpenglow.

The next person to join us was one of the Fox and Hound partners, Dion, looking sweaty and uncomfortable in a purple silk shirt one size too small. His round cheeks looked even fuller above the too-tight collar, but his smile was as bright as ever.

"I don't dress fancy that often," Dion said in his deep baritone voice as he unbuttoned the tight purple collar. "I might have put on a couple of pounds since the last time I wore this shirt. I've been stress-eating like a madman."

"Running a business is challenging," I said. "How do you like owning a pub? The Fox and Hound always looks busy whenever I've been there. You must be doing well."

"Business is good," Dion said. He asked what line of work we were both in, and didn't offer further comment on what he'd been stress-eating over.

We made small talk about the view for a few minutes, then Franco and Della arrived. Franco wore a novelty T-shirt, black with a printed design of a tuxedo on the front. The shirt was large and hung loosely on his thin frame.

Della wore a very short, form-fitting dress that showed off her curves and smooth skin. Her gleaming black hair fell artfully over her bare shoulders. She was the picture of a young star, and Franco, in his silly tuxedo T-shirt, looked like her seedy manager.

Marie came out to make sure people were getting their drinks. She said, "How is everyone? Dion, you look great in purple. Franco, I'm so glad to see you got dressed up."

Franco smoothed the front of his T-shirt and pretended to straighten the printed-on bowtie.

Marie turned to Della and started to say something, but choked on her words. Sputtering, she looked the girl up and down, from cleavage to bare legs and back to cleavage again. Then, mumbling about something burning, Marie turned on her heel and left for the kitchen.

Della didn't seem to notice, much less care. If anything, she looked bored, and kept checking her phone.

The group's conversation returned to the view, and the notion of further tourism development on the mountain. Franco and Dion joked about opening a second Fox and Hound on a neighboring peak.

While the others talked, I whispered to Jessica, "You're right about Marie carrying a torch for Franco. I don't get it. What's the appeal?"

"Franco's got the whole rebellious thing going on. He's in his forties, but he's still a bad boy."

"Bad? I guess so. Like bad yogurt or bad cottage cheese."

Jessica snorted. "Oh, Stormy. You know what my grandma says. *If you don't have anything nice to say, come sit beside me.*"

A new person entered the dining room, and some of the others yelled, "Benji!"

Franco said, "The chemistry geek has arrived! Benji, are you going to whip us up some magical martinis that won't give us hangovers?"

Benji had sandy-brown hair, plain glasses with silver frames, and a high-tech, expensive-looking watch peeking out from the sleeve of an ill-fitting and out-of-style brown suit.

Jessica caught my eye and shrugged. I sensed she'd been hoping the ninth and final person to join us would be cute and single, but Benji was far from her type. He was so shy that when she shook his hand, he looked as if he was melting.

Christopher arrived a few minutes later, wearing a sport coat with dark jeans and a pair of Vans sneakers. He avoided eye contact with me and stuck close to his cousin.

The wine flowed freely, and the group seemed to be coming together nicely, despite the twenty-year age difference between the oldest, Franco, and the youngest, his girlfriend Della.

Watching the interactions between the three guys who'd been part of the treehouse gang, I guessed their group dynamic hadn't changed over the years. Franco was the cool guy, the leader who came up with the ideas. Dion was his sidekick, his right-hand man. And Benjamin was the geeky one, the book-smart kid whose homework they copied.

Marie returned with a tray of appetizers. She would have been the girl they always hung out with, yet didn't see as a *real* girl. I felt sorry for her as she held up the tray, practically begging to be noticed, while they scooped up food by the handful and kept talking.

She squeaked, "How is everything?"

Benji, who'd been relatively quiet, loosened his too-short tie. "The food is more than satisfactory. Thank you for inviting us, Monsterpants."

Franco and Dion laughed like hyenas.

Franco shook Benji by the shoulders. "Benji, you haven't changed at all, you geek. And I totally forgot about Monsterpants."

Butch gave the guys a quizzical look. "Monsterpants? Is that a nickname? Marie told me she's never had any nicknames." He turned to his wife. "Monsterpants?"

Her face as red as a summer radish, she choked out, "Those stupid big sweatpants! They were way too big for me, so I had them in a bag, because I was going to return them. And then these two idiots climbed into them at the same time." She pointed at Dion and Franco, who were howling with laughter.

Marie stamped her foot. "I am not a monster!" She shot them all scathing looks, then left again for the kitchen.

Butch cleared his throat and silenced the laughter with a stern gaze. "That's my wife you're talking about. Do you really want me to toss you over the side of the mountain?"

The three looked guiltily at each other while Benji stammered that he'd meant nothing by it.

Butch said, "And she's also the chef. Unless you plan to miss tomorrow morning's crepe buffet or the other meals she has planned, I suggest you stop calling her Monsterpants." He walked toward the kitchen, calling back, "You'd better show my wife the respect she deserves."

Once Butch was gone, Dion said, "It's all on us if she poisons the food."

"Naw, she's fine," Franco said. "Marie, always did have a good sense of humor. She's quiet at first, but she's got that big laugh."

"As big as those sweatpants?" Dion asked.

Franco grinned. "Nothing could be as big as those sweatpants." He explained to young Della, at his side, "She wasn't returning them. She wore those sweatpants constantly. What Marie *says* she did and what she *really* did rarely match up."

Della pursed her full lips, her face taking on a catty quality. "You mean she's a liar?"

The three guys looked at each other for a moment, then Benji said, "Marie is our friend."

Franco chuckled. "Sure. Our *good* friend. Remember the stories she used to tell about what she and Benji got up to in that old car of his? The one with the full bench seats?"

Benji's cheeks reddened. He'd refused wine, taking a can of cola instead, and now drank from his can in gulps, as though his mouth was dry. Either

Benji suffered from underdeveloped social skills or he had something to hide. Or, judging by the way he was sweating, both.

Dion asked Benji, "What ever happened to that old car of yours? It was a Plymouth Volaré, right? Why didn't you sell it to me? I loved that car."

Benji gripped his cola can tight enough for it to crinkle. "The Volaré went to Mean Gene, at the junkyard."

"When?" demanded Dion, getting more interested by the second. "And why? You know I would have bought it off you, man. Especially with that sweet stereo. I would have paid book value or better."

Christopher jumped in to say, "You never sell a used car to a friend. Loan them a million dollars, sure, but never sell them a depreciating asset."

Benji looked down at his scuffed shoes, avoiding eye contact. "The Volaré was written off. I had a fender bender, and twisted the frame."

Franco interjected, laughing, "It was no fender bender. Listen, I was sworn to secrecy at the time, but the statute of limitations has got to be worn off."

Benji said tersely, "Shut up, Franco."

Franco didn't shut up. Gleefully, he said, "This genius here, Benjamin Biggs the physics and chemistry whiz, our class valedictorian, was trying to park his car when he smashed it into the back wall of his own garage."

Benjamin Biggs? I knew that name.

Christopher straightened up and made eye contact with me. We both raised our eyebrows.

While the guys razzed each other about who was the stupidest of the gang, I raised my hand to get their attention.

"Excuse me," I said to Benji. "Are you Benjamin Biggs, of Biggs Foods? The company that makes Rainforest Delight?"

Everyone fell silent. Benji's nostrils flared and he glanced around as though marking the exits.

Cautiously, he said, "Guilty as charged. I am Benjamin Biggs."

CHAPTER 12

THE RAINFOREST DELIGHT OUTBREAK hadn't just been the talk of Misty Falls, Oregon. Word had spread nationally, with outbreaks in several other states as well.

Jessica had read us the latest information during our long drive up to the lodge.

News outlets were reporting the hallucinogenic substance as an unspecified fungus. The public relations firm working for Biggs Foods kept issuing statements, hinting that the contaminant was something organic that had spontaneously shown up in one of the batches of Rainforest Delight. They claimed to be cooperating with the FDA, and said they were participating fully to discover the cause of the outbreak.

Everything about the company's statements set off my lie detectors. They claimed to have no idea what the contaminant was, yet they had laid out a perfect connect-the-dots report, leading reporters to the fungus theory.

I hadn't allowed myself to get too curious, because I didn't think I would ever get access to the

California processing plant or anyone at the company.

But now I was at a remote mountainside resort with none other than the owner of Biggs Foods himself, Benjamin Biggs.

Something similar must have been going through Jessica's and Christopher's minds as well. They watched him closely.

Benjamin Biggs became even more socially awkward, his hands moving jerkily across his suit jacket, over the left upper pocket in particular.

He said, "Judging by the way you three are looking at me right now, something is wrong." He was breathing heavily. "You might even be familiar with my company's smoothie product. I hope you're not customers."

Franco punched his geeky friend on the shoulder. "Dude, Dion wanted to call and warn you, but I wouldn't let him. The redhead here had one of your drinks and climbed a tree. I saw the whole thing on the news." He let out a mean laugh.

Benji wiped the sweat forming on his forehead. "I would have appreciated some warning."

Franco, standing in the middle of the group, ran his hands over his silkscreened faux tuxedo and said, "Where's the fun in that?"

Jessica exclaimed, "Fun?" She poked Franco on his back repeatedly, like a woodpecker at a skinny tree. "Hey, jerkface. If you think setting your friend up for a fight is *fun*, you're a real piece of work."

Franco turned around slowly, amused by Jessica's feistiness. "Typical redhead," he said with a lascivious grin. He grabbed her hand and raised it to his chest. "Now do the front. Rat-a-tat-tat. I kinda like it."

"You're gross." She yanked her hand away.

I signaled for Christopher to grab her arm before she upgraded to punching him. He nodded and gently corralled her outside of the circle.

Della left Franco's side to stand beside Jessica. "She's right, Franco. Sometimes you go too far. Your friend Benji has enough problems without you two picking on him. You think you're so funny, but your jokes are mean."

Franco grabbed her wrist and tugged her back toward him roughly. He growled, "You love it when I'm mean."

Della just rolled her eyes and pulled out her phone, ignoring him but remaining at his side.

Christopher walked Jessica over to me. He said, "Keep her away from Franco, will you?"

"For his safety, sure."

The group divided, and Benji came over to join us.

With his head hanging, Benji said to Jessica, "I am so very, truly, deeply sorry. I apologize for Franco, but most importantly, I apologize for the Rainforest Delight."

"Stuff happens," she said calmly. "I'm no worse for wear, and neither's Christopher. He had the other smoothie."

Benji looked from Jessica to Christopher and back again. His body swayed unsteadily. He looked as if he might faint, or fall to his knees before them to beg forgiveness.

"We're both okay," Christopher said. "No need for any more problems. We're all up here as friends of Butch and Marie. I don't speak for Jessica, but, personally, I can get over a few hallucinations. When I was growing up, my parents didn't let me off the leash that much, so it was actually an interesting experience."

Jessica chimed in, "I'm over it as well. You seem like a nice enough guy, so I'm sure you didn't do it on purpose."

Benji choked out, "I didn't. I swear."

Franco called out from the other half of the divided group, "What's next? A sloppy group hug? Benji *seems nice* to you, so he's off the hook? No drama? No hair-pulling?"

Della reached up and tugged on Franco's dark hair, where it fell over his eye like a wild horse's forelock. "I'll pull your hair, baby."

He growled, "Is that so?"

"Sure, baby. But first you have to stop being a jerk to the other guests."

"Or what?"

She made a spanking gesture.

Dion said to Franco, "Would you mind toning it down with my baby sister when you're right in front of me?"

Franco stuck out his chest. "Get used to it."

Dion glared at his business partner. "No need. It's not going to last."

"If you think that, then you don't know your sister."

"I know her better than you do. And I care about what's best for her."

Just then, Butch returned to the dining room to announce that dinner would be served as soon as we sat down. Between the news about Biggs Foods and all the bickering, I'd almost forgotten we were there to eat.

Christopher caught my eye. "Are you and I okay?"

"Of course we are. I'm sorry if I overreacted in the cave."

"Good," he said. "The three of us need to form a strong alliance if we're going to make it through this dinner, let alone the whole three days."

"Agreed," Jessica said.

"Agreed," I said, and we shook on it.

Butch clapped his hands and called out like a circus barker, "Places, everyone. Mind the place cards my wife has set out. Please take your assigned seat, and keep your arms and legs inside the ride until it comes to a complete stop."

The central round table had been set with a gleaming white cloth and sparkling place settings. Overhead was a smaller version of the candy-colored glass chandelier we'd seen in the lobby.

We took our seats, adhering to the handwritten place cards. With five men and four women, the seating was mostly boy-girl-boy-girl, with me between two men, Franco and Benji.

Marie circled the round table, setting out individual plates of green salad decorated with citrus chunks, toasted almonds, and pomegranate jewels.

We began eating, and I angled my body away from Franco so I could talk to Benji. He seemed skittish, so if I wanted to get to the truth about the Rainforest Delight, I would need to bide my time and build up a rapport.

"So far, so good," I said. "The salad, anyway. I've always loved pomegranates."

Benji replied, "I guess this is the part of dinner where I ask you what you do for a living and pretend to be interested."

"We don't have to talk about our careers."

"No, I think we should. I may be strange and geeky, but I can roleplay being a normal businessman, visiting a mountainside resort. That is what Marie wants." He gave me a quick robotic smile before returning his attention to separating his salad into its different components—citrus in one pile, pomegranate seeds in another. In a sing-song voice, he said, "Tell me, what do you do for a living?"

"I run a gift shop, Glorious Gifts. The place has been around for years and years. I bought it from a woman who's on a world cruise right about now."

He replied, "What a fascinating coincidence. I don't regret this conversation after all."

I waited, unsure whether he was sarcastically mocking me, or genuinely interested.

He continued, "In my teen years, I had a part-time job working at Glorious Gifts. The pay was twelve percent better than working for my aunt and uncle at the B-Mart Stop and Shop, plus I enjoyed the diverse retail activities." He finished sorting the salad and glanced up at me, his eyes trained on my mouth. "Tell me something. Did the store ever sell the last of those tiki heads with the red eyes, or are they still lurking in the stock room?"

"You know about the tiki heads?" I laughed, happy to be finding things in common. "Benji, give me your address and I'll gladly put them in a box and ship them to you."

He shied away from me. "Certainly not." He turned his shoulder, signaling our conversation was over, and went back to sorting his salad.

I looked across the table, at Christopher and Jessica, who were both happily chatting with Della about her singing career.

For the next few minutes, I focused on eating my salad. The pomegranate seeds were tricky, and I had to chase them around the plate with my fork.

Marie came around to clear the salad plates. Butch was right behind her, dropping off plates with man-sized T-bone steaks, accompanied by double-baked stuffed potatoes.

The men let out a chorus of appreciative sounds. Even Jessica, who kept to a vegetarian diet except for occasional indulgences, made cavewoman grunts over the seared beef.

"You can thank Cousin Butch for the T-bones," Butch said.

In unison, Jessica and I said, "Thank you, Cousin Butch."

He beamed proudly. "This lodge is going to be a success. I can feel the love in the air. Now, dig in, everyone."

Marie warned the group, "But not too fast. We're a long way from any medical help, and we don't want anyone choking."

Jessica said, "Don't worry, Marie. With the way my brothers used to wolf down their food, I was doing the Heimlich maneuver once a week."

* * *

My T-bone steak was delicious to the last morsel. I'd worried it was too much dinner for me, but a good portion was bone, plus I snuck a few bits into my purse for my cat.

After Butch and Marie had cleared the dinner plates and left for the kitchen, Franco leaned back in his chair and reached around me to poke Benji on the shoulder.

"I know your secret," Franco said.

At the mention of a secret, my ears couldn't help but tune in.

"It's not a secret anymore," Benji said. "The whole Biggs Foods empire went from a valuation of five million to zero, overnight. I'm broke. If you want to kick me while I'm down, get in line."

Franco said, "Not about that, genius. I know about the fender bender with your Plymouth, and why you swore me to secrecy. I just put it all together."

His voice cold and hard, Benji said, "Stay out of that matter. Trust me."

"You're bluffing, and you were never a good bluffer. That's why we loved playing poker with you."

"Let this one go," Benji said. "Can't we make one last memory with the gang all together without you ruining it?"

"One last memory? What do you mean? Is someone dying? Are *you* dying?"

"I'm not exactly living," Benji replied.

The sadness in his voice alarmed me, so I turned to him, concerned. He hunkered down over his perfect cubes of carved beef, avoiding my eyes.

* * *

After our dessert of miniature no-crust cheesecakes with three different fruit toppings, we enjoyed specialty hot drinks with our favorite liqueurs. Jessica and I both chose the deceptively-named blueberry tea, with amaretto, orange liqueur, and not a blueberry in sight.

The conversation had faded into silence when Jessica proudly announced, "Stormy is working toward getting her private investigator's license."

Christopher said, "Tell us more about that. I'm curious to hear what led you to this new career path. It can't possibly be the compensation, so what is it?"

The others leaned in, equally curious, except for Franco, who said, "Bah! Who needs a detective these days? All you need is an internet connection."

I gave him a sweet smile. "Care for a demonstration?"

"For free? Sure. Hit me with your best shot." He crossed his arms.

"You didn't have wine, and Marie brought you beer in the bottle, so you could read the label. Most commercial beers contain trace amounts of gluten, but that particular brand is popular with people who have celiac disease, because it's made without wheat. You have a serious gluten allergy, and trust issues when it comes to your food. Your friend Marie knows that about you, and she also cared enough to prepare this entire meal without gluten—except for the bread rolls, which you haven't touched."

Franco started clapping a sarcastic, slow clap.

"Too easy," he said. "And who cares about someone's food allergies? Show me something useful. A genuine secret."

"A genuine secret? You would have to check your friend Benji's inner suit pocket, on the left. The room's gotten quite warm, and he's the only man who hasn't removed his jacket. Plus he keeps touching that area of his suit. See? He's doing it right now."

All eyes turned to Benji, who jumped up so fast, he toppled his chair over.

"Not cool," he said to me, scowling. "Extremely not cool."

Franco stood. "What's in your pocket, Benji? Are you going to show us, or do I have to make you?"

"Mind your own business."

"Show us what you've got," Franco said. "We're all friends here. How bad could it be?"

While the two of them squared off, I gave Jessica a wide-eyed, innocent look. I hadn't been sure of either of those things until I'd said them, and I honestly hadn't expected Benji to be hiding anything other than his cell phone.

Christopher caught my eye. In a judgmental tone that echoed his mother's voice, he said, "Stormy-Lou, you never could back down. This is how you're always getting yourself in trouble."

I answered him by quoting Shakespeare. *"Thou poisonous, bunch-back'd toad."*

He had no response for that.

Behind me, Benji let out an exasperated sigh.

"Fine," he said. "Everyone wants to see what's in my pocket? Here you go. Take a good look."

He pulled a zipper-sealed plastic bag, sandwich-sized, from his jacket pocket and dropped it in the center of the table. The bag contained about a quarter of a cup's worth of fine, white powder.

CHAPTER 13

DION LUNGED FORWARD and grabbed the bag from the center of the table. His effort caused a button to pop off the chest of his too-tight purple shirt.

Grinning, he said, "Benji, you sly dog. Cocaine? The Peruvian Marching Powder has been the downfall of many. Since when did you take up the booger sugar?"

As everyone else looked around in confusion, Dion opened the seal on the bag, licked his finger, and stuck it into the white powder.

Benji let out a startled cry and ran around the table. He grabbed Dion by the wrist before he could lick all the dust from his finger, then plunged Dion's hand into a nearby pitcher of ice water. Dion howled and yanked his hand free, their movements knocking over the pitcher.

Dion lunged for the plastic bag again, and Benji tackled him bodily. The two wrestled, rolling around on the gleaming new hardwood until Butch and Christopher separated them.

Franco didn't bother getting up from his chair until the end of the scuffle, to take a photo.

Meanwhile, Marie had seized the plastic bag, using two cloth napkins as gloves. She re-sealed the bag, then held it gingerly.

She scolded Benji. "How dare you bring a bag of coke to my beautiful resort?"

"That's not coke," he said.

"Then what is it? And why did you jump all over Dion for trying to taste it?"

"Because he could have died." Benji pulled himself away from Christopher's hold on him.

"That's the contaminant," I said.

Everyone turned to face me. I almost laughed at the trusting looks on their faces. Suddenly, I was the expert on whatever Benji had in his pockets, all because of a few keen observations I'd made earlier.

Since I had the stage, so to speak, I stood and continued, "That's the same substance that poisoned a batch of Rainforest Delight. Marie, you hang onto that bag. Make sure it's sealed and don't inhale any of the dust. Benji, we'll give it back to you, but first you need to answer a few questions. First of all, why did you bring the powder here?"

"For safekeeping."

I nodded. "Fair enough. Second question: How did the powder get into the Rainforest Delight?"

Benji circled around the table and took his seat again, next to me. "By accident," he said. "One of the workers at the plant spilled a bag of vitamin mix and decided to replace it with one of the bags in my office, rather than get in trouble with the shift supervisor." He put his face in his hands. "I was so stupid, leaving my office unlocked."

I glanced around at the others, who looked stunned and curious, as well as more than happy to let me continue the questioning.

"Third question: What is it?"

Benji crossed his arms. "You wouldn't believe me if I told you."

"Try me."

He held out his hand and gestured for Marie to return the bag. She looked to me for guidance.

Benji said, "I'll answer your third question, but that's all, and only if you give it back to me for safekeeping."

Christopher jumped in. "Speaking of safekeeping, we could call the police and get them up here."

"No," Marie said. "Benji's too soft for prison. I'll dump this whole bag down the sink if anyone so much as dials the number nine."

Butch walked over to stand next to his wife. "We don't want any controversy associated with the resort. Do you have any idea what a scandal would do to our opening?"

Christopher made a face. He looked as if he had a lot to say and was fighting to keep it down.

Marie leaned across the table and placed the bag in Benji's hand. "Answer the third question," she said softly. "What's the white powder?"

Benji tucked the bag into his pocket, licked his lips, and said, "Toadanhydrotetrodotoxin."

Jessica stared across the table at him with her blue eyes wide open. "Toad-and-hydro-tet-tet-what now?"

"Toadanhydrotetrodotoxin," Benji said. "I've been calling it TDX for short."

Dion said, "I know that drug. It's used for a variety of treatments, from psychotropic therapy to painless euthanasia. It's extracted from the venom of animals… who live on the planet Toadonx."

Everyone looked around the table and began talking at once.

Planet Toadonx?

"You geek," Dion said, laughing. He picked up the button that had popped off his purple shirt and tucked it into a pocket.

Jessica said, "I don't understand what's happening."

Dion explained, "We all loved reading this one sci-fi series, *Tales from Planet Toadonx*. I remember reading the paperbacks in the treehouse." He laughed some more. "Good one, Benji. You totally got me. If that had been actual TDX, and you'd let me eat it, I'd be in big trouble right now."

Franco said, "You would try to steal someone's spaceship and get yourself shot with a phase pistol."

Marie said, "Was that the one with the big worms, in the sand?"

Dion said, "You're thinking of Dune, which was more focused on politics and betrayal, and not nearly enough space battles and explosions."

I returned to my seat and turned to Benji. "Why are you messing with us? This isn't funny."

"Actually, this is quite funny," Benji said as he patted his pocket. "It's just icing sugar. I was hoping to trick Dion into snorting a line of it later, but this was so much better."

"You're a bigger jerk than Franco," I said.

He pretended to be hurt.

* * *

Once everyone had settled down from Benji's prank with the bag of icing sugar, Marie invited us to the lodge's recreation room. We were slow to rise from our chairs, full from our meal, but she promised us hand-made chocolates, so that got us moving.

Compared to the dining room, with its high ceiling and huge windows, the recreation room was a cave, with its low ceiling and dark, windowless walls. Even the smell was different—musty and ancient.

"We're in the original hunting lodge," Marie said. "This room's next on the renovation list."

Butch said, "But we're not changing much. This is a man's room, and it's staying that way. There's a gym on the other side of that wall, so we might put in a door, but that's it."

Christopher walked over to one of the room's two pool tables and lifted up the dust cover. "These tables look vintage," he said. Dion, Franco, and Della started uncovering the second table.

Butch said, "Those pool tables are original to the old rustic lodge, and as solid as the mountain we're currently tucked inside."

Jessica asked, "We're inside the mountain?"

A sly smile stretched across Butch's face as he craned his neck to look up.

We followed his gaze. Instead of a normal-looking ceiling, above us was solid rock, smooth enough that it hadn't caught my eye at first. We were inside a cave. Below us was a regular flat floor, covered in a dark carpet, and the gray-brown walls on four sides were flat and man-made, but we were definitely inside the mountain.

"Wild," Jessica said. "We're in a cave. Like bats."

Marie said to her husband, "See? We need better lighting in here, at the very least, so people can appreciate where they are."

Butch snorted. "You don't have to control everything. You've got your million-dollar kitchen, and your fancy glass chandeliers. If you ask me, the guests want to see something rustic at a lodge, like wood or antlers, but I'm too nice and I always let you have your way."

"You let me have *my* way?" Her face grew red and her voice rose higher. "Excuse me, but who put up the money for this place? Not you." Her voice cracked with emotion. "You'd rather see all my hopes and dreams destroyed before you'll even consider asking your family for help."

Christopher swooped in like a vulture at the mention of help and money. "What's wrong? How can I help?"

I gave him a dirty look as I put my arm around Marie's shoulders protectively. "Let's go put on some coffee," I said to her gently. "Plus you mentioned something about chocolates."

"Go ahead," Butch said to her. "Your friends can play a game of pool while I get the sound running on the karaoke system. By the time you get back, I'm sure Della will be treating us to the concert of a lifetime."

Della looked up from the pool table, where she'd been racking up balls, and tossed her dark hair over one bare shoulder. "I've never played a cave before, but I'll do my best. I take requests, so start making a list of your favorites from the seventies, eighties, and today!" She laughed at herself. "Sorry, did that last part sound like a speech? I've only said it a million times."

Marie gave her a tight-lipped acknowledgment, then turned and left the recreation room. As I chased Marie down the hallway, I heard her muttering, "Of course Della will turn out to be the big star, with her big bobblehead and her big eyes, and her big… empty brain. That's exactly who the public wants to see on their TV while they eat their microwaved food."

I caught up with her and listened to some more muttering about bobbleheads before she went quiet.

"You don't have to do everything alone," I said. "When I was working for Fairchild Capital, I guided a lot of people through their business startups. Sometimes it helps to talk."

"I talk to my friends."

"Those jokers? Franco and Dion didn't exactly come to your aid when you started arguing with Butch. And your friend Benji seems to have his hands full already."

Marie shot me a bewildered look, her puffy eyes tiny behind her thick glasses. "The guys are not the best, but they're all I have."

"You've got me and Jessica for the next few days."

We entered the kitchen, where Marie immediately relaxed, back in her domain. The handmade chocolates were still in their cooling trays, waiting for finishing touches. She set out clean plates and showed me how to pipe the fillings in and seal the two sides.

In addition to the chocolates with soft fillings, Marie had also prepared several with whole nuts, sugared citrus peels, and delicate sprigs of mint on top.

She told me I had to taste what I was working with, in order to do the job right, so I obliged, tasting everything from creamy fruit fillings to more exotic blends of nuts and hot chilies.

While we worked, I asked her what it had been like to have her own TV cooking show.

She brightened up as she described how she'd been discovered while working at a hotel, and been given the opportunity of a lifetime. Creating a show concept and getting the pilot filmed hadn't been easy, but the process sounded fascinating.

She said, "I could tell you about the early mornings and long days, sore feet and wardrobe problems, or all the back-stabbing politics at the network, but I won't. I can't complain. The truth is, being on that show was magical. Every day was an adventure, and oh, the creativity!"

"Coming up with all of those recipes and themes must have been tough."

"Not really, because once I started being creative, it was almost like a muscle, and every day I got even more ideas—more than enough for ten shows. The best part was, I had an incredible support staff. They could turn my wildest dreams into reality. If I asked them for the best baking apples, they'd bring in a hundred varieties and run tests to find the perfect taste and texture." She glanced around the empty kitchen, as though she was nervous about telling me a secret. "Most people will swear the Granny Smith is the one and only apple for pies, but my special trick is to blend two varieties, for tart flavor plus sweetness. I like Honeycrisp and Pink Lady."

"That's a good tip. I'll have to tell Jessica."

The kitchen doors swung open and Jessica walked in. The timing was so perfect, Marie and I both started laughing.

Jessica said, "I see the real party is in the kitchen."

"We were just talking about Marie's TV show."

"Your show was adorable," Jessica said. "I loved those segments on how to modify pre-made foods, especially the one about using store-bought puff pastry to make pizza popovers."

Marie's happy expression fell into sorrow. Tears welled up in her eyes. "That wasn't my show. That was Mia Del Rosso, and her Italian Country Kitchen."

Jessica's pale face reddened. She looked to me for guidance.

I quickly said, "Jessica, you must be confused. Mia Del Rosso is literally unwatchable. She has that annoying voice. The worst personality. Terrible show."

Marie sniffed. "She really is the worst."

I agreed, "If I turn on the TV and it's her big bobblehead, I click it right off." I didn't dare say much more, given the fact I'd never heard the woman's name before, much less seen her show.

Marie laughed through her tears. "Franco hates Mia Del Rosso's voice. Sometimes we watch her newest show at the same time and send each other text messages about how horrible she is."

Rather than commenting on what a strange activity that was for a grown man, or how perhaps it wasn't healthy to keep watching a show they both hated, I simply said, "Franco is a good friend."

* * *

With the chocolates loaded up on the trolley, we wheeled our way into the recreation room.

The karaoke system was fully operational, and Della's voice filled the space. The gray-brown walls were covered in fabric-like acoustic tiles, not wallpaper, so the sound quality was excellent, considering we were inside a cave.

Jessica was right about Della being entertaining. She took requests, and worked up the small crowd with her soulful renditions of classics, plus some new songs that were popular on the radio. Her visual show was as captivating as her audio, thanks to her very short dress and her jiggling dance moves.

The men seemed captive to her charms, except her brother, who nodded along, listening with his back turned to her. He claimed he was a better voice coach that way.

Della finished her song. "Thank you so much," she said into the microphone. "But tonight isn't just about me. It's about this beautiful mountaintop retreat, where all of us are stars. Please give a warm welcome to our next act, the dreamy and steamy Christopher Fairchild, who will be singing a duet with his dear friend, the brilliant and charming Stormy Day."

Everyone cheered. I shook my head at Christopher, but got up on the little stage and took the second microphone.

He grinned. "Once more for old times?"

"We're on stage now," I said. "We might as well put on a show."

The music started, and we sang the mid-eighties Bryan Adams classic, "Summer of '69." We'd sung it together many times before—any time we happened to be somewhere with karaoke, or whenever it played on the radio. We fell into harmony easily—not perfectly, but the audience didn't hold back their cheers, and sounded much bigger than seven people.

When we finished and stepped off the stage, we discovered the crowd was down to six, because Butch had curled up on a sofa at the edge of the room and was fast asleep.

Jessica said to Marie, "He must have been exhausted. It's so loud in here."

Marie said, "Whatever you do, don't wake him. My husband has very unusual sleep habits. We actually met at a sleep laboratory. I was there for treatment of my insomnia, and he had… well, he's just a bit odd. Leave him on the couch. Trust me."

Della had taken the stage again. She called on Jessica to come up and help her sing the Motown classic, "Please Mr. Postman."

Christopher took a seat next to me, and during the girls' cheeky rendition of "You've Really Got a Hold On Me," he asked if I was having fun yet.

I had to admit I was having the time of my life.

CHAPTER 14

IT WAS NEARLY nine o'clock when I excused myself from the karaoke party and Marie's never-ending parade of exotic, mouth-watering chocolates.

The night was still young, but something about having eaten my weight in sweets made me crave a soft bed and privacy, where I could change into stretchy pants and check my digital messages.

Back in my room, I found Jeffrey sitting on a chair, staring at the door as though he'd been expecting me.

I gave him some attention, but he was more interested in sniffing the contents of my purse than getting petted and hearing about my evening.

"You can thank Cousin Butch for this T-bone," I said as I served up the small morsels.

While he ate, I changed into some comfy loungewear—a striped shirt and dark gray pants that didn't show gray cat fur—then cracked open the patio door for some fresh air.

I settled on the bed and closed my eyes, just for a moment.

* * *

Jessica gently shook me awake.

"Stormy, you can have my bed if you prefer, but we should probably wash your makeup off."

"Good idea," I said as I peeled myself off Jessica's bed. She knew how much trouble my combination skin gave me if I didn't do my end-of-day cleanse.

When I came out of the washroom a few minutes later, she was pulling her emerald-green bathing suit from her suitcase. It was one of the few items of clothing she had that wasn't pink. She'd chosen green because pink on a swimsuit made her feel naked, even with the brighter shades.

"There's a pool?" I asked. "Or a hot tub? I must have missed that on the tour."

"No, but some of us are going to try out those new sensory deprivation tanks. Not right this minute, because Della wants to try a few new songs, but things are winding down."

"Shouldn't you just go to bed? Oh, never mind. It's not that late after all." According to the room's digital alarm clock—cleverly disguised as a sleek wooden box, with the numbers glowing through a thin wood veneer—it was barely half past nine.

My knockout nap had been a short one, but I felt invigorated, possibly due to the second wave of the chocolates kicking in.

"You should come try the float tanks," she said. "There are only three of them, but you can share mine, and we can take turns."

"I wouldn't trust myself to stay conscious. I would sure hate to wake up drowned," I joked.

"Waking up drowned does ruin one's day," she said with a smile.

She gathered up a couple of towels, then rubbed her forearms and looked through the glass doors, at the darkness of the valley. The room was breezy from the narrow opening at the door.

She said, "Did you let Jeffrey out? We should call him in before the local animals get his scent."

I'd only had the door open wide enough for fresh air—or so I thought. Jeffrey was nowhere to be seen.

"That little stinker squeezed out?" I ran to the glass door and slid it open wider. I leaned out, looking for tracks in the nearby snow. I didn't see any paw prints, but I did feel something furry brush my leg as Mr. Seize The Opportunity shot past me and into the darkness. He hadn't been outside before, but he was now.

I quickly pulled on a jacket and boots while explaining to Jessica that, in my caution, I'd actually set the cat loose.

She reached for her pink jacket. "I'll help you catch him. If he's up a tree, you know I'm the woman for the job."

"I can handle this one. You go and have a good float in those funky tanks. I want a full report when you're done. Don't wait for me, because I would probably get in the water and cramp up from all those chocolates Marie forced on me."

She arched her red eyebrows. "All those chocolates she *forced on you*?"

"Also, I didn't bring a swimsuit, and this isn't a nudist resort."

* * *

Outside in the mountain air, I was more awake and alert than ever. The weather was surprisingly warm for late February, and I didn't even need to zip my jacket.

The resort's landscape lighting wasn't completed, but enough lamps were in place for me to track Jeffrey by his kitty paw prints. As I walked, the snow condensed squeakily under my boots, partially melted. The temperature had risen above the freezing point, and Jeffrey's tracks ran through both snow and patches of mud.

Jeffrey's gray form zig-zagged ahead of me without a sound. The night was silent, except for owls hooting in the distance. He jumped on top of a sturdy boulder and tilted his head to look at me sideways. I approached calmly, and just as I reached for him, someone opened a patio door. In the relative silence, the click of the lock and the whoosh of the door sliding was enough to startle Jeffrey. He jumped straight up, onto a low-hanging tree branch. His butt swung clumsily before he caught his balance and started climbing the tree.

I hissed up at him, "Jeffrey McFluffy Trousers, get your furry pants down here."

Two minutes passed.

"There's more T-bone."

No response.

I called up, "You'll be staying there all night, because I'm not climbing this tree to get you."

Ten minutes passed, and he showed no sign of coming down.

"You're making a liar out of me," I grumbled as I slipped out of my jacket, set it on the boulder, and started climbing. It was my second tree in two days.

At a height of about eighteen feet, I paused to catch my breath and admire the view. On one side, the dark valley stretched out forever in the moonlight. On the other side, the individual rooms of the lodge were lit up like display cases. Below my eye level was the lower floor, where all the guests were staying, as well as Butch and Marie. They'd said the upper floor wasn't ready yet, nor the staff quarters.

If nobody was staying on the upper floor, why was the corner suite lit up? Had the workmen left the lights on?

The room was twice the size of ours, and instead of shades of slate and bark, it was decorated in shades of honey and rose petals. Was it a honeymoon suite? The walls were bare, but I spotted framed artwork leaning against the closet door, ready to hang. The art was a series of tasteful nudes.

Forms inside the room moved. My breath caught in my throat. The suite wasn't empty. I held very still as two people stepped out onto the balcony.

Even in silhouette, backlit by the light inside the room, the two were easy to identify as Marie and her crush, Franco.

Franco said, "Is there a raccoon in that big tree? I feel like we're being watched."

"A raccoon?" Marie leaned out over the railing, peering in my direction. "I see something sort of striped. It could be one of the other wild things that live up here."

"Must be a zebra," Franco joked.

Marie laughed loudly, then sighed. "Franco, you always could make me laugh, and it feels good to laugh."

"Save some laughs for tomorrow," Franco said. "Thanks for showing me the room. Have a good night." He pulled away from the railing and walked back into the room.

Marie stood alone on the balcony, saying to herself, "Marie, you can do this. Yes, you can."

She turned and ran into the room after Franco, not bothering to close the sliding glass door.

"Franco, wait!" She grabbed his hand and pulled him over to the bed. He followed, but slowly, as though conflicted, or playing hard to get.

Marie climbed on the bed, and said something I couldn't hear.

Franco took a step back and said, "Really? You poisoned your husband?"

"No, no, it's not like that. I just gave him a sleeping pill instead of the medication he uses to stay awake. He'll be out for a few hours. Franco, this is our chance. Just one last time, for real, to remember forever."

He took a step closer. "Just one time?"

She reached down to the hem of her dress and pulled the gray garment up over her head in one movement. Underneath the plain dress, she wore an elaborate contraption with black lace and garter belts. She took off her glasses and shook her hair out of her ponytail.

Franco let out a low whistle. "Damn, Marie. You've been hiding that hot little body all this time."

"And it's all yours." She put her hands on her hips and beckoned for him to join her on the bed.

Meanwhile, outside their room and two stories up a tree, I decided I had no business watching that particular show. Jeffrey must have had the same feelings, because he walked across my shoulders on his way back down the tree.

I moved to follow him, but one of my feet had fallen asleep, and my first step down resulted in me losing my balance. The branch I reached for snapped dryly, the cracking sound causing the two people in the honeymoon suite to whip their heads in my direction.

I held very still, hoping they hadn't seen me.

Within seconds, their focus was back in the room again.

Marie cried out, "Don't go! Franco, don't you dare walk out of this room or you'll be sorry."

He stepped back from the bed, away from her reach.

"Now is not a good time," he said. "You always had the worst timing."

"Because of Della? You're too good for her. She doesn't appreciate you."

"Never mind her. The bad timing is about tonight. I'll meet you here tomorrow night, same time. Right now, I've got to talk to Benji about something."

"What are you talking about? What does Benji have that's more important than... us?"

"He's still got money. I'm going to help him out by holding some of it for him before he goes bankrupt."

"Holding it? How are you going to do that?"

"I'm going to pretend I'm blackmailing him. I figured out what happened with his old Plymouth, and I'm going to use that to get his money."

"His Plymouth? I don't understand. That was over twenty years ago." She crawled to the edge of the bed and reached for him, but he stepped back again. "Franco, don't tease, and don't lie to me."

He chuckled. "You're right. I'm going to keep the money. There'll be enough to go around. Maybe I'll share some with you, if you're nice to me." He shook his finger at her. "But you need to cool it for tonight."

She grabbed his hand and proceeded to lick his finger.

He gave in and stepped up to the bed to kiss her, his hands all over her body. They embraced for only a moment before he pulled away and went for the door.

"Don't go," she begged.

Without a word, he left the room and closed the door.

Marie slowly got up, her shoulders slumping and her arms dangling at her sides. She closed the glass patio door, picked up her dress, but then dropped it and threw herself on the bed, face first. I couldn't hear any sounds, but I could see by the shaking of her body that she was grief-stricken.

Despite witnessing her attempt to seduce Franco, I couldn't help but feel sorry for her.

* * *

Jeffrey enjoyed short excursions outside in the evening, but he always returned home before my bedtime for Kitty Playtime Hour.

He'd beaten me down the tree, so there was a chance he would beat me back to the room. I called his name and whistled for him as I walked back toward my patio, through patches of mud and crunchy snow.

Most of the rooms on the ground floor had their curtains drawn, but Christopher, in the room next to ours, had left his curtains open. His television was on, flickering blue light in the room. Christopher was crashed on the bed, eyes closed, asleep on top of the covers with his clothes on.

"Marie and her chocolates," I said to myself, triggering a more worrisome thought. Our chef had admitted to swapping her husband's medication in order to get him out of the way. How many sleeping pills did the woman have? And how far was she willing to go?

I stepped over the low shrubbery surrounding my room's patio and froze. There was someone in my room, looking at my things on the desk. A man.

CHAPTER 15

IF I HADN'T just seen Christopher in the adjoining room, I would have thought the sandy-haired man in my room was him.

Standing just outside the wide-open patio door, I cleared my throat. "Mr. Biggs, I believe you may have wandered into the wrong room by accident."

He dropped my book on the desk and whirled around, his hands raised. "I wasn't snooping."

"You're in my room, looking at my things. Mr. Biggs, that is the textbook definition of snooping."

"I was returning your cat."

He pointed to Jeffrey, who sat on the room's armchair, hind leg daintily pointed in the air while he performed his one-cat show, Watch Me Lick My Unmentionables.

I stepped inside and closed the door so he wouldn't dart out again.

"How did you know the cat was mine?"

"You're not the only one observing people's behavior. I saw you putting steak in your purse, so when the cat sauntered into my room and squawked at me that he was lost, I knew he was yours."

"Oh, you speak cat as well?"

"Enough to get by." He put his hands in his pockets and leaned over my books again. He looked boyishly young, with his suit jacket off and his shirtsleeves rolled up.

He kept looking at my big book on the criminal code—the one so thick, I hadn't yet dared to crack the spine.

"You seem interested in that one," I said. "Would you like to borrow it for a few days? I have plenty of others."

"If you wouldn't mind, sure." He held the tome to his chest like a shield. "I'll get out of your way now. I'm going to raid the kitchen for a can of cola."

"Sounds fun," I said. "I'll come with you."

He seemed perplexed by my offer, but didn't refuse the company.

I gave Jeffrey a pat goodbye, then we left. Benji started toward his room, then stopped. "I probably can't get in that way. My keys are back inside, and I left by the patio. I'll have to go around through your room when we get back."

"That's fine," I said.

He breathed heavily while we walked, as though something was bothering him. "I'm not trying to get into your room for anything else," he said.

"I believe you."

His breathing gradually returned to normal.

"Your cat is really nice," he said.

"I'll pass that along to him."

We arrived at the kitchen and started looking around for anything resembling cola. All but a few safety lights had been switched off, and the space felt cavernous in the dark.

I asked Benji, "When you guys were growing up, what was Marie like?"

"She was nice, just like now."

"Did you two ever date?"

"I always liked Marie more than she liked me. She said our chemistry wasn't right. That's one of the reasons I got so interested in chemistry. I wanted to make something that could help guys like me, to be more like Franco."

"You wanted a drug to change your personality?"

He looked surprised that I'd understood what he meant. "Exactly."

I smiled warmly. "I hope you eventually realized that your personality is just fine how it is, and you stopped trying to change it."

"No, I didn't give up. Chemistry isn't astrology. It's a hard science, and our minds can be easily manipulated. Science will never stop, so why should I? We're on the brink of discovering compounds that can improve all of humanity. Maybe bring us closer together."

"Benji, are you talking about chemicals that make people fall in love?"

"Of course not. That wouldn't be ethical."

"But changing someone's personality is ethical?"

He kept checking cupboards as he answered, "There are countless chemical reactions happening in the brain at every moment. Some of those events can be manipulated, either by thoughts and actions, or by the introduction of artificial compounds."

Laughing, I said, "Benjamin Biggs, tell me the truth. Have you or have you not used your genius chemistry skills to invent a love potion?"

"Of course not," he said with annoyance. "Would I be here by myself if I had?"

"You tell me. Are you in love with Mar—"

"No," he said, answering before I could even finish her name. "She's with Butch now, and even if she wasn't, she would never look at me the way she looks at Franco."

"How do you feel about that?"

"Sad for her, because Franco didn't even want her hanging around back when we were kids. She got into the group because her parents owned the lumber yard, and we got free wood to build the treehouse." He paused, then his voice shifted to a happier tone. "That old treehouse is looking rough these days, according to the photos the guys took on the weekend, but you should have seen it twenty-five years ago. We loved to sit up there and read books and talk about the future, and how great it would be. I thought the future would have solutions to all my problems, and drug manufacturers would have pills to make me more like…"

Just then, Franco came into the kitchen, and Benji stopped talking.

Franco glanced around the kitchen. "I'm looking for Dion. Did he come through here? He wants me to go float in those tanks with him and the redhead chick. I think he's into her."

"I haven't seen him since I left the karaoke show. Your girlfriend is really beautiful, by the way."

Franco sneered. "Beautiful and high maintenance." He pointed a finger at Benji while backing out through the swinging doors. "We're going to talk about that thing, with the money. I help you, you help me, and we all help ourselves."

Benji nodded slowly. "You can have everything. I don't need it."

"Remember, you brought this on yourself," Franco said, and then he was gone.

I checked the door to make sure Franco wasn't standing outside listening.

"Benji, I work with a lawyer in Misty Falls. He might be able to help you in ways your corporate lawyers can't."

Benji finally found the cola and opened a can. He took a long drink, then set the can down slowly. Solemnly, he said, "Your lawyer friend won't be necessary. I have a solution. Everything is going to be all right."

"What does Franco have on you? Is it worse than what's going to happen with your company? At dinner, you said you were worth five million, and it's gone down to zero."

"Franco's got nothing," Benji said. "He's chasing a ghost."

* * *

Back in my room, I played with Jeffrey, tossing some makeshift toys around the room while I worked on composing a message to send Logan.

If I wanted to tell him about my first day at the lodge, where would I even start? I didn't want to say how Christopher had tricked me into exploring the caves with him, then tried to kiss me. I started to describe the food Marie had been making, but deleted it for being so boring in text format, especially compared to the juicy gossip about her trying to seduce Franco, and drugging her husband. I couldn't send that sort of information by text. Also, I didn't want Logan to think the trip was some wild swingers' convention.

Would he be interested in hearing that the owner of Biggs Foods was up at the lodge? Possibly. How about Benji's prank, pretending he had an imaginary drug from the Planet Toadonx? How would I even start relaying that anecdote?

My day had been so interesting, it literally defied description.

After a dozen false starts, I finally typed: *We're having a good time. Wish you were here.*

I sent the text to Logan, then read through my other messages and got ready for bed.

Undressing, I noticed some grime on my shirt from the tree-climbing adventure. To prevent the stain from setting, I hand-washed it in the bathroom sink. Although the lodge wasn't officially open for business, the washroom was stocked with complimentary supplies, including the cutest miniature box of lavender-scented powdered laundry soap.

Jeffrey sat on the bathroom counter, supervising.

I asked him, "Should we wait up for Jessica, or hit the hay?"

He ignored me, fascinated with the laundry soap bubbles popping in the sink.

"It's getting late," I said. "I'm starting to worry. If she doesn't show up soon, we'll have to form a search party."

Jeffrey swiped at the bubbles, licked some off his paw, then sneezed.

CHAPTER 16

I WOKE UP to a bright room full of spring sunshine. My bedroom window seemed bigger than usual, the size of an entire wall. After a few seconds of disorientation, I remembered I was at the Flying Squirrel Lodge.

Jessica had returned the night before around midnight, so I hadn't needed to assemble a search party after all.

We got showered and dressed, talking about how quickly the weather had turned beautiful. Summer was coming early, and it looked as though the melt was underway.

By the time we returned home, the waterfall that Misty Falls was named for would be roaring with the mountain run-off. Unlike some of Oregon's other spectacular falls, ours didn't dry up in the summer, due to being fed in part by an underground spring. The falls were breathtaking year-round, but at their thunderous, roaring best in the spring.

Jessica was telling me about local cliff-diving sites when we stepped out into the hallway.

She stopped talking about cliffs and asked me, "Do you smell something?"

I sniffed the air. "Something fermented. Beer?"

"Franco," she said. "What a jerk. The lodge isn't even open yet, and he already stunk up the hallway."

"Marie did want to put the lodge through a test run. Now she can test the carpet cleaning supplies."

* * *

We entered the sunny dining room and stopped in reverence of the snow-dusted mountains beyond the picture windows.

I reached for the back of a chair to steady myself. After a lifetime of looking up at mountains in the distance, looking out at them at eye level gave me the sense of being a bird in flight, soaring over the landscape.

The scent of food brought me back to reality.

Marie stood at one end of a buffet table, serving golden crepes straight from circular flat griddles. The guests were to walk their plates along a vast range of sweet and savory fillings, from poached peach slices and slivered almonds to pale yellow clouds of scrambled eggs and rounds of crispy back bacon.

I was drizzling maple syrup over my banana-chocolate creation when Dion bumped into my elbow on purpose and gave me a knowing look.

With a rich, baritone voice, he said, "Someone's been making up for lost time."

"Are you teasing me about my two crepes?" I asked. "That doesn't seem fair, considering you have four."

"I'm talking about you and your ex, Christopher, making up for lost time. I heard *everything*."

"You must be mistaken. All I did last night was sleep."

Dion waggled his eyebrows. "Not at five o'clock this morning," he said, then he left the buffet with his crepes.

Christopher came over and asked, "What was that all about? Is he hitting on you? I heard he liked Jessica."

"He said you and I hooked up last night, and that he heard everything."

Christopher scratched his head. "We hooked up? You'd think I'd remember something like that."

"If you need a hint, apparently it was at five o'clock this morning."

Christopher said, "Five? This morning? Wasn't me."

"Dion's room is between yours and Franco's, so it must have been Franco and Della."

Just as I said her name, Della entered the dining room. She wore a short dress that was barely appropriate for daywear. Her gleaming black hair was pulled back in an artfully messy bun, and an oversized pair of dark sunglasses covered her eyes.

She yawned, in the manner of someone who might have been awake since five o'clock.

Christopher leaned in and said, "Case closed, Detective Day."

Butch came around to the crepe station and asked Marie if she needed anything, then he asked me if I was finding my favorite crepe toppings. He seemed nervous, his eyes flitting around while he rubbed his hands and told Christopher, "You name a topping, I will make sure you get it. How about pineapple? The Fairchild men all love pineapple. Try the pineapple-cherry sauce, with a little ham, on one of Marie's savory crepes. You'll think you're in heaven."

Della slipped up behind Butch and put her manicured hand on his tattooed arm. "In heaven? Tell me more."

Butch made a gurgling noise, yanked his arm away from her, and fled as though he was on fire.

Della laughed. "Silly Butch. Such a big, tough guy on the outside." She pushed down her sunglasses and watched him run into the kitchen. "Such a cute little butt on him, too. Lucky Marie." She gave me a knowing smile, then pushed her sunglasses back up and walked over to the coffee station, her hips swinging, thanks to her very high heels.

Christopher stared after her, transfixed. I playfully pushed his jaw up and told him to stop drooling, then I walked over to join Jessica at her table.

Unlike the previous evening, when we'd dined at a central round table, the dining room had been arranged to encourage smaller groupings.

I walked past Benji Biggs, who sat alone, gazing out of the window, lost in thoughts—unpleasant ones, by the expression on his face.

I sat next to Jessica, who was watching Benji at the next table. She shook her head. "That poor guy has the weight of the world on his shoulders. I wish we could cheer him up."

"You're not angry at him, Jess? His company, Biggs Foods, did poison you. And we still don't know how it happened."

"True, but I'm not like you, Stormy. I don't get worked up over stuff, and I don't obsess. Maybe it was the way I was raised."

"You think I'm obsessive? I'd argue with you, but that would just *prove* I'm obsessive."

"I didn't mean it as an insult," Jessica said. "You were raised by a cop, and you have a very strong sense of justice. When you obsess, it's for the right reason. I really admire that about you. But while your family was talking about crime scenes at the dinner table, my mother was teaching us about finding peace and letting go."

"Didn't your mother go off to be a monk or a nun for a while?"

"She went on some retreats, but she always came back." Jessica smiled at the memory as she dug into her fully-loaded crepe. "My mother was singing the merits of *letting it go* long before the Disney song came out and made it seem like a new concept."

"Thanks," I said with a huff. "Now I've got that song in my head."

She stuck out her tongue. "You're welcome."

We both dug into our food. I considered telling her about seeing Marie trying to seduce Franco, but then Christopher joined us, and I didn't want word to get back to his cousin, Butch.

I scanned the dining room to see if Marie was behaving strangely toward Franco, but he wasn't there. Della sat with her brother, Dion, while Benji sat alone. Marie stayed at her buffet station, making ten times as many crepes as the group could eat.

The three of us were debating a second trip to the buffet when Dion came over, turned around the chair next to Jessica, and straddled it.

"Hey, Red." He waggled his eyebrows, the movement causing his densely-curled hair to roll forward and back.

"My name's still Jessica," she said, a trace of amusement on her lips.

He picked a crumb of food from her plate and put it in his mouth. "Did Butch say anything to you about the float tanks? I bumped into him this morning, and he said he was shutting them down to do maintenance."

She batted her eyelashes. "He didn't say anything to me."

His voice deep and throaty, he replied, "I hope they get fixed right away, because I can only think of one thing more relaxing than floating in those tanks with you."

She put her hand on his chest. "Not in front of my friends," she squealed. "Have some decency."

He winked at her, then got up from the chair and re-joined his sister.

I said to Jessica, "Anything you want to tell me?"

She rolled her eyes. "You guys, it was nothing. We were both really relaxed when we got out of the tanks, and we had one little kiss in the hallway. That's it."

Christopher and I exchanged a look. There'd been a lot of romance happening at the lodge overnight. What would tonight bring?

* * *

The three of us voted, and the result was unanimous. A second trip to the crepe buffet was in order.

I'd started with a sweet one, so I helped myself to one of the sugar-free savory crepes, loading it with scrambled eggs, chorizo sausage, plus some fried green tomatoes Marie insisted I try. The local ones weren't in season yet, but hers had come from a greenhouse she was sampling as a new supplier.

"We're here to test things for the lodge," I said as I stacked my plate. Jessica repeated the same mantra.

Della came up to Marie and asked if there were any gluten-free crepes for Franco.

Marie snapped, "Why doesn't he ask me himself? Why's he hiding in his room?"

Della said, "I think Franco might be sick. He smelled funny, and he wouldn't get out of bed. I told him he was stinking up the room, and he just grunted and told me to get lost. I only came to breakfast because I couldn't get the patio door open for fresh air."

"Sorry about that," Marie said. "The door on the room at the end is defective. Butch should have told you when you checked in. Don't worry, we'll have it fixed before the grand opening, and I'll have Butch check the ventilation."

"Do you think I should bring a doggie bag to Franco?" Della asked.

"We'll make him a nice one." Marie grabbed a plate and whirled around the buffet, piling the plate with gluten-free options for Franco, and explaining the ingredients of each item as she went.

Della accepted the full plate and said to Marie, "You're a nice lady. I mean that, for real. I want you to know, no matter what goes down, that I really respect you."

"Thanks," Marie said, looking equal parts confused and satisfied.

She was handing cutlery to Della when a thunderous sound cracked through the dining room.

We all silently looked around at each other. Then everyone started talking at once, asking what the noise had been. We gathered around Butch and Marie for answers.

"Was it a hunter?" Christopher asked. "I'm no outdoorsman, but that was a rifle, wasn't it?"

I said to Marie, "It's Monday today. What time is your construction crew getting here?"

She answered, "That wasn't my crew. They've got the next few days off, so we can relax in peace."

Christopher said, "We won't be getting much peace if we've got rednecks shooting up the place."

"The lodge is totally safe," Butch said vehemently. "Let's nip these rumors in the bud. The land is all marked off with big signs saying No Hunting."

Marie turned to him, her eyes wide behind her thick glasses. "But that noise…"

"Don't you worry, little darling. It's not even big game season until the fall. That crack must have been the mountain letting off a little steam."

"Steam?" Marie's chin trembled. "You mean like a volcano?"

Half of the group gasped. Were we on an active volcano? People started talking evacuation plans.

Butch raised his arms and yelled for everyone to shut up. Once we were quiet, he said, "We're not on a volcano. I don't have the maps handy to give you all a geology lesson, but you have to trust me on this one."

Dion said, "It might not have been a big game hunter, but could it have been someone shooting wild turkey?"

Butch rubbed his chin. "Shouldn't be. Not enough grain seed for turkeys on this rocky terrain."

"But it's possible, right?" Dion asked.

Butch turned to Christopher. "Let's say that thunderous crack was a hunter. How about you and I head outside and give some redneck the scare of a lifetime?"

Christopher looked at me with his eyebrows raised, as though he was asking me for my permission, or a good excuse.

"Have fun," I said cheerfully. "Wear something bright so nobody mistakes you for a turkey."

CHAPTER 17

AFTER OUR THIRD helping of crepes, Marie finally cut us off.

Sounding like a mother, she said, "Get outside right now and enjoy this perfect weather. You're here to test-run *all* the amenities. This morning, Butch has you scheduled for snowshoeing."

There weren't many takers. Christopher and Butch were still off in search of rifle-wielding hunters, Dion said he'd already promised to test the gym equipment, and Della had disappeared to her room with the plate of food for Franco. That left only Jessica, Benji, and me.

Benji tried to get out of it, pleading, "I've got my work with me, case studies about Psilocybe semilanceata, and other… boring chemistry stuff you wouldn't care about."

"I'm a chef," Marie said. "We're both chemistry geniuses, in our own ways. The difference is I get to chop things. Getting my hands and body moving is what keeps me sane. I know you're going through a rough patch, but you've got to keep going. Get your skinny butt off that chair and go snowshoeing, right now."

She clapped her hands and literally shooed him out of the dining room, along with Jessica and me.

* * *

I hadn't been snowshoeing since a winter trip in high school, when we'd used huge snowshoes that looked like tennis rackets and smelled as if they were made of animal parts. By comparison, the sleek, modern snowshoes we found in the trekking hut beside the lodge resembled something you'd connect to your laptop. The gear was fashioned from lightweight aluminum and neoprene, sorted into different sizes calibrated for various body weights.

Jessica, who had been snowshoeing many times, explained, "Men and women have different thigh bones. See how Benji's thigh comes straight down from his hip, whereas our thighs curve inward?"

"What?" He looked down at his leg, then at ours, then his, then ours. He had a very serious expression.

"This won't be on the final exam," Jessica joked as she socked him on the arm. Benji wasn't expecting her tomboyish punch, and fell back onto some unpacked cardboard boxes.

Jessica helped Benji up and continued, "Because of that curving thigh bone, women have a narrower stride. That's why the women's snowshoes are shaped differently."

"So, I shouldn't wear these cool red ones?" I set down the red snowshoes I'd been planning to wear, from the men's section, and chose yellow ones from the women's section.

"Now you're cooking with fire," Jessica said.

Benji picked up the red snowshoes and studied them as though the components were a logic puzzle.

The snowshoes had adjustable straps, so they fit a variety of footwear. While Benji stared at his, I used my hands on mine. Through trial and error, I figured out how to get the straps around my waterproof hiking boots. He was still examining the bindings after I was done and ready to go.

"Benji, lighten up," I said. "Life isn't a chemistry equation you can solve by thinking. Marie's right. We could all stand to get out of our heads and live a little."

"I'll try," he said, then he put on the snowshoes.

We all borrowed some hats and scarves from the trekking hut, then set off on our way up the mountain.

Once we made it past the muddy patches around the lodge, the modern snowshoes worked like a dream, floating us on top of the snow. We climbed toward the peak, on a path marked by orange arrows fastened to the majestic trees that stood tall on either side of the trail. Crisp mountain air invigorated us to casually race each other, competing to see who could stay in the lead.

I was puffing, but happy. After weeks of working on the computer or in my car, I loved stretching my legs in such a gorgeous winter wonderland.

We'd been trekking more or less straight up for thirty minutes when Benji staggered off to the side and hugged a tree.

Jessica, who had barely broken a sweat, teased him. "Is that all you've got? For someone with such a health nut business, I expected a little more competition."

"I know," he said between gasps. "I'm a total fraud. I don't deserve to live." He leaned forward and put his face in his hands.

Jessica grimaced at me and asked quietly, "Is he crying?"

"We broke him," I said.

She went to his side and patted his back. "Don't be sad. I'm sorry I offended you. I have a weird sense of humor and I'm always rough on guys. Honestly, it's not great for my dating life."

He wiped his cheeks and looked up at her. "But you're so beautiful," he said. "And the more you act so nice toward me, the worse I feel about poisoning you with the Rainforest Delight."

"But you didn't do that on purpose, did you?"

He was slow to answer. "The lawyers... they say... I shouldn't admit to any wrongdoing until there's evidence, but I don't know if I can lie if I have to take the stand."

Jessica glanced at me, then said, "You knew." She took a step back. "You knew there was a problem, a fungus in the batch, and you didn't issue the recall until people started getting sick."

He didn't answer.

She lunged forward and shoved him on the shoulders. "Admit it. You knew, and you didn't do anything." She shoved him again, harder.

He fell backward into the snow. He shot me a guilty look as he got up again and stumbled away, tripping over the snowshoes. He continued to run, downhill, back toward the lodge.

I went to Jessica and put my hand on her shoulder. I could feel that she was shaking.

"Are you okay?"

"Give me a minute." She closed her eyes and breathed deeply.

After a moment, I said, "What happened to letting things go?"

She gave me a bewildered smile. "Maybe you and your thirst for justice are rubbing off on me. Did you see that? I really went after him!"

"Should we go catch him? I'll hold him while you shove snowballs down his pants."

"Let's give him some time to think about what he's done."

"Sure," I said.

She bit her upper lip and stared at the trail leading back down for a moment, then suddenly pushed me —not hard enough to knock me down, but enough to upset my balance.

Laughing, she called back over her shoulder as she bounded up the trail, "Last one to the top is a rotten egg!"

* * *

Even with our narrow, modern snowshoes, we staggered back to the trekking hut as bowlegged as first-time cowgirls, tired but smiling.

Benji had made it back already and returned his equipment. We wiped down our gear, returned everything to its right place in the hut, then went back to the lodge.

We stopped in the room to check on Jeffrey and freshen up. Christopher wasn't in his adjoining room, so we went in search of him.

The recreation room was empty, but we heard people talking in the next room, the gym.

We stopped just outside the door, when we heard Dion and his sister fighting.

"You need to date someone your own age," he said.

She yelled back, "So what if I prefer older men! I like someone who'll take care of me. That's not a crime. And I don't appreciate you going around to Franco behind my back and poisoning him against me!"

"What?"

"You told him about me and Butch, didn't you? I don't even know how you found out, but you did, and you told Franco this morning, and you ruined everything."

"What's this about you and Butch? What are you talking about?"

"Franco was furious! You should see the damage he did to the room. I'm not paying for it, either. This whole thing, it's all on you."

"What are you even talking about?"

"Don't lie to me!" she wailed. "I know what your liar face looks like. I know you better than you know yourself, and that's your *liar face*."

"Della, calm down. Start from the beginning. What happened this morning?"

Instead of calming down, she swore at him as she stomped her way toward the gym's exit. "I'm leaving this stupid resort! You and Franco can get your own ride back into town! Don't try to stop me, either, because I'll punch anyone who gets in my way!"

Heeding her warning, Jessica and I dove toward a door across the hallway. On the verge of giggling, we let ourselves into a small room to hide from her. We waited, listening to the sound of Della's stomping heels fade away as she left the wing.

Jessica started laughing. "Am I hallucinating, or are we actually hiding inside a utility closet?"

"By the look of all the fiber-optic cables and panels, we are definitely in a utility closet. Maybe we're both hallucinating."

She pinched my arm.

I pinched her arm.

We both giggled like teenagers.

"Stormy, I can see why you like detective work. This is fun."

"Will it still be fun when you find out we're locked in here?"

Her blue eyes widened, and she reached for the handle. The door opened and she breathed a sigh of relief.

I smiled, because I'd known the door wouldn't be locked. It was against code to have doorhandles installed so people could accidentally lock themselves in supply rooms and janitorial closets, never mind what you see in comedy movies. Stairwells, however, were another story entirely. I'd found that out the hard way while working on a case for Logan, and since then I'd made it my business to become an expert on doors.

We let ourselves out and continued our search for Christopher. Our next stop was the lobby, where we found Dion and Butch standing by a stack of construction materials.

Butch rested against the pile of wood, his elbow propped up casually. He said to Dion, "I don't know what you heard, but sometimes I sleepwalk. If someone saw me in a place I wasn't supposed to be, I must have been sleepwalking."

"Were you sleepwalking last night after midnight?" Dion asked, his baritone voice hard with aggression. "Or this morning, around five o'clock?"

Butch shrugged. "How would I know, if I was asleep?"

"You have keys to all the rooms, don't you?"

"I do, plus there's a full set over there at the check-in counter. Anyone could—" He turned to point at the reception desk and stopped talking when he saw us. "Hello, ladies. How did you find the snowshoe adventure?"

"Super." I gave him two thumbs up.

Jessica said to Dion, "What's going on with Della? She mentioned something about leaving the resort."

"Good," Butch said. "I mean, no, she can't go. Did she say why?"

Dion stepped back and swayed from side to side. "Uh… maybe we should go check their room. Della said something about Franco making a mess."

"A mess?" Butch straightened up from his casual pose. His nostrils flared and his shaved head flushed a shade of pink.

He moved toward the northeast wing, rolling his shirtsleeves up over his tattooed, muscular forearms.

I started to follow, sensing trouble, but Jessica stayed in the lobby.

"I'll keep looking for Christopher," she said.

I nodded as I left her. That was one big difference between us. She'd also sensed trouble, and had the opposite reaction.

I ran to catch up with Butch.

155

CHAPTER 18

Butch banged on the door to Franco and Della's room.

Della yelled through the door, "Go away!"

Her brother, who'd come with us, said, "Leave her alone for now. She'll cool off."

The door handle jiggled as she locked it from the inside.

Butch pulled a large ring of keys from his pocket and unlocked the door.

"I can't be part of this," Dion said. "I'll go see if Marie needs help with lunch."

He turned and left, but not before I noticed his eyes were open wider than usual. He'd struck me as a stoner from the moment we met, because of his droopy eyelids. They looked anything but sleepy now. I watched him as he walked away, glancing back at us every few paces.

Meanwhile, Della was trying to block the doorway with her body. "Don't be mad." She took off her sunglasses and batted her eyelashes at Butch as she shifted into a provocative pose within the doorframe. "I swear I didn't have anything to do with this."

"Let me see him," Butch said. "You wait in the hall with Stormy while I go in and deal with it."

"He's not in here," Della said.

"Get out of the way." His voice got gruffer. "Della, get out of the way, you little brat."

She slapped him across the cheek. "How dare you talk to me like that! I can't believe I thought you were cute." She slapped him a second time.

He didn't flinch any more than a man carved from granite would.

"Slap me all you want." He reached under her armpits and lifted her out of the way, then went into the room.

Della glared at me and spat, "Don't make that face. I don't need your pity."

Inside the room, Butch called out, "Where is he? Where's Franco?"

I walked in, Della close behind me. The room was breezy and cold. Clothes lay everywhere, the pictures on the walls were askew, and the formerly-crisp lampshades looked as though they'd lost a fight.

I commented, "Someone's been redecorating."

Butch surveyed the mess, then started yanking the covers off the bed. Next, he pulled off the entire mattress. If the room hadn't been a mess before, it certainly was now.

"Where's Franco?" Butch demanded.

"Did you look out there?" Della pointed to the patio. The room was near freezing because it had no door. Pebbles of broken safety glass lay along the patio door's track.

Butch tossed the bare mattress back on the bed frame and walked with me, over the glass and onto the patio.

I pointed to the empty door frame. "This was the bang we heard at breakfast. It was this huge pane of glass breaking."

"Couldn't have been," Butch said. "That crack sounded like a shotgun blast."

"A big panel of safety glass can make an awfully loud noise," I said. "That's why skilled thieves don't break them if they can avoid it."

Della stepped out to join us. She tucked a stray tendril of glossy black hair into her loose bun and gave me a wary look. "You're doing that detective thing again, aren't you? Do you think he was fighting with someone in here?"

"If he was fighting, it wasn't with one of the eight people who were in the dining room. Franco's the only one of us who wasn't there when we heard the bang."

She watched me out of the sides of her eyes. Her voice high, she said, "But someone could have broken in. See how all the glass is inside the room?"

I crouched over the track frame. The pattern of the broken glass, sprayed largely across the interior, did suggest the patio door had been broken from the outside. What roused my suspicion, though, was Della's transition from spitting venom at me in the hallway to being the helpful Watson to my Sherlock Holmes.

"Hold that thought," I said. Their eyes were on me as I walked back into the room and went to the bedside table. Like the one in my room, the nightstand held an alarm clock that resembled a block of wood, and a heavy lamp with a stone base. The shade of the lamp had been crushed badly. Using my fingers, I located something embedded along the seam.

I held up a bead of safety glass. "Whoever broke the patio door did so with this lamp, which means, unless these lamps grow on trees in the surrounding forest, the glass was broken from the inside." I locked my eyes on Della. "Either there was a vacuum inside this room, or someone swept up that glass and sprinkled it inside. Any idea why someone would do that?"

She stepped into the room and crossed her arms. "Franco's stupid. He might have a genius IQ, but when he gets mad, he's like a caveman. I'm always having to clean up his messes around the house. One time, he threw the toaster at the smoke detector."

Butch went to the stone lamp and picked it up. "These are heavy," he said. "Did Franco happen to let on what he was upset about?"

Della sat on the corner of the bare mattress and made eye contact with Butch. In a sultry tone, she said, "He might not have been sleeping after all, when you wandered into my room at about half past four this morning."

"I was sleepwalking," he said.

She smirked. "You did more than *walk*."

He turned to me and repeated, "I was sleepwalking."

I raised my eyebrows and said nothing.

Butch stuttered at me, "Are y-y-you calling me a liar? Hook me up to a lie d-d-detector, if you're so sure. In fact, it's about that time of the year, give me a free c-c-colonoscopy while you're at it. I can drop my trousers right now. Grab a flashlight and have a good look. You might even find a dollar or two that hasn't gone into this stinkin' money pit."

I held my hand up, palm out. "Butch Fairchild, I don't care what sum of money you keep in your dark recesses, and I can assure you, I have neither the tools nor the inclination to search for it."

* * *

After leaving Butch and Della alone to sort out the mess, I returned to my room to find it had also been redecorated—in shades of white. Toilet paper white.

Without his outdoor access, Jeffrey had been hit by cabin fever. His search for entertainment had resulted in the destruction of several rolls of toilet paper. I picked up shreds of white fluff while he watched with curiosity.

I told him that despite the mess, he was actually one of the better-behaved guests at the lodge.

Jessica returned to let me know she'd located Christopher.

I asked, "Does he have buckshot in his rump from the turkey hunters?"

"Actually, thanks to his bright green jacket, he made it back unscathed." She surveyed the room's confetti. "You had a party without me?"

I flung a handful of shredded toilet paper over our heads. "I needed to amuse myself somehow. I was going to start a torrid affair with the owner of the lodge, but it looks like Della beat me to it."

She gasped. "Della is having an affair with Marie? Sort of a love-hate thing?"

"I meant with Butch." While she picked the flecks of toilet paper out of her red hair, I told her about the trashed room and broken glass door, how Franco had gone missing, and how I was ready to pack up my things and leave immediately.

She gave me a pleading look. "But I'm just starting to have fun."

"We'll stay for now, but I swear, if one more weird thing happens, I'm out of here."

"Sure. One more weird thing and we're gone." She leaned over to check the time on the room's clock. "Oops. I'm supposed to be in a yoga class right now. Christopher is teaching."

"Christopher is teaching a yoga class? Pack your bags! I said *one more weird thing*, and I meant it."

She ignored me, and started changing into her pink workout clothes. She offered no further explanation about how Christopher had gone from being a person who made fun of yoga to one who taught it.

She asked, "What are you going to do while I'm at yoga? You're not going to hide out here alone, are you?"

"I'm not alone. Jeffrey is here, and we have a busy afternoon planned. Next on the agenda is dining on tuna, followed by drinking water from the toilet bowl, even though there are five bowls of perfectly good water spread throughout the room."

"Come to yoga. We could put some toilet water in a bottle, if you'd like."

"Send everyone my regards, especially Guru Christopher, but the meditation I'm craving involves quiet time with my email."

She wished me luck with my email, then left the room.

Unfortunately, I still didn't have the password for the network. I picked up the room's phone and pressed zero, not expecting to reach anyone.

Marie answered. "Lunch will be late," she said. "Around two o'clock."

"Actually, I just wanted the network password so I can check my business email."

"We're not set up for that yet."

"But I can see the network with my laptop."

There was a long pause, then she gave me the alphanumeric code. "Don't give that password to the others," she said. "I think it's the access to the whole network."

"You're the best," I said, then settled in to do some work. There was nothing new from Logan, but my inbox held some tasks that needed attention, so I got busy.

I was deep in the flow of things when someone knocked on the door.

I checked the peephole, just in case it was Della in a punching mood or Butch with a flashlight.

It was Marie Fairchild, in another drab gray dress, paired with her red clogs.

When I opened the door, she was wringing her hands.

"The password worked," I said.

She pushed her glasses up her nose and looked around me, into the room, before asking, "Stormy, would you say you're a *good* detective?"

CHAPTER 19

Was I a good detective?

Marie wanted to know, and since she'd asked me so directly, I felt she deserved an honest answer.

"I'm the best detective on this mountaintop," I said.

She didn't laugh. "I need to hire you."

"How about a lawyer? Sometimes people think they want a detective, but what they really want is a lawyer."

"Why would I need a lawyer?"

As I sometimes do with difficult questions, I answered with a question of my own. "Why do you need a detective?"

She took that as an invitation to enter my room. She had a gray handbag with her, and she pulled out a matching gray checkbook. "What do you charge? And will you take a post-dated check? I promise it should clear in a few days."

"Marie, I can't take your money."

She slumped against the room's dresser, looking fragile.

I quickly added, "Because you're practically family. I can't take your money because I won't charge you."

I cleared the clothes off the room's chair. "Have a seat and tell me what I can do for you."

She took a seat and crossed her legs primly. "Butch is up to something."

I sat on the bed and leaned forward in anticipation, but then corrected myself and leaned back again. If I was going to be her detective, I couldn't be her gossip-seeking girlfriend. As a professional, I've learned that the best way to keep things moving forward is to remain neutral.

"What exactly makes you think Butch is up to something?"

She pushed her glasses up and blinked three times before saying, "He called our insurance company this morning, several hours before we knew about the broken door in Franco's room."

"And?"

"That's it. Why? Have you noticed anything else?"

I deflected her question by inviting her to tell me why it was suspicious that he'd talked to their insurance company.

While she spoke, I took notes using the lodge's stationery. She explained that he told her about the patio door shortly after we discovered the mess in Franco's room. They'd argued over money—an ugly fight—and he told her that she could deal with the insurance company, since opening the lodge was all her idea.

"When things aren't going well, this place becomes *my* lodge," she said, shaking her head. "He tossed me his phone to call them, and when I did, I saw he'd already called them once today."

"And why's that suspicious?"

"He hates dealing with the insurance company. He *always* gets me to call. I was surprised he even had the number in his phone. The call he made this morning lasted twenty-two minutes. He's hiding something, and he doesn't want me to know. I have a bad feeling about this. What should I do now?"

"This one's easy," I said. "You just want to know what he was calling about?"

She nodded vehemently.

I held out my hand and asked to borrow the phone.

Private investigators, licensed or otherwise, have rules governing their fact-gathering methods. We're not allowed to pose as police officers, for example. However, we can and do get creative.

I have two secrets to getting information on the phone.

First, people are rarely listening closely, and they'll blank out the first part of what you're saying, such as your fake name, and focus on the words you end with, which should be a simple request— something that's easy to say *yes* to.

Second, if you sound bored enough, people assume you're just doing your job.

When the Fairchilds' insurance agent answered, I said, "This is Susan Squirrel, calling on behalf of Mr. Butch Fairchild. I'm sorry to bore you with this, but my boss has misplaced his notes. The darn guy would lose his head if it wasn't attached. Would you mind repeating back to me what you told Mr. Fairchild this morning, during your conversation?"

There was a pause, and I worried that my brazen use of the name *Susan Squirrel* was too showy, but then the man on the other end of the call started talking. Talking and talking. About risk management, appurtenances, and liability.

I scribbled notes as quickly as I could, pausing only when the man said, "Unfortunately, accidental death or dismemberment on the premises could exceed your coverage."

Every fiber of my body tensed. My mouth went dry. *Accidental death or dismemberment?* Was there a dead body somewhere on the premises, waiting for me to stumble over it? I glanced out the window, past the patio, where every lump and bump of snow could be hiding something sinister. Why couldn't spring come faster?

"And that's why you need those signs," the man concluded.

"Signs?"

"You tell your boss, Mr. Fairchild, that no matter how ugly his wife finds the warning signs about medical conditions, they're very important. When I come up there for the grand opening, I want to see those signs on all the doors leading to those crazy things you have, those *float tanks*. We can't prevent people from expiring on the premises, but we can reduce our exposure to litigation and investigation."

I thanked him, ended the call, and relayed my findings to Marie.

She let out a long sigh of relief. "That's all? He wants us to put up those ugly warning signs? I can do that." She took back the phone and got up to leave. "Please don't tell Butch about this, will you? I feel so paranoid, with these crazy suspicions popping into my head."

"I know the feeling. Let me know if you need anything else."

"Here's hoping I won't." She stopped to give Jeffrey a chin scratch. "There's probably another perfectly good explanation for why Butch was reviewing the security camera footage from the hallway, so I won't waste your time with that."

She thanked me again as I walked her out. When I glanced up at the hallway ceiling, I spotted the dome for the security camera immediately.

Back in the room, I pulled Jeffrey onto my lap and mulled over the facts.

Butch's call to the insurance company could have been nothing, but the timing seemed odd. Why ask about accidental deaths on the premises now? Had something happened recently? Or was something going to happen?

Where was Franco, anyway? Butch had seemed so certain he would find him in the trashed room, in or under the bed.

Had Franco gotten ill during his stay? From the food, or something in the lodge? And if Butch knew, was he trying to sweep it under the carpet? I'd seen him get upset over the threat of people spreading rumors about the lodge.

And what had the security camera captured in the hallway?

Marie had quickly lost interest in the footage, but I hadn't.

Getting the footage was something I could do on my own. I'd already been inside the building's electrical room once that day, and I'd seen the brand-new sticker from a security system manufacturer. I just had to pop into the room again, get the name of the maintenance company, then call customer support to help me access the camera footage.

When Marie gave me the password so I could get on the internet, she inadvertently gave me access to the entire computer system.

She probably thought I was through helping her, finished as of that one phone call. Little did she know that when you hire Stormy Day to investigate a mystery, the job doesn't stop until everything's uncovered and somebody's in trouble.

* * *

I left my room and started toward the stairwell, then stopped. I could feel the security camera on me, recording my hesitation.

Something about my meeting with Marie smelled fishier than the seared tuna steaks Jeffrey had been feasting on.

I'd learned a bit about Marie and her three childhood friends over dinner. They'd called themselves geniuses because they'd all scored high on conventional intelligence tests. That didn't guarantee they were smart in all aspects of life, but it meant I shouldn't underestimate any of them.

Why would she be so concerned about a twenty-two-minute phone call to an insurance agent, but lose interest in the more suspicious behavior of her husband reviewing camera footage of their friends?

It was almost as if she'd wanted me to hear that specific information from the insurance agent. And right after she'd given me full access to the resort's computer system.

Was I being set up?

My gut was trying to tell me something.

Who was being paranoid now?

I needed somewhere quiet to think, so I turned and crossed to the opposite end of the hallway, to the doors for the spa.

Inside the in-house spa, the air had a refreshing aroma—like the scent of my gift shop, but simpler. Huge pillars of white scented candles placed throughout the space smelled of tea tree oil and mint.

The construction crew hadn't finished, so the walls had only a patchy coat of chocolate-milk-colored paint. Overhead was a tangle of exposed electrical and plumbing, not yet hidden by a drop ceiling.

I found the perfect place to think, in a reclining leather pedicure chair, positioned to take in the view. The spa was directly below the dining room, with the same outlook.

Off in the distance, gray storm clouds were gathering.

I squirmed in the leather chair. I puzzled over my meeting with Marie, and all the layers of what she might have meant, but I kept thinking the same pesky thought: I really didn't like pedicures.

Just sitting in the chair made me twitch. Over the years, I'd been talked into getting a few pedicures. Every time, I'd been excited about the "treat," only to dread every minute of the foot-tickling torture, gritting my teeth to keep from jerking my foot and kicking some well-meaning spa attendant in the face.

That was all I had? Just my gut telling me not to get any more pedicures?

I slid out of the chair, my thinking session over. I would go upstairs, get the name of the security company, then satisfy my curiosity about the hallway footage, even if I was falling into some devious genius trap devised by Marie.

Something nearby made a whooshing noise. It sounded like an office chair having its height adjusted—a hydraulic whoosh.

I heard someone cough, and then the whoosh again.

My skin prickled.

I wasn't the only one in the spa.

CHAPTER 20

MOST PEOPLE'S EARS are sharper than they think.

That creepy sensory awareness, of knowing when someone's in a dark room with you, isn't from any psychic sixth sense. The warning in your head comes from your hearing, detecting a change in the hum of the room because a soft, clothed body is dampening ambient sounds.

People aren't that different from bats, who emit chirps and use echo-location to map their surroundings. We don't have wings or fly around at night catching tasty bugs, but we can use sound to see. Some blind people use tongue-clicks to map their surroundings well enough to ride a bicycle.

I clicked my tongue against the roof of my mouth.

Nope, I didn't have bat powers. Someone was in the spa, but I couldn't sense where.

"Hello? Is anyone else down here?"

Nobody answered.

I started checking the individual treatment rooms.

"Hello? Free pedicures for anyone in the spa. My treat."

Still no response.

The washrooms were empty, and the supply closet held only towels and lotions. After opening every door and cupboard in the place, I arrived at the back of the spa, at the last room, the one with the sensory deprivation float tanks.

The overhead lights were dimmed. Three white pods sat in the middle of the room, glowing blue from built-in lighting, like the furniture of an alien space ship.

The sleek pods were not the sensory deprivation tanks of the seventies, with their boxy design and industrial rivets. They were fiberglass and pill-shaped, gleaming like something from the future. Even their positioning in the room—arranged like the petals on a three-leafed flower—conjured up images of science fiction, with its theories about altered consciousness and astral projection—the idea of transporting one's self to another place and time, free floating outside the body.

The high salt content in the water allowed tank users to float silently and without effort, achieving ultimate relaxation. If the makers of the tanks were to be believed, floating in the saltwater would improve mental alertness, decrease pain, facilitate healing, improve sports performance, wash your car, do your taxes, and clean the clutter out of your attic.

All three of the wondrous pods were closed, their lids down. I ran my hand over the smooth white surface of the nearest one. The mechanism for the lid's hinge was hidden, but it could have been responsible for the whooshing pneumatic sounds. If someone was in the spa with me, the only place left to look was inside the pods.

"Hello? Is anyone experiencing improved mental alertness in here?" I glanced around the dim, blue-glowing room. "Or floating around outside their body?"

Nobody answered, but that didn't mean I was alone. The tanks had layers of soundproofing, since their purpose was to block outside stimuli.

I tapped on the lid of the nearest one. "Anybody home?"

Still no answer.

I located the handle and popped open the lid on the first one. The tank was empty. Completely empty. There wasn't even any salty water.

I walked to the second one and prepared myself. My heart was racing like crazy. After you've stumbled across a dead body or two, your imagination gets a little more active about visualizing bodies inside body-shaped spaces.

Butch had been asking his insurance agent about deaths on the premises. It wasn't unreasonable for me to expect to find a body inside one of the tanks.

I took a deep breath and lifted the lid.

Empty. No body, no saltwater. Just a single, long red hair. It was the pod Jessica had floated in the night before.

I went to the third pod and flipped it open, just to be thorough. It contained a large, bald man.

His eyes flew open.

I yelped.

He let out a surprised noise that sounded like a Saint Bernard woofing, then hoisted himself upright, tattooed muscles flexing under his rolled-up sleeves.

He grumbled, "Miles of unpopulated space all around, and still a man can't find a quiet place to think."

"Were you sleeping in there?"

He frowned. "Why would I sleep in there? It's for relaxing."

"I'm no expert, but you're doing it wrong. There's supposed to be saltwater in here so you can float. It's about floating. Hence the name, float tanks."

"I know what they are," he said grumpily. He started to climb out.

I stepped back to give him some space. "Why'd you drain all the tanks? Are they malfunctioning?"

He cracked his neck left and right, then tucked his shirt back into his trousers. "What makes you think the tanks are malfunctioning? What have you heard?"

"Just that they were closed for maintenance."

"And that's my job. Maintenance." His tone was crisp, bordering on aggressive. "If you must know, I've been up since four and I've had a busy day. I just hammered up some plywood in that room with the broken door, and now I'm inspecting the tanks. I can clean up these messes. I don't need a helper, and I sure don't need a supervisor."

I stepped back, hands up. "I didn't say you did."

"See you at lunch." He turned and left, shutting off the lights in the other treatment rooms as he walked, leaving me in the darkness.

I jogged to catch up with him.

"Butch, has anyone seen or heard from Franco?"

Gruffly, he said, "How should I know?"

We exited the spa, and Butch stopped at the door to his room. "Anything else?" he asked.

"I didn't tell Marie," I said softly. "You need to talk to your wife, but just so you know, I haven't said anything yet about you and Della."

He kept his back to me. "There's nothing to tell. It's real simple. I accidentally sleepwalked into her room, and she took it to mean more than what it was. She jumped on me like a rattlesnake, wrapping herself around my body. I didn't want to disturb Franco, so I took her out into the hallway to talk some sense into her. All of that wasn't more than ten minutes, tops."

"Nothing happened physically?"

He turned his head just enough to make eye contact over his shoulder briefly, then returned his gaze to his door.

"I can't say I was perfect for all of those ten minutes, but I'm only human."

"Your wife's not perfect, either," I said. "None of us are. But the lodge is beautiful, and everything's going to work out."

"You figure? I told Christopher we weren't ready for guests, but my cousin doesn't take no for an answer."

"What? Christopher implied that you'd insisted…" I trailed off, because Butch had already disappeared into his room and closed the door.

I clenched my fists. "Christopher," I hissed.

The door at the other end of the hallway opened, and Christopher came through, followed by Dion, Benji, and Jessica, all with damp hair and towels over their shoulders. Dion was grinning, his round cheeks giving his face a diamond shape. Benji's expression was grim, his eyes downcast behind his foggy glasses.

"You're the man," Dion said as he clapped Christopher on the shoulder. "I didn't think I could do a headstand, but the way you walked me through it made so much sense, and there I was. Doing a headstand. I feel like a new man."

Jessica laughed. "You were a new man for all of thirty seconds before you fell on top of me."

"That was my big finale," Dion said. His deep, booming laugh filled the hallway.

"You guys wanna see a big finale?" Jessica asked.

Christopher and Dion were enthusiastic in saying yes. Benji hung back a few paces, looking as miserable as the others were happy.

Jessica waved to me at my end, then gestured for me to move to the side of the hallway. She took a breath, raised her arms to center herself, then ran toward me. Once she hit speed, she did not one, not two, but three forward flips in a row, sticking the landing near where I stood.

She waggled her eyebrows at me. "I've still got it."

"You always could cheer circles around me," I said.

"But everyone loved seeing you on top of that pyramid." She grinned. "Do you still have your cheerleader underwear, with the letters on the back?"

Christopher walked up to us. "What underwear? What letters?"

"Never mind," I said.

The other two men had disappeared into their rooms to shower. Jessica slipped away next, leaving me alone with Christopher in the hallway.

I had a bone to pick with him, and now was as good a time as any. "Christopher, remind me again, why are we up here? Was it really because your cousin Butch wanted a trial run before the opening?"

"What did Butch say?" Christopher wiped his face with his towel and nodded for me to step into his room.

I followed him in. "Don't you dare answer my question with a question."

"Fine," he said. "Butch told me he had everything under control, but I didn't believe him." Christopher ducked into his washroom, turned on the shower, and returned without his shirt. I caught an eyeful of muscles I'd never seen before. I'd seen them on fireman calendars and sometimes in my imagination, but never on Christopher.

"Family helps family," Christopher said. "You can't be angry at me for trying to help the guy, can you, Stormy-Lou?"

I heard him, but I wasn't listening. I couldn't take my eyes off his muscles. "Are you taking steroids?"

He slapped his taut abdomen. "The only drugs I've taken were in that smoothie, and that was an accident. This is all me, all natural."

Steam billowed from the bathroom door behind him, enfolding us in warm fog.

I pointed at the indentations and ridges between his muscles. "Is this why you brought me up here? So I could see your new muscles and see what I'm missing out on?"

He slipped his arms around me and kissed the top of my shoulder.

"That shower's nice and hot," he said. "Let's keep talking in the—"

I pulled away from him, grabbed the door handle, and was back out in the hallway in three pounding heartbeats.

I'd barely caught my breath when someone said, "There you are."

Della.

She looked furious. She grabbed my forearm with the daintiness of an eagle helping a salmon up the river. I twisted my arm free and demanded an explanation.

"You have to move your car," Della said. Her dark sunglasses covered her eyes, but I could feel them flashing rage at me. "Get your keys and move your car, or I'll move it for you."

CHAPTER 21

I DID ALWAYS enjoy the feeling of my keys in my hand, the jingle and heft that meant I was on my way to something.

After Della changed her tune to a more polite one, I agreed to get my coat and keys so I could move my car for her. She wanted to leave the lodge, and I wasn't about to stand in her way.

As we walked down the hallway, I squeezed the ring of keys in my hand. I didn't need them, since my car had keyless entry and ignition, but they would serve as a substitute for brass knuckles in case Della decided to slap me the way she had Butch.

We passed Marie in the lobby. She was sitting on a pile of wood, drinking wine.

"Now what?" Marie said. Della didn't stop to explain. I followed her through the main doors, outside.

A blast of wind-blown pain smacked me in the face.

Sleet. The sort of semi-frozen rain that's all corners and sharp lines.

In the time since I'd seen a handful of dark clouds gathering, a storm had whipped itself into a frenzy.

The downpour of needle-like rain obliterated the remainder of snow around the building, exposing a stretch of mud between us and the parking lot.

With one arm up to shield my eyes, I picked my way across the muck under the punishing sleet. It was barely mid-afternoon, but the sky was dark and ominous.

Della needed me to move my car because her green Volkswagen Beetle had been boxed in by trailers full of building materials and tools.

We reached the cars, and I said, "Della, you shouldn't leave alone." I tried to be as reasonable as I could with icy water pelting me in the teeth. "What about Franco? You can't leave him."

"I won't. He's probably out there on the road, walking into town. He's stubborn like that, and he was mad. You saw the room."

"But this storm is bad, and your little car barely made it up here in good weather."

"I'll come back," she said over the howling wind. "I just need space right now, but I promise to come back."

While we were talking, Marie emerged from the front door and ran toward us, her red rubbery clogs splashing through the mud.

"Now what's the matter?" Marie demanded. Her words were slurred, and her eyes unfocused.

"She wants to leave," I explained. "I'm going to move my car so she can go."

Marie slapped the keys out of my hand, into the mud.

She snarled at Della, "What's wrong with you? Are you pouting because you're not getting enough attention from all the men? Why even wear a dress at all? Why not prance around here naked?"

Della turned to me and whipped off her sunglasses so she could glare directly into my eyes. "You told her about me and Butch."

I tried to signal Della to calm down, to let her know that I'd done no such thing, but we could all barely keep our eyes open with the stinging sleet.

Marie jumped in with a drunken, "Stormy's the best detective around, and she's my friend. She tells me everything."

Della wiped a layer of rain from her face and squared up to Marie. "I know about you and your crush on my man. You think I don't check his phone? Maybe if you weren't so busy sending Franco messages about some TV chef you're jealous of, you could be taking better care *of your* man." She leaned forward, getting her face right in Marie's. "If you kept a tighter leash on Butch, he wouldn't be sneaking into *my* bed."

Marie recoiled, drew back her right arm, and tried to punch Della. Luckily for Della, she missed. Unluckily for me, she punched me right in the solar plexus. I'd been on guard for blows from Della, not Marie. I sank down into the mud.

On the plus side, I found my keys.

What happened next sounded like a dozen tomcats fighting in an alley, and ended with Marie falling on top of me. In my struggle to get up, she mistook my movements for aggression, and started wrestling me. She had the upper hand, and shoved me face-down into the mud, one arm twisted behind my back.

From that position, I watched Della rev her car and drive it right into my bumper. She backed her

Beetle up, then rammed my car repeatedly until it rolled forward enough for her to squeeze by.

I flung Marie off my back and got to my feet just in time to watch Della's taillights disappear around the bend.

CHAPTER 22

I RETURNED TO the room caked in mud, looking like some wild forest creature in search of a human victim.

Jessica took one look at me and said, "New spa treatment?"

"Hah! We'll see how funny you are when I'm eating your brains."

"What happened? Did you fall down the side of the mountain?"

I groaned and rubbed my ribs. "More like the mountain fell down on me," I said. "Actually, it was Marie. She might look harmless, but she gets *mean* when she's drinking."

Jessica helped me into the tub so I could get undressed without messing up the room. I told her about my day so far. She already knew about the smashed patio door and extra-marital activity between Butch and Della. I filled her in on Marie's suspicions regarding Butch's calls to the insurance company about liability for accidental deaths on the premises, and the existence of security footage from the hallway outside our room.

She held her hand to her mouth. "You'll see me kissing Dion if you watch that footage."

"I'll fast-forward the mushy stuff," I promised, then I told her about finding Butch in the empty float tank, and how he swore his body contact with Della had been minimal. By contrast, Della had painted a much more shocking image when she'd gotten into the catfight with Marie. I didn't know who to believe.

Jessica asked, "Why would Della even feel threatened by Marie? So what if she and Franco were sending messages about cooking shows. You and I do that sort of thing all the time. It's what friends do."

"But a friend doesn't lure a friend up to the honeymoon suite on the top floor, then whip off her gray dress to reveal some very complicated underwear."

Jessica's bright blue eyes widened. "Marie did that?"

"Last night. I was outside chasing Jeffrey up a tree when I saw them in the upstairs room and heard everything."

She blinked. "Everything?"

"Franco left before things got X-rated, but he promised he would meet her up there again tonight."

She took my clothes as I passed them to her and rinsed them in the sink while I started the shower.

After a few minutes, she said, "I think everything around here has gotten weird enough to justify going home early."

"We can stay if you want. You and Dion are looking cute together, and I wouldn't want to pull you apart."

"He is sweet, which is a good reason to try that whole hard-to-get thing. If he wants to take me out, he can do it back in Misty Falls."

"We're going?"

"We're going. I'll talk to Christopher. I can tell him everything, right?"

"Sure, but before you do, there's one more thing." I peered around the shower curtain at her. "Christopher made a move on me."

"Of course he did."

She didn't look at all surprised.

She left the washroom to go talk to him and get our things packed.

I took my time washing the mud out of my hair.

Christopher wanted me back. He'd been sweet and fun, hardly irritating at all, during the whole trip. And now his face was connected to the body of a swimsuit calendar model.

Yes, things had gotten very weird, indeed.

* * *

Christopher and Jessica were both packed when I emerged from the washroom in clean clothes. Even Jeffrey was ready to go, sitting on my closed suitcase, grooming his ears.

I grabbed him in my arms. We all left the room, walking fast. We didn't see anyone in the hallway. We found Marie in the lobby. She was sitting on a pile of construction materials, and still caked in mud. If it hadn't been for the glass of wine moving to her lips, she could have been a sculpture.

"You can't leave now," she said.

We set our room keys on the reception desk, thanked her for the hospitality, and apologized for ducking out early.

"You'll be sorry," she said. "The roads are probably in ruins, just like my marriage."

Christopher said, "If you cared so much about your marriage, why were you trying to sleep with your buddy Franco?"

She gasped and sloshed the wine from her glass at him. She'd worn herself out wrestling with me in the mud, though, so the white wine fell six feet short of us.

Jessica chided Christopher for opening his mouth about the attempted tryst. "That was for your information only," she said as she whacked him on the upper arm. "How does anyone trust you with corporate secrets if you can't keep something under your hat for ten minutes?"

"Butch is family," he said.

"That's right," Marie slurred. "Family."

"We should be going," I said.

Marie refilled her glass and held it up. "To the Fairchild family." She paused dramatically. "You all suck."

As far as toasts went, it wasn't the most artful one I'd heard, but what it lacked in poetry, it made up for in emotion.

On that note, we left.

* * *

The roads were muddy and difficult to see in the sleet.

Our pace was barely faster than walking, but I felt better with each mile between the resort and us. After every tight corner, I expected to see Della's green Beetle stalled on the edge of the road, but there was still no sign of her when the sun set.

Conversation in the car revolved around neutral topics, such as how much pizza we were going to order when we got home. We'd missed lunch, partly because the chef had been too intoxicated to make it, and we'd missed dinner as well.

Christopher sat in the back seat with Jeffrey, who was on his best car behavior—yowling only every seven and a half minutes.

We had just divided up the Junior Mints from my purse when I heard a familiar digging sound behind me.

Christopher groaned. "Your cat needs to use the bathroom."

"That's what the box is for," I said.

"Oh no," he groaned.

Jessica said, "Don't make eye contact with him."

Christopher clamped his hand over his eyes. "Is it happening?"

Jessica leaned over the seat. "Hang in there, Christopher. It's nearly over. He just has to bury it."

"The smell," Christopher said. "I'm gagging. Pull over. I'll walk home. Let me out."

I pulled the car to the side of the road. The rain was still coming down, but it had eased to a light sprinkle. I suggested he remove the problem from the litter pan rather than give up on the car entirely.

He hopped out with the plastic bin and set it on the road, in the glow of the headlights, then stared down at it.

Jessica said, "He's never had a cat, has he?"

"No, but he is really smart. He'll figure it out."

"What's he doing now? Oh, he's harvesting something from that tree. A pine cone? What's he going to do with that?"

"Not much," I said after a moment. "Look, now he's thinking. He's getting himself a branch. That'll work."

"It's a shame he didn't get a forked sort of branch, like from that pine tree. That's just a long, straight stick. What's he doing?"

"He's using it like a skewer."

"No, he wouldn't!"

"Jessica, take a picture. Yes, he is. And look, now he's holding it up for us, like a prize. Doesn't he look proud?"

She took a photo with her phone, then I lowered my window to tell him to speed it along. The sound of thunder rolling through the mountains obliterated my words.

Christopher took one look over his shoulder, then waved his free arm wildly as he ran back to the car and threw himself in.

"Hit the gas!" he yelled over the endless thunder.

Small pebbles pelted my car's roof, followed by medium-sized pebbles.

Jessica yelled, "Mudslide!"

Christopher yelled, "Drive!"

Jeffrey just yelled.

I threw the car in reverse and hit the gas. The road was even more challenging in reverse, with everyone screaming, but I kept us on the narrow path until we were beyond the mudslide warning sign we'd passed when the sand-digging had begun.

I stopped the car and we waited until the rumbling ceased. The night became quiet. Everyone had stopped yelling. The rain hit the roof with a pleasant pitter-patter.

We drove forward again, but didn't make it far before we encountered a muddy pile of destruction. The road was impassable, covered in dirt, rocks, and old-growth fir trees, snapped and split like kindling.

Without a word, I did a multi-point turn and headed back to the lodge.

Everyone was quiet, even the cat.

Maybe the mudslide wouldn't have killed us, or maybe if our timing had been different, we would have been well past the danger zone. But none of us were ready to admit that a stinky cat poop had just saved our lives.

CHAPTER 23

THE MOOD IN the car was tense as we drove back toward the lodge. We made some phone calls to report the mudslide as well as that Della had been on the road, in her little green Beetle.

The dispatcher Jessica spoke to said there was nothing to worry about, that Della would likely turn up in town, and the roads would be cleared shortly. None of us felt reassured.

I sped up each time we passed through another mudslide zone, then slowed to a safer speed after we were clear.

When we reached the generic sign that promised lodging ahead, I broke the grim silence. "Did you guys see that sign? Lodging in three miles. Maybe they have a room for us."

Jessica played along. "On this mountain? I think I've heard of an old hunting shack up here, with a funny name, like the Perturbed Badger."

"Do you mean the Slightly Damp Hedgehog?"

"Maybe it's the Flapping Raven," she said. "Or the Banjo-Playing Owl."

"I hope it's half as nice as the Baritone Weasel."

She gasped theatrically and held her finger in the air. "I looked at the map earlier, and I remember now. This place up ahead is a five-star lodge called the Gargling Peacock."

"Are you sure? I've been on this mountain before and have a souvenir matchbook for the Nocturnal Parakeet Who Tweets at Midnight."

"You may have visited before they renamed it. They did that a few times. At one point it was called the Salty Salamander Who Has a Dragon Tattoo."

"Isn't that in Sweden? This place, if it's the one I'm thinking of, has a more American-sounding name, and it's definitely a type of rodent."

"The Flatulent Hamster?"

"Yes, that's it! I hope innkeepers will put us up for the night at the Flatulent Hamster."

Behind us, Christopher groaned.

* * *

Everyone hushed when we pulled up to the Flying Squirrel Lodge. The external landscaping lights were out, and the dark building jutted from the mountain like a modernist mermaid on a boat headed into battle.

With Jeffrey tucked inside my jacket and our luggage in tow, we ducked our way through the rain, circling wide around the worst of the mud. The front door had been left unlocked, and the lobby was empty and dark.

Overhead, the elaborate blown-glass chandelier, which had been so cheerful in the day, hung over us like a sea monster with darkly gleaming tentacles.

"The power must be out," Christopher said.

I re-opened the front door a crack. "Do you two hear that hum? It must be the emergency generator, running the safety lights and bare essentials."

"Darn," Jessica said. "Karaoke night is canceled."

"And tonight was Beatles night," I said.

Christopher hunted around the vacant check-in counter and found our old room keys.

Before retiring for the night, we looked around for Butch and Marie. They weren't in the kitchen or any of the other common areas, nor was anyone else.

We'd been in the car for several hours due to the poor road conditions. It was nearly nine o'clock—too late for dinner, but strangely early for everyone to have gone to bed.

We knocked on the doors of the other guest rooms, but nobody answered. The owners and other remaining guests were hiding from us, sleeping, or… checked out.

"Marie had those sleeping pills," I said. "What if she put the others to bed so she could meet Franco in the honeymoon suite for their planned tryst?"

None of us relished the idea of catching them in the act, but we went up to the suite anyway and knocked on the door.

Nobody answered, but Christopher swore he could hear movements inside the room.

Jessica said, "Marie's probably just passed out in there."

"Call her phone," I suggested, so Christopher did.

A ringtone sounded on the other side of the door, then went silent.

Christopher knocked again. "Marie, it's just us. The roads are blocked by a mudslide, and we need a place to stay. We've got the keys and we'll be in the same rooms as before."

I added, "I'm really sorry things have gone sideways." No response. "Marie, I'm basically an expert on things going wrong with Fairchild men. Let me know if I can help with anything." I rubbed my sore rib, bruised from our misunderstanding in the parking lot. "And I'm not mad about what happened earlier. I know you didn't mean to hurt me."

We waited another minute. Christopher got a text message from her on his phone: *You can stay as long as you need. I'm okay. Just let me have some space.*

We were halfway down to our rooms when she sent a second message: *In the cooler is some sliced roast beef that would make nice sandwiches.*

* * *

We all enjoyed the roast beef in the comfort of our room, in the warm glow of the single safety light by the door plus some candles Jessica had brought.

We humans had our beef in sandwiches with lettuce and horseradish, and the cat had his just how he liked it—dragged onto the room's only carpet, which was the bath mat.

We still hadn't seen the other guests, and there were no more messages from Marie.

As the hour drew closer to midnight, Christopher lingered on our side of the adjoining rooms.

"Why'd you bring candles?" he asked Jessica.

"My mother always brought candles on trips," she said as she lit more votives on the room's dresser. "We traveled on the thrifty side, and cheap motel rooms smell like a hobo's armpit."

"Those candles must be gardenia," Christopher said, smelling deeply. "Gardenia is my mother's favorite. I'd pass along the travel tip about the candles, but she'd never set foot in a motel, and she prefers to travel light, anyway."

"Traveling light is a luxury of the rich, who can ask the concierge for supplies. My mother didn't just pack candles. She had first aid supplies with extra bandages, laundry detergent, crisp bills straight from the bank teller for vending machines, and a wrapped mystery item for emergencies, to keep me and my brothers occupied—usually a travel-sized jigsaw puzzle."

"Sounds like fun," Christopher said, sounding wistful. "I'm an only child." He laughed at himself. "As if it isn't super obvious by how I am."

"You're okay," Jessica said. "If you manage to woo Stormy back, do you want to have a big family?"

I grabbed the nearest thing—a pillow—and chucked it at her. She caught the pillow and tossed it right back at my head. "Let him answer the question," she said.

We both looked at Christopher.

He swallowed and pulled out his phone. "I'm going to try Butch again." A minute later, he reported, "Still not picking up."

Jessica checked her phone. "Coverage is patchy up here on the mountain. If he's in the part of the lodge that's embedded in the rock, he's probably cut off."

I starting cleaning up, stacking our plates. "I'll take these to the kitchen and do another round of the lodge to find him."

Jessica put her hand on my arm and gave me a worried look. "Or we could stay here in the room until morning and *not* go running around a dark lodge during a power outage."

Christopher walked to the patio door and peered out at the darkness. "Maybe they're all outside."

"Even better," Jessica said sarcastically. "Let's go outside in the dark and split up, all the better to be picked off one by one."

Christopher turned and looked into my eyes. "We don't need to split up. We could be together." He blinked. "Looking for the others."

CHAPTER 24

IT WAS A dark and stormy night when Christopher and I set out into the rain wearing garbage bags over our coats. We stopped at the trekking hut to upgrade our outfits to real rain gear, and picked up two lanterns.

Jessica had stayed behind in the room, running our base of operation. She would be making follow-up phone calls about the mudslide, getting the power back on, and finding contact information for the local search and rescue, should we need it for anyone we couldn't locate. Franco hadn't been seen since before breakfast, twelve hours earlier.

"I'll go on my own to check the caves," Christopher said as we closed up the trekking hut. "You follow the sound of the generator and check that area."

"You get the dry caves while I take the rain?"

"We can cover more ground if we split up."

"And if we're alone, it'll be easier for the serial killer who lives in the woods to pick us off one by one," I joked. "You're stuck with me, for now."

He shot me a teasing grin. "What if I have to take off all this rain gear, and you see me in nothing but a wet shirt and get all flustered again?"

"Strip naked and do the Chicken Dance for all I care. And what makes you think I was flustered? You can't fluster me with a mere sexy shower invitation."

We entered the cave, turned a corner, and followed the tunnel deeper into the mountain.

We searched through the connected caverns, taking turns calling out for the others. Christopher had the map with him, but the cave system was simple enough that we didn't need it.

Our search was fruitless. The caves were as lacking in people as the lodge was lacking in karaoke, at least until the power came back on.

As we stepped out of the caves and into the rain, I told Christopher that if he ever did get one of those secret cave maps, he had to share it with me.

He said, "Whenever I see anything interesting, you're always the first person I think of."

"Good. I'm particularly interested in maps of the caves closer to Misty Falls."

"You want those gold doubloons." He grabbed my arm as I stumbled over a soggy branch. "Careful now."

"How do you know about the gold? I thought that was just a local legend people tell in town."

"You're forgetting I've been around your father a time or two, and after enduring a few six-packs of that beer he drinks, he starts with the local legends. Then his accent gets thicker, and he moves into the old Irish legends." He chuckled. "There's always poetry to be recited."

I laughed with him. "And ballads to be sung."

"What's that one song your father loves, about the guy being shipped off to Australia after a woman sets him up for a theft? She's got eyes like diamonds?"

"'The Black Velvet Band.' One of Dad's favorites."

"We had some good times," he said with a sigh.

"You and my father got along well enough, after the initial breaking-in period. And you handled my sister like a champion."

"Sunny is a lot like you, and I had plenty of practice with you."

I snorted. "She's not like me. We're polar opposites."

"Just keep telling yourself that."

We reached the lodge and circled our way around to the guest rooms. From the outside, all the rooms had the same eerie glow from their single safety light, except the one Franco and Della had been assigned, which had a patchwork of wood keeping out the elements.

We knocked on the glass doors for two of the other rooms, looking for Dion or Benji, but both had their curtains drawn and nobody answered our knocks.

We checked in with Jessica and let her know we were going to find the generator next.

"Have you guys been outside this whole time?" she asked. "I heard noises, like water running in the pipes. I popped my head into the hallway, but I got too creeped out to leave the room." She waved one hand, fanning her face as her eyes welled up. "I think my blood pressure dipped. My vision got kind of distorted, and I thought I was going to faint."

"Are you okay now?" I stepped into the room and hugged her. "I'm sorry we left you."

"I'm okay," she said. "I got on the bed and Jeffrey walked on my back. It made me feel a lot better."

Christopher was still on the patio, in the rain. "You two stay here and hold down the home base," he said. "I'll check the generator and be right back."

I started to argue with him, to insist on going, but the look on Jessica's face convinced me to stay. At least the room was far less wet than the dark forest. It wasn't much warmer, due to the heat being off, but it was dry and came with a cat who could barely wait for me to sit down before climbing into my lap.

While we waited for Christopher's return, Jessica filled me in on home base operations. The local ranger, Rory, had been very helpful. The torrential downpour had caused not just one mudslide, but three of them in the area. Rory had surveyed the damages with a fly-over.

"The ranger has a helicopter?" I clapped my hands. "When are we getting rescued?"

"Don't get too excited. It's one of those remote-control things."

"A drone? Darn. A drone might be able to airlift Jeffrey, but that's all. And he wouldn't even appreciate it."

Jessica nodded knowingly. "He thinks riding in the car is bad. He would lose his mind over flying."

"But it would be adorable. Imagine him in a little rescue sling."

Jeffrey looked up from where he was curled on the bed and gave us suspicious eyes. He always knew when we were devising new ways to embarrass him.

Someone tapped on the patio door glass. Christopher had returned, and he had Dion with him.

"Look who I found," Christopher said. "The generator's fueled up and running fine, from what we can tell."

Dion ran his hand over his curly black hair and gave us a sheepish look. "We didn't know you three were coming back."

They stepped inside, and I was so happy to see another guest, I hugged Dion.

He backed away from me, looking confused. "Why are you being so nice? You should hate me right now, because of what my sister did to your car. Marie told us everything."

"You're not to blame for what Della did." I glanced over at Christopher, who was busy taking off his rain gear, then asked Dion, "Speaking of Della, have you heard from her? There were some mudslides on the road, and we're all worried about her getting home safely."

"Christopher told me," he said. "Della didn't even know about the mudslides. They must have happened behind her. She sent me a message about punishing Franco for making her worry about him."

"He's back in Misty Falls? She picked him up hitch-hiking after all?"

"Sounds like it." He leaned over the bed and gave Jeffrey a head pat. "Here's the fellow I've been hearing about. He is a cute one." Jeffrey twisted onto his back, inviting Dion to touch his tummy. Dion knew better than to fall into the trap, and stuck to the face.

"What about Benji?" I asked.

"He's probably asleep already," Dion said. "I saw him in his room about an hour ago, right after the power went off. He said he was a dead man walking. I think he meant he was tired. Benji always was an odd duck. When we were kids, he asked his parents to give him a curfew, so he could blame them when he left parties early."

He patted Jeffrey's head one more time, then walked to the door leading to the hallway. "I suppose I'll hit the hay as well, unless I could interest anyone in a nightcap, something special I brought up for celebrating." He grinned at Jessica. "You can always trust the owner of a bar to have a bottle of something good."

"Sure," she said. "If you have enough to share with all of us."

He said he did, and he wasn't kidding about it being good. When Dion returned with a bottle of vintage port, even Christopher was impressed.

Dion poured the dark red liquid into four tiny glasses and handed them out. I inhaled the scent deeply in preparation for tasting.

"Declared vintage," Christopher said as he inspected the bottle's label. "You must really like us."

Dion smiled proudly and explained to Jessica, "Only the finest blends from the winery's three estates are declared. They age beautifully. This one is thirty-three. A very good age. Seasoned and also young."

Jessica smiled at his not-so-subtle flirtations.

As for the vintage port, it was heavenly, and just sweet enough to be satisfying. To really understand the flavors, though, I would need a second glass.

The four of us loosened up with each sip, our faces lit by warm candle glow, and our hearts warmed by sharing funny stories about growing up in Misty Falls.

We all got drowsy and comfortable. Both of us women reclined on one bed, Christopher lay on the other, and Dion stretched out on the floor with some pillows and a cat who insisted that nobody else *ever* paid him any attention.

We fell asleep in those positions, in our clothes, and didn't wake up until first light, to the sound of a rooster crowing.

A rooster crowing?

Jessica groaned and pulled her pillow over her face. "Not funny," she said. "Who's making rooster noises?"

"Too early," grumbled Dion, still stretched out on the floor.

Christopher was already awake, doing yoga poses in front of the window.

The rooster crowed again, louder.

"Somebody hit the snooze button on that rooster," Jessica said.

"That's not a rooster," Christopher said. "You wouldn't believe me if I told you."

"It's your wild turkey family, come to call you back to your nesting grounds."

"Nice one," he said. "Get out of bed and come see for yourself."

CHAPTER 25

WE JOINED CHRISTOPHER at the open door just in time to see Benji run across our patio, jump on top of a boulder, and cry, "COCK-A-DOODLE DOO! I'm alive!"

He struck a comical pose with one hand on his head in the shape of a rooster's comb. His form was dark, silhouetted against a light blue sky. The storm clouds had rained themselves out overnight, and now countless birds chirped about the glory of spring.

"COCK-A-DOODLE DOO!"

Dion stepped out to talk to his friend. "Benji, dude, have you lost your mind?"

Benji shot us a wild-eyed look, grinning as if he'd just broken out of a cell. His brown hair frizzed in a messy halo, his glasses were askew, and he wore mismatched shoes under his too-short trousers.

He answered, "I lost my mind, and I feel great! Come with me, man. Let's watch the sun rise."

"The sun's already up." Dion turned to us. "He's snapped like this at least once before. He'll come around, but I should probably go have a chat with him."

"Go ahead," Christopher said. "We'll see you at breakfast, assuming there is one."

"Power's back on," Jessica reported. She flicked the room lights on and off. "That means we have hot water. Stormy, do you want the first shower?"

I told her to go ahead, and pulled out my laptop. Christopher returned to his room to get ready.

* * *

After a quick trip to the electrical room for the security company's phone number, I gave them a call.

The night's power outage was the perfect cover to get the information I needed. I knew the system ran on a battery backup, but pretended I didn't. The guy on the support line explained the backup system to me, then walked me through how to access the video feeds.

As I expected, the password was the same one Marie had given me for the network.

I thanked the guy—but not sweetly enough to rouse his suspicion—then got down to watching the footage I'd been interested in since the previous afternoon, when Marie had mentioned it.

The lodge had only three zones set up so far. One camera covered the gym, another the front lobby, and the third was the lower floor hallway—the one just outside my door.

I scrolled the feed back by sixty hours, to Sunday night, when we'd first arrived. Using the variable speed replay, I raced through footage until I got to midnight, when Dion had walked Jessica back to the room and kissed her.

After that, the hallway was empty for hours, until Butch and Franco showed up. I smiled at the appearance of Franco's novelty T-shirt on the video. With the lighting and resolution, it looked as though he wore a real tuxedo.

Franco looked drunk, his arm around Butch's shoulders as he leaned on him for support. His other arm swung wildly, beer spilling from the bottle in his hand. That explained the beer smell we'd detected in the hallway Monday morning.

Butch helped Franco into his room and was back out again within minutes, by himself. That happened at three o'clock in the morning. I backed up the footage to be sure.

I fast-forwarded to five o'clock, the time when Dion claimed he'd heard the sounds of a couple carrying on. Minutes after five, Butch appeared again at the end of the hall. He walked slowly down the hallway.

Was he sleepwalking? I was no expert, but he was moving unusually, taking small steps and rocking from side to side. He got to Franco and Della's door, and entered the room. Three minutes later he stumbled out—with Della. True to his description, she was wrapped around him, her legs around his waist and her body barely covered in a short nightgown.

They kissed for two minutes, then went back inside the room. He was out again within seconds, seemingly stunned, standing still. He slowly turned his head and looked directly at the camera.

I paused the video and studied his face. He looked miserable, and he also looked wide awake. I leaned in, the screen inches from my face, and replayed the footage.

Just then, someone banged on the patio door.

I slammed my laptop shut guiltily.

At the glass door stood the man I'd just been watching on my screen, only now his smooth head looked anything but shiny. His head was smeared with mud. His face was equally grimy, and so were his clothes.

I opened the door. "Butch, what's with the new look? Is that a mineral mask you're trying out for the spa?"

"Cold, cold, cold." He took small steps, barely able to lift his boots over the ridge of the door frame.

I grabbed his hand and helped him to the chair. "What happened?"

He mumbled that he didn't know what happened. His words jumbled together over his chattering teeth. He kept mentioning a rooster, how he'd woken up to a rooster and followed the sound.

"Butch, we need to get you warmed up. I'll get you into the tub, into hot water."

"No water," he said through chattering teeth. "Hell, no."

"You must be related to Jeffrey," I said. "That's exactly what he says about baths."

At the mention of his name, my curious boy jumped up onto the arm of the chair and sniffed the mud caked across Butch's brow.

I cranked up the room's thermostat. Butch was shivering and in rough shape, showing signs of mild hypothermia, but his breathing was strong and he didn't seem confused when I asked him where he was.

I started getting him out of his soaked and muddy clothes. His cuffs and collar were soaked, but the water-resistant outer shell of his jacket had kept his upper body dry. His jeans hadn't been so lucky.

Jessica finished her shower and came out of the bathroom to find me on my knees, tugging off Butch's jeans by the cuffs.

"Holy snickerdoodles," Jessica said. "Butch, you dirty old hound dog. You need to sign yourself up for a three-day workshop about keeping it in your pants. Keep waggling it around and you're going to get it confiscated."

Butch yelped and covered the front of his boxers with both hands.

"Jessica," I wheezed over my laughter. "This isn't what it looks like."

"That's what they all say." She grabbed the nearest thing—my colorful bathrobe—and pulled it on over her towel. "Why are you covered in mud?"

I grabbed the blankets from the beds and wrapped them around Butch while I explained to her what I knew, which wasn't much.

She got Butch a glass of water and apologized. "You can see why I jumped to conclusions," she said. "It's because of your misbehaving that this vacation has gone off the rails."

"I deserve everything bad that happens to me," he said glumly while flicking the drying mud off his head. "I should be dead of exposure. I should be dead right now, after spending the whole night outside."

Guiltily, I glanced at the empty bottle of vintage port on the dresser. "We thought everyone was accounted for last night," I said. "Marie didn't say you were missing."

Jessica brought a washcloth from the bathroom and started cleaning his face. "Let's hope you learned your lesson," she said. "Treat your wife better so she actually notices when your big, dumb, shiny head isn't on the pillow next to hers."

The color was returning to his face, and his words came out clear but soft. "Last thing I remember, I was checking on the generator. I was tired. Sometimes it comes on fast, especially in times of intense stress. I'm awake one minute and asleep the next."

"This could be dangerous," I said. "Somebody needs to be keeping an eye on you if you do this regularly."

"Like a sitter," Jessica said. "Or a nanny. But not a cute one that you would try to make out with, obviously."

"I don't need a babysitter," he grumbled. "I've got medication to manage my condition."

"About your medication," I said. "Hypothetically speaking, is it possible your bottle of pills has expired and lost potency? Or that somebody who handles your medication mixed up your wakefulness dose with a sleeping pill?"

I was careful not to spell it out for him, that his wife had been swapping his pills to get him out of the way, but he needed to be warned. I had to speak to Marie as well. If he'd died of exposure in the woods because of her actions, she could have been criminally liable.

"Marie swaps my pills from time to time," he said. "She thinks I don't notice, but I always do, and I play along. The secret to marriage is letting the other person think they're getting one over on you."

"And how's that working out for you?"

"Not great," he admitted.

Jessica leaned over Butch to examine the back of his head. "You've got a big goose egg back here. Did somebody whack you upside the head last night?"

He reached up and touched the red lump. "I might have slipped and fallen. It was awfully slippery out there in the rain."

She looked into his eyes. "Did Marie hit you?"

"Of course not," he snorted. "My sweet little Marie? She's as nice as pie."

I scoffed. Nice as pie? Pie had never wrestled me in the mud, but the man had survived a rough night, so I let it go.

* * *

We stopped by Butch and Marie's room, two doors down, so Butch could trade his blankets for clothes. He opened the door without using his keys.

Jessica frowned at the lock, then ran over to check our door, which she found was also unlocked.

She asked, "Don't hotel doors lock automatically?"

Butch had already gone into his room, so it was just the two of us in the hallway.

"Usually they do lock," I said. "Maybe the rules are different in a lodge. All the better for people to sneak in and out of each other's rooms."

I looked up at the dome covering the security camera.

"While you were showering, I got access to the hallway footage," I said.

"You sly fox," she said.

I told her about what I'd seen on the video, from her chaste kiss with Dion, to the kissing between Butch and Della, five hours later.

"At least it was just kissing," she said. "He could probably use that footage to exonerate himself."

I rubbed my chin and stared at the dome again. Maybe he already had. Could he have altered the footage to change the timestamps? No, he didn't strike me as the hacker type, and even if he were, it wouldn't have been easy.

"What do you think of Dion?" Jessica asked.

"What do *you* think of him?"

She looked down and pointed her toes together. "Stormy, I didn't tell you this before, but before Christmas, I had an appointment with Voula Varga, to talk about my love life. She sold me one of her dolls and promised a man would come into my life soon. A man who was so smart, his friends all called him a genius."

"Voula Varga was a con artist."

"Sure, but what if she really was psychic? They always say psychics can't see their own future anyway, so what happened to her doesn't mean she couldn't be right about other things."

"Benji is also a genius," I said with a smile. "Maybe Voula was right about you catching a genius, but you went for the wrong one."

She rolled her eyes, smiling. "Something about a man running around pretending to be a rooster doesn't do it for me. And why are his pants so short? Wasn't his company worth five million dollars?"

"That's why he was rich. He was working on his chemical formulas and not worrying about the length of his trousers."

"The way he was crowing out there, I think he might have been testing some of his chemical formulas on himself."

"Maybe he figured out what was in the Rainforest Delight. It could have been a natural fungus, like the ergot that grows in rye. That stuff has caused mass hysteria more than a few times throughout history."

"But it wasn't ergot," she said. "I've been reading up, and I didn't have the burning skin or convulsions."

"You seem okay now. How are you feeling?"

She smiled. "In the light of day, everything's great."

"How about at night?"

She didn't answer, and then Butch emerged from his room.

* * *

Christopher had beaten us to the dining room. He sat alone at a table by the windows.

"Dion's in the kitchen helping Marie," Christopher said. "Benji's still outside, communing with nature. Butch, if you hear a rooster crowing out there, it's your wife's friend Benji."

"Is that so? What a geek." Butch took a seat next to Christopher.

I found it odd that Butch didn't check in with his wife in the kitchen, but it was just the latest in a series of odd things, and I was finding it difficult to keep being shocked.

We had a carafe of coffee, plus ice water and grapefruit juice at the table, so all was well in my world.

Jessica broke the morning's news to Christopher. "Your cousin Butch decided to earn his Boy Scout badge for sleeping in the freezing rain without a tent."

Christopher frowned. "They give badges for that? It seems a bit irresponsible."

Butch guffawed, then told Christopher about his cold night sleeping in the woods. He was showing off the big bump on the back of his head when Benji Biggs came running into the dining room, gasping for breath.

Jessica and I exchanged a glance. *The rooster was back.*

Benji didn't crow, though.

Still panting, he exclaimed, "He's dead!" He leaned forward, his hands on his knees. "Franco is dead."

CHAPTER 26

THERE ARE THREE things you need to know about the Darwin Awards. First, they are only awarded posthumously. Second, nobody wants to get one. Third, originality and style count, so simple stupidity isn't enough to make one a winner.

Personally, I never liked the idea of mocking those whose terrible ideas got them killed and thus removed from the human gene pool. No matter how rash, they were still people. However, if a new Darwin Awards list happens to come across my inbox, I'll give it a scan.

Unusual deaths make us curious, thanks to self-preservation. We make thousands of choices every day, and we hope they're the right choices. Only through our shared stories—even the silly ones we send around by email—do we learn about other people's choices and consequences.

I may enjoy a superior smirk at the idea of some fool using a lighter to check for a gas leak, but I will read the whole list in earnest, filing away facts, just in case. You never know when you might need to steal the metal cables from an elevator, and it's a good tip to not attempt this while inside the elevator box that's held up by those same cables.

When Benji showed us pictures he'd taken of Franco Jerico's body on the ledge, wearing that silly tuxedo-print T-shirt, I feared Franco had done something worthy of a nomination for the Darwin Awards. He certainly was dressed for it.

I stood back from the group while Butch, Christopher, and Jessica comforted Benji and pressed him for more details.

His story came out in spurts. He'd been on his walk, enjoying nature, when he heard some crows making a racket. He peered over the edge of a steep crag and spotted Franco on a ledge, on his back, facing up.

He thought Franco was joking around, but then he saw what the crows had been squawking over. In tears, Benji described how he'd thrown rocks at the birds to drive them away. He ran straight back to the lodge to get help bringing Franco inside.

"But you can't move the body," I said.

Everyone turned and stared at me as though I was a monster. They all assumed it was an accident. Apparently, I was the only paranoid person thinking the mountain ledge could be a crime scene.

"He'll get picked to the bones," Butch said. "We can't leave a man out there."

The others murmured in agreement.

Christopher had Benji's phone, and was examining the photographs. "He must have fallen, maybe hit his head. Is that dark spot around his head blood, or just a shadow?" He tried to show Jessica for a second opinion, but she covered her mouth and stepped back.

"Might have been a cougar," Butch said. "They sneak up behind you and then it's one quick bite to the spine." He gave Benji's shoulder a soft pat. "It would have been quick and painless."

Benji took his glasses off and rubbed his eyes. "Franco loved animals. He always talked about owning exotic pets, like snakes or tigers. I can see him now, trying to make friends with a cougar." He choked back a sob. "You idiot. Franco, why'd you have to get yourself killed? You had so much to live for."

Jessica sat next to Benji and put her arm around him.

Christopher came over to me. "We need to call the police, and someone has to break the news to Dion and Marie."

"You call it in, and I'll talk to those two."

He nodded appreciatively. "You always were better than me at breaking bad news."

"You're the good news guy."

"We made a great team." He glanced at the door to the kitchen. "Good luck in there."

I thanked him and slipped quietly into the kitchen.

Dion was smiling as he laid slabs of streaky bacon on the grill. He said to Marie, "Rule number one? I know that already. Never fry bacon naked."

Marie laughed. "Rule number one of being a chef is you have to get all your ingredients set out before you start cooking. It's called *mise en place*. That's French for *everything in its place*."

"More like French for *boring*. You've gotta loosen up, girl. Chillax. That's chill plus relax."

Marie stopped stirring her pancake batter when she saw me standing there. We hadn't spoken since we'd tried to talk to her through the door of the honeymoon suite, and she didn't look pleased to see my face.

"Everything's under control in here," she said tersely. "If you're starving, go ahead and take that fruit platter out."

Dion looked up from the grill and asked, "Have you ever had pancakes with bacon cooked right into them? You'll die when you taste these."

He took the bowl from Marie and poured strips of oblong pancakes over the crisp bacon, then wiped the edge of the bowl with his finger and licked it.

"Interesting," he said to Marie. "These are gluten-free?"

"Mostly rice flour," she said. "It's my own recipe."

My throat tightened. I had to tell her that the friend she'd made pancakes for was dead. There was no way to make it easy, but I could make it fast.

"Dion, Marie, I'm sorry, but I have some terrible news."

Dion pointed his spatula at me. "My sister has returned!"

"Not that I know of. This news concerns Franco."

Marie reached for an enormous knife and used it to skewer a whole cantaloupe. "Tell Franco he's not welcome for breakfast until he apologizes and pays for the broken patio door."

"He should definitely pay for that," Dion agreed.

"Flip those pancakes," Marie said. "The batter bubbles are popped."

Neither of them seemed terribly concerned about their friend, but I pressed forward and broke the news as gently as I could.

While I talked, Marie stared at me in disbelief. She kept asking me to repeat myself. Dion repeatedly asked where the body was.

I answered their questions, giving the same limited amount of information over and over.

Once it seemed the news had sunk in, I said, "Christopher is talking to the police. They'll inform Della." I looked at her brother, who stood as still as a statue while the pancakes smoked on the grill. "Dion, someone should be with her when she gets the news. Could you call a family member who's in town?"

He reached for his phone, then put it away. "I need a minute," he said. "Poor Della."

"Poor Della?" Marie clutched the sides of the stone-topped prep table, her knuckles turning white. "Poor Della?"

Dion gave her a confused look. "We'll get through this, Marie. Everything's going to be okay."

She gripped the table as though she was trying to pick it up. In an eery, otherworldly tone, Marie said, "She killed him. Della murdered Franco and then left the rest of us to pick up the pieces."

"My little sister did no such thing!" Dion exclaimed. "She's innocent. She's just a girl. A sweet, innocent girl."

"You're blind," Marie said through clenched teeth. "She killed him, and we're going to find the evidence to put her away. Stormy Day, I'm officially hiring you as my detective. You're going to prove that *sweet, innocent Della* is responsible for this."

"Easy now," I said. "We're all upset, but accusing people isn't going to help."

"Stormy's right," Dion said. "Knowing Franco, he probably did this to himself."

"He wasn't suicidal," Marie said. "Not like Benji, with his morbid talk last night about his last will and testament." She gave me a hopeful look. "Are they sure it's Franco's body out there and not Benji's?"

"I told you, Benji's the one who found him. He was out walking and saw the body."

"Outside?" Marie looked so confused. I would probably have to tell her everything all over again in a few minutes.

Dion looked straight at me. "My sister didn't hurt Franco. She loved him. They were going to get married."

"And you weren't happy about that," I said. "Were you?"

His lips moved, but no words came out.

"Your pancakes are burning," I said.

He stared down at the grill as though he had no idea where he was. Marie pried the spatula from his hand.

"Dion, I didn't mean it," she said. "Della cared for him, in her own way."

"What's that supposed to mean?" His usual joking demeanor was gone, replaced by something colder. "My sister's just a kid, with a bright future. You always put her down because you know she'll be a star, and you're a failure."

She recoiled as though slapped. "Is that how you really feel?"

He shot me a guilty look, then apologized to Marie. "I have a big, stupid mouth," he concluded.

"We're still friends until the end," she said. "Even if there's only three of us left. Friends forever."

The door hinges squeaked behind me as Butch and Benji came in. Butch walked toward his wife with open arms.

She stepped back, avoiding his embrace. She asked Benji, "Is it true?"

Benji's mouth twitched into a tight frown. "Franco is dead."

Marie let out the saddest wail I've ever heard. She pushed past her husband and launched herself into Benji's arms.

* * *

Butch took over in the kitchen, starting with fresh pancakes. He said that no matter what happened next, we would need food, even if it wasn't fancy.

We sat in small groups in the dining room, solemnly discussing what needed to be done next.

Jessica spoke to the local ranger again, about getting a mountain rescue team for the body.

"Bad news," she said after she ended the call. "I couldn't get a timeframe for the road, and we're on our own as far as retrieving the you-know-what." She was pale, and struggling to not be sick. Avoiding the word *body* seemed to help.

Christopher relayed the details from his conversation with Officer Peggy Wiggles. She wanted to talk to Benji and take his statement using a video call on his laptop. We were not to disturb the body, but she did want us to protect the scene from wild animals by covering it with tarps and taking turns keeping watch.

Butch didn't like the sound of that. "If there's an angry cougar out there, I'm not going to sit around a tarp waiting for a snap on my neck. Especially not after whatever might have snuck up on me last night."

Christopher asked me, "What did Finnegan say?"

"My father? I haven't talked to him."

"You can use my phone." He held his phone out as though making a dare.

I declined the offer. "No need to worry my father, or get him overexcited. Besides, there's a handy version of him inside my brain, giving advice."

"You always were Daddy's girl," he said. His voice had a confrontational tone. "No other guy could ever come close."

I glanced over at Jessica and Butch. They were preoccupied, and had missed Christopher's attempt to lure me into a fight.

His timing was perfect, as always. We were in the midst of a terrible, stressful situation, and naturally Christopher felt powerless. Strange as it was, making me angry was his coping mechanism. I'd never seen it so clearly before.

I crossed my arms and kept breathing calmly, refusing to bite into his bait.

Butch got up from his chair and walked around to put his hands on Christopher's shoulders.

"Those roads might be blocked for days," Butch said to his cousin. "Tarp or no tarp, we're not going to take shifts sitting next to a decaying corpse. What would a couple of Boy Scouts do?"

Christopher answered, "My mother wouldn't let me join Boy Scouts."

"Then what would your mother do in this situation? Let's say she's at a resort and there's a dead body."

"She would call the concierge and demand he do something."

Butch patted Christopher's shoulders. "As the owner of this establishment, I hereby appoint you the *concierge*. You're coming with me to get the body and carry it back here."

"But the police said—"

"No excuses. We'll make a Boy Scout out of you yet. Meet me at the trekking hut in ten minutes."

Butch left before Christopher could wiggle his way out of it.

Christopher gave me a pleading look. "He can't be serious."

I told him, "You'd better wear a bright jacket again, so nobody mistakes you for a turkey."

* * *

While the Fairchild boys went off to get the body, Dion and Marie started emptying the lodge's second walk-in cooler. Benji got the network password and returned to his room for the video call on his laptop.

I took Jessica back to our room. She wasn't feeling well and preferred the bathroom, where she could sit on the cool tiles.

She called out from the bathroom, "I don't know how you handled seeing the you-know-whats that you saw. Just the idea is making me…"

"You'll feel better soon. And didn't I tell you that being sick is normal? Everybody throws up. I've decorated the snow at crime scenes more than once."

She groaned and ran more water.

I sat on the bed and played with Jeffrey, glad to have my stowaway cat there for company.

There's nothing quite like an unexpected death to make you feel as if you're falling into a pit with no end in sight.

If there were a hole through the center of the earth, falling to the other side would take around forty minutes. A person traveling through this theoretical tunnel would have to grab onto something quick when they popped out the other side, or they'd fall right back again and keep looping, keep falling.

An hour after learning of Franco's death, I couldn't shake the sensation I was in that tunnel, falling and falling again.

* * *

Jessica had just climbed into the tub for a bath when my phone rang.

The woman on the line got right to the point. "How well do you know this Benjamin Biggs fellow?"

"Peggy?"

"Of course it's me. I haven't spoken with you in two days and I missed the sound of your voice."

"Some people say I have a not-unpleasant singing voice. I was hoping to belt out a few more tunes in the lodge's karaoke lounge, but this whole death thing has put a damper on the festivities." I quickly added, "Not that I'm complaining. Franco's having a much worse vacation."

"He didn't look so good in the photos Mr. Biggs sent me. What do you know about him? He says he didn't touch the body, but I've got some doubts. Can he be trusted?"

"Benji? I'm not sure I could make that assessment."

"Would you let him look after your cat?"

"No."

"Just as I suspected. First his company's smoothie mix sends the town into a frenzy, and now he's turning up bodies. Trouble follows this man wherever he goes."

"I only said I wouldn't let him look after my cat because he's odd, in that absent-minded-professor way, and he'd probably forget."

"What's his state of mind been like over the last two days?"

"Up and down. He played a joke on his friends, but then he made some comments that suggested he was considering suicide. Maybe he's got a mood disorder. This morning, before he found the body, he was running around pretending to be a rooster."

There was a stunned silence, then Peggy asked, "Have you observed him clucking like a chicken?"

"Not personally. He was making rooster sounds. Cock-a-doodle-doo."

"I don't like the sound of that."

"Neither did Jessica this morning. But before we arrest the guy, have you looked at the girlfriend? Della tore out of here in a hurry last night, and Marie's suspicious of her."

"That's not good. You need to manage that situation before folks up there start lighting torches and grabbing pitchforks."

"Everyone else is leaning toward it being an accident. Either he fell, or a cougar got him. Franco wasn't a big guy. He wouldn't have stood a chance against a wild animal attack."

Peggy asked if I'd seen any wild animals during my stay so far. I hadn't, but we talked over all the details I did know, for a solid hour. I had to charge my phone partway through.

The more she heard, the more frustrated she sounded. "Stormy, I'm busier than a one-eyed cat watching two mouse holes, but I've got half a mind to lace up my hiking boots and climb that mountain."

"Hiking boots? That must be your subtle way of letting me know the roads won't be cleared any time soon."

"If I had better news on the road situation, I wouldn't be asking you to start an investigation on my behalf."

"An investigation?" I swallowed hard. Franco's death wasn't a simple research job like the ones I'd been doing for Logan. If I accepted the case, my work would be scrutinized by everyone at the Misty Falls Police Department. If I screwed up, nobody would let me forget it. And if I did a great job, that could be even worse.

I mumbled, "I suppose… but then again…"

"You sound like a woman trying to talk herself into something and out of it at the same time, like me, when my friends were all playing cops and robbers with their grandchildren, and I decided my late-in-life calling was playing cops and robbers for real."

"Peggy, I want to help, but you should know I don't have my license, or even half the hours."

"I can't think of a better way for you to get your hours."

"Then I'm on the case. I'll start working on a timeline. The last person to see him was Della. What's she saying?"

"That you're a real mean five-letter-word who blocked in her car and got what she had coming." Peggy snorted. "Don't worry. I didn't believe her about that. But I do believe her when she says she has no idea what happened to Franco after she left the room yesterday morning."

"Poor girl."

"Don't you worry about Della. I'll keep an eye on her. As for your investigation, let's keep this between us for now. Find out anything and everything you can, within reason."

"Anything and everything," I repeated. "Within reason."

She ended the call before I could clarify what she meant by *within reason*.

Butch and Christopher would be back soon with the body, and Peggy had mentioned her suspicions about it having been compromised.

I pulled out my laptop to review the notes from my online course in the basics of forensic pathology.

Sometimes it's better to beg forgiveness than ask permission.

CHAPTER 27

EVERYONE'S GOT SECRETS, big or small. Some secrets lurk beneath the human heart, some are written in password-protected computer diaries, and others are kept in plastic canisters inside the bathroom medicine cabinet.

I tapped on the door to Benji's room. "How are things going in there?"

No answer.

I knocked again, harder. "Benji, I'm worried about you. It's okay if you don't feel like talking, but could you make a noise to let me know you're alive? Give me one of your now-famous rooster noises."

The door opened. Benji hadn't changed his clothes since breakfast, and smelled of body odor. His glasses were so smudged by fingerprints, I was surprised he could see through them.

With no trace of humor, he said, "I don't usually go around making rooster noises."

He didn't invite me in, but I went in anyway, coughing and pointing at my throat. "Water," I croaked.

He stood aside and let me into his washroom. Still coughing, I closed the door and turned on the taps.

I'd made some notes before dropping in, and my first goal was to see if he was taking any medications that would explain his mood swings. Just like a bad party guest, I rifled through his things. Benji's shaving bag contained a razor, products for sensitive skin, vitamin D, a crinkled and empty tube of foot cream, but no prescription medicine.

I left the washroom holding a full glass of water. He was trying to tidy the room, stuffing clothes into a suitcase.

"Don't clean on my account," I said. "Jessica's getting tired of my company, so I thought I'd kill some time by checking in on you." Uninvited, I took a seat on the room's chair, positioned with its back to the patio door.

He shot me a wary look and continued packing. I fought the urge to confiscate his smudged glasses and clean them for him.

"You must be shaken up," I said. "Seeing a body is shocking, and it can play tricks on your head. I've been through it a couple of times myself."

"My head's okay," he said. "I wanted to pack anyway, so I can leave the minute I'm able."

"Did you drive up? Which car is yours?"

He slowly folded a shirt while staring at my mouth instead of my eyes. Benji wasn't an eye-contact sort of guy, so that wasn't out of the ordinary for him.

"You're asking a lot of questions," he said. "Just like that cop. She's acting like this is a murder. Now you're in here asking me things. You must be after something."

"I want the same thing everyone does." I sipped my water slowly, giving the impression I had all day.

"I want to understand what happened. What possesses a man to throw a lamp through a sliding glass door, and then wander into the forest alone? Franco must have had a reason for going out there. You're his friend. What do you think happened? Did he have a fight with Della, or did someone call and tell him something upsetting?"

Benji kept staring at my mouth. "I couldn't possibly know what happened," he said. "I wasn't there. We were all at breakfast."

"How about later in the day? You didn't see Franco when you were on your way back from snowshoeing with me and Jessica?"

"No." He turned his focus up to my eyes briefly, then down to the floor.

"You're a smart guy. Do you have any theories about what happened?"

He met my gaze and held it, his eyes piercing behind the smudged lenses. "No."

"Was it always just the four of you who were best friends? Was there anyone else? Someone who didn't get invited to the reunion?"

He whipped his head and looked out at the patio. "Someone else could be up here. They could have done everything." His voice betrayed his excitement about this new idea. "It wasn't one of us."

"Who's out there, Benji? Who popped into your head just now?"

"Nobody." His posture crumpled. He sat on the edge of the bed, looking down at his feet, at the hole in one of his socks. "For a second, I had a person in mind, but it was vague, like the scary killer in a slasher movie. There's nobody out there. Nobody with a name."

"The gang was always just the four of you. Like the four tree frogs on your Rainforest Delight."

"We weren't exactly popular."

"I bet you guys had some fun together."

"We did. We were so young when we built that treehouse." Benji smiled at the memory.

With patience, I asked him about those early days.

He told me how Marie's parents had supplied the lumber, and he'd drawn up a blueprint for the treehouse, but Dion and Franco had been too busy clowning around to follow the plans. They were more interested in banging nails into things than getting wood cut to the right length.

The treehouse was between their four homes, and they met up constantly, without having to call each other. "You showed up whenever you wanted to be alone, or have some company, and it always worked out," he said wistfully. "We kept a bunch of our books in there, and sometimes other kids went inside, but they didn't wreck anything because they were afraid of Franco."

"Franco used to intimidate other kids? Like a bully?"

Benji abruptly got to his feet. "Thanks again for stopping in." He reached for the two books on his nightstand. He chucked the sci-fi paperback into his suitcase, then handed me the other one—the thick book about criminal code that I'd loaned him. "Thanks for the book. I found it very interesting. I read some chapters during the power outage. I'll finish packing, and maybe I'll meet you and Jessica in the recreation room to play a board game later."

I accepted the book, but wasn't ready to go. Buying time, I flipped it open to the middle page.

The book let out a very loud, very telltale crack.

Benji flinched.

"That was the spine cracking," I said. "This book has never been opened, which means you just told me a lie." I crossed my legs and my arms.

He got flustered immediately. Nobody likes being called on their lies, especially not people who desperately want to be adored by others.

Rubbing his forehead, he hyperventilated, seemingly on the verge of swearing, then spat out, "Franco was trying to blackmail me."

"Was he after one of your chemical formulas?"

"No. Money."

A moment of silence passed. "Did Franco have something on you? Some crime from your youth? Is that why you were interested in the criminal code book? To see how bad whatever you did was?"

By Benji's stunned expression, I knew I was on the right track.

His voice cracking, Benji said, "I didn't look in the book. I decided to pay him, even though I didn't do anything wrong. I'm innocent. If people would listen to me, they'd know."

I uncrossed my legs. "I'm right here, and I don't have anywhere else to go. I promise to listen with an open mind."

I relaxed my posture, leaned back, and nodded to let him know he could unburden himself without interruption.

He took a deep breath. "Franco was wrong, but he still thought he could get some money before it was all gone. He said he knew about my old car, the Plymouth. He came to my room on the first night, not long before your cat wandered in."

He stopped talking, so I gently asked, "What happened with the car? At dinner, the story was that you'd smashed it into the wall of your garage while parking. Is there more to the accident?"

"What happened wasn't what Franco thought, I swear. But he might have told someone else." He paused and pushed his smudged glasses up his nose. "What do you charge for investigations?"

"I'm not taking new cases at the moment."

"I just need to know one thing. What happened to Butch last night? He says it was no big deal, but he has that lump on his head. He's hiding something, or he knows something. Someone tried to get rid of him."

"He's too tough to get rid of easily. What did you see outside yesterday evening, during the storm?"

"Nothing. I was right here in my room. All night. I have proof." He pulled his laptop out of his suitcase, tapped away for a moment, then turned it to show me a video of himself. The sound was off, but he appeared to be alone, talking to his laptop.

"Here's my alibi," he said. "I started making a video, but then I got distracted when the power went out. The laptop switched to battery backup, and the recording ran for hours. If somebody was outside last night, knocking out Butch, this proves it wasn't me."

He fast-forwarded through a couple of hours of himself sitting on the bed reading a paperback sci-fi novel, using his phone as a flashlight. He slowed the video to regular speed and zoomed in on the narrow gap between the curtains covering the patio door. A face appeared in the darkness. My face. It was me, knocking on doors the night before, after the mudslide.

"I'm your alibi," I said. "That's pretty solid. It's too bad you were hiding in here and didn't answer the door. We might have stopped whoever it was before they whacked Butch and got to Franco."

Benji hung his head. "I know. I feel terrible."

"Della was already gone by that point, so that clears her, unless she hit Butch on the back of the head before she left, maybe suspecting that he told Franco about the two of them kissing." I shook my head. No, that wasn't likely. She'd left in the late afternoon, so it would have been a long time for someone to be knocked out in the storm, even a tough guy like Butch.

Benji said, "Marie hates her husband right now."

"Sure, but Butch also could have been fighting with Franco, or even Dion."

"Or Christopher."

"My Christopher? He was with me in the car, then we checked the caves…" And then he went out to the generator by himself. But why would Christopher hit Butch? It made no sense. A good investigator keeps an open mind, but that was just too far open.

"How does this work?" Benji asked. "Do I pay you by the hour, or by the day? Name your fee. Someone should get a piece of Biggs Foods before the lawyers rip it apart."

"Let me think about it." I got up to leave.

"I need you," Benji pleaded. "You and that cop both think someone murdered Franco. You're already investigating me as a suspect, so let me pay you to look wider."

I pursed my lips and cursed myself for being so obvious. Benji was a genius, after all. "How did you know?"

"You're good, but I heard the click of the medicine cabinet when you were in my bathroom. Before that, I heard the high-pitched ring of your phone through the wall, right after I finished my video call with the police. It was Peggy Wiggles phoning you, right?"

I moved closer to the door.

Benji pleaded, "Help me."

"I don't know if I *can* help you."

"You can't make things worse. Please. I'm not good at asking for help, but here I am, asking."

Time passed. I heard my father in my head. *Stormy, it never hurts to have one more friend. He* typically used it as his excuse for flirting with every woman he encountered, but it was still good advice.

Benji's eyes looked so sad behind his smudged glasses.

"Sure," I said with a long exhale. "But you can't tell anyone I'm working for you, and I don't guarantee results."

He rummaged through his suitcase for his checkbook, then wrote me a check with no dollar amount. I accepted the check with no intention of cashing it. I was already working for Peggy, and I would only pretend to be working with Benji to ensure his cooperation.

"Benji, is there anything else I should know? Any information you've been holding back, for any reason?"

He looked me squarely in the eyes and said, "No."

I thanked him and let myself out. In the quiet hallway, my hand trembled as I reached for the door handle to my room. I'd remained calm under pressure while questioning Benji, but it had not been easy. When he'd asked about Peggy, I'd fought a powerful urge to flee.

Benji seemed harmless on the surface, but he had lied to me at least three times. I'd caught him on the lie about the book, but he still had information he wasn't telling me. Both times I'd asked him about theories, he'd answered while looking me directly in the eyes instead of his usual habit of focusing on my mouth or the floor.

Had I just been alone in a room with a killer? It wouldn't have been the first time.

I let myself into my room so I could make notes and report back to Officer Wiggles.

The curtains were drawn to block out the afternoon sunshine, and Jessica was under the covers in her bed. Without waking her, I left the big book with my other things, checked on Jeffrey, then quietly let myself out again.

What next? Christopher wasn't back yet with the body, or he would have messaged me.

The hallway was quiet, except for a sound similar to water trickling. The sound was coming from down the hall, from the open door leading to the room that had been Franco and Della's.

CHAPTER 28

FROM A DISTANCE, the sound of fingers tapping on a computer keyboard mimics the sound of trickling water.

I stopped by the half-open door of Franco and Della's room and listened.

There were no voices, just the sound of fingertips on a keyboard.

Somebody was up to something. Quietly, I pushed open the door and crept in.

Dion sat with his back to me, at the room's desk, which was pushed up against the wood covering the smashed door. He was focused on the laptop screen and didn't acknowledge me.

I read over his shoulder, scanning an archived article from the Misty Falls Mirror. The date wasn't visible, but the headline was clear: Police Admit No Leads in Mysterious Hit and Run.

I didn't need to read the text to know what the article was about. I'd been seven years old, young enough that my father was reluctant to share all the details of cases, but old enough to ask him questions. I wanted to know—and the whole town wanted to know—if the local police would ever solve the case.

A male victim had been struck while crossing the street. The driver of the vehicle fled the scene, scraping other cars and even knocking over a mailbox.

Luckily for the pedestrian victim, his injuries weren't fatal. He suffered a broken leg, and that would've been the end of it, but a local reporter seemed bent on turning the investigation—or lack of one—into a huge scandal. As a child, I was too naive to understand the issues. One night, I told my father that he could make the whole thing go away if he would just track down the bad person driving the car. He paced the kitchen for a while, then promised me ice cream for a month if I never brought up the topic again.

The ice cream bribe had worked, and I hadn't thought much about the case until seeing Dion's screen.

Accompanying the article was a photo of the pedestrian, with the same dark eyes and curly hair as Dion.

"That was your father," I said. "I didn't know."

Dion jerked around, startled. He closed the laptop. The computer's lid was covered in stickers and rhinestones, spelling out the name *Della* in swirly cursive.

"And your father was the investigator," he said. "I try not to think about it, so even when I heard your last name was Day, I didn't put it together until now."

"My father was troubled by that case. It was the first time he brought his work home with him. We had boxes of statements in the living room."

He scoffed. "For all the good it did."

"My father did everything he could to track down that driver," I said. "It was a terrible time for him."

"Was it? Did he go on painkillers for his broken leg and get hooked on the drugs? Did he have lingering nerve pain the doctors couldn't treat, pain they said was all in his head? Did your father drink himself to death within a year? Because mine did."

"I'm so sorry."

He looked at the laptop as he traced the rhinestone letters with his finger. "Don't be sorry. It wasn't all bad. My father wasn't that great. When he took that final dose, everyone's life started getting better. My mother remarried, and then Della was born. In a way, my father died so that she could live."

"You seem to really love your sister. How is she doing? How did she take the news?"

"She's not returning anyone's phone calls, so the sooner we can get ourselves out of here, the better."

"Do you need some help packing up her things?" I glanced around the gloomy room. In her haste to leave, she'd left not just her laptop, but also clothes, toiletries, and platform shoes. In light of her boyfriend being dead, she probably wouldn't care about any of those things for a while, but getting them to her was the right thing to do.

Dion thanked me, and said he could use my help.

Together, we went over the entire room and bathroom, picking up all the items that belonged to either Della or Franco. We used the room's pillowcases as temporary bags.

While we tidied, we talked about growing up in Misty Falls. I mentioned Benji's blueprints for the treehouse, and Dion relaxed with a big laugh.

"He wanted to put in a working elevator," Dion said. "You should have seen his schematics, with pulleys and levers and counterweights. The guy was already over-thinking everything. If we could get him to laugh and lighten up once a week, it was a miracle."

"It sounds like he was careful, even as a kid."

Dion smiled as he slid Della's laptop into the pillowcase. "He was always wound up so tight. You know how Superman squeezes a lump of coal into a diamond? We used to joke that one day Benji would get a C-minus on a science exam, and there would be a little crackle sound, then he'd be gone, and there would just be a diamond sitting on his chair."

I laughed. "That doesn't sound like the kind of guy who would drive his car into the wall of his garage. What year did he do that, anyway?"

Dion's expression turned serious. "I don't remember."

"Doesn't matter. We all do dumb stuff when we're kids." I laughed. "I was a cheerleader. You should have seen me and Jessica in those days." I gave him a warm smile. "She seems to like you."

He grinned and looked away. "She's really nice."

We finished packing up the things, and I reached for the pillowcase with the laptop. "You'll be coming in my car back into town, right? Jessica will probably insist. I've got room in my bag, so I'll pop this in there for you."

He looked as though he might object, but I backed my way out of the room quickly.

* * *

Back in my room, I sat cross-legged by the door so I didn't disturb Jessica.

Della didn't have her computer password protected, which I had expected, given that her brother had been on it.

I was able to pull up the history for the computer and check the files that had been opened recently.

The Misty Falls newspaper article had been accessed recently by Dion, probably from the same link in the browser history that I could see. The article about the hit-and-run had been accessed first on Sunday night, with that laptop.

At the same time, someone had been going through photos of the clubhouse gang, in their youth. The laptop had an archive of photos from before Della was born, so either it was actually Franco's laptop or the couple shared it.

Except for the gleaming metallic braces on her teeth, the Marie in the photos looked the same as the Marie at the lodge. She had her brown hair in a ponytail and wore glasses in the style of the day. She wore a pair of large sweatpants in several of the pictures. I could understand how she'd earned the nickname of Monsterpants.

Dion had a big smile and wore his curly hair longer in those days, fanning out in a wide oval. Benji wore too-short trousers in every picture, and sported a haircut that looked as if his mother had put a bowl on his head and snipped around it. Franco always stared defiantly into the camera lens with one eye, the other covered by a dark forelock of hair.

I couldn't tell how long each photo had been looked at, but I could see through the history on the slideshow application that the ones accessed for a larger view all contained a boxy, dark blue car—Benji's Plymouth Volaré. It wasn't the sexiest, its shape resembling the police cruisers on the road in those days, but the kids seemed to enjoy posing in or on top of the vehicle, even decorating it for parades.

Benji's Plymouth was absent from all photos dated after the unsolved hit-and-run accident. From that point, the kids posed with a station wagon driven by Marie.

I closed the laptop and ran my finger over Della's rhinestones.

I'd interrupted Dion before he'd gotten to the photos with the car, which meant that he might not have put together the puzzle of what Franco was trying to blackmail Benji over.

Whether it was true or not, Franco, or someone else using Della's laptop, had connected the hit-and-run of Dion's father with the disappearance of Benji's car.

When I returned to Misty Falls, I would need to speak to my father about the accident, but in the meantime, I would keep it to myself. If Dion found out while we were all trapped at the lodge, no good would come of him accusing Benji of hitting his father.

On the positive side, now I understood what was going through Franco's head on Sunday night.

On the negative side, the facts didn't look so good for Benji, who had a powerful motivation to get rid of his blackmailer.

Before I could dwell on my discovery too long, my phone buzzed with an incoming message.

Christopher was letting me know they were back with the body.

I quickly stuffed Della's things into my suitcase and pulled out a cardigan to wear inside the walk-in cooler.

245

CHAPTER 29

IF YOU NEED to store a corpse without freezing it, the optimal temperature is between 36°F and 39°F. Not so coincidentally, this is the same range at which you'd keep your home refrigerator, to prevent spoilage of pork chops and other meats.

If you won't be getting to your pork chops or your corpses for a long time, you'll want to go for negative temperature storage, at 14°F or colder. That'll freeze your stored items and seriously slow down decomposition.

The Fairchild cousins were preparing to load the body of Franco Jerico into a 37°F cooler when I arrived in the kitchen.

Butch looked up at me and deadpanned, "A good friend will help you move, but it takes family to help you move a body."

Christopher gave me a pained look. "Butch has been practicing that line for the last half hour."

"How'd it go, other than the bad jokes?"

Christopher answered, "We didn't see any cougars, but the birds followed us all the way back to the lodge, flitting from branch to branch and cawing. I felt like I was in an Edgar Allen Poe story."

"On the bright side, you've both earned your body-moving Boy Scout badges. Good job getting him back here in one piece." I reached for the edge of the blue tarp covering the body, then paused. "He is still in one piece, right?"

They assured me he was. They'd used a stretcher from the safety supplies in the trekking hut and strapped him to it for the hike back. Once they reached the lobby of the lodge, they loaded him onto Marie's rolling kitchen cart, then wheeled him into the kitchen on the makeshift gurney.

The secondary walk-in cooler had been emptied of food supplies in preparation for its temporary use as a morgue. Christopher opened the silver door, but his cousin seemed reluctant to wheel the body into the chilly space.

I asked Butch, "What's the matter? You got him this far. Are those last ten feet too cold, or too creepy for you?"

He answered, "More like the payment on that piece of equipment is too recent. It was a custom job. The manufacturing alone was a fortune, let alone the installation."

I patted him on the shoulder. "The cops aren't going to take the cooler as evidence. We'll put that extra tarp underneath, to cover the floor, but the whole reason for refrigerating him is so that he won't putrefy and leak fluids all over."

At the word *putrefy*, Butch had already started fleeing the kitchen.

Christopher didn't look so eager to hear about leaking corpse fluids, either.

"Let's wheel him in," I told Christopher. "The guy's not going to get up and walk himself into the morgue."

With his lips pressed tightly shut, Christopher took hold on his side and we rolled the body in.

We stood inside the walk-in cooler, the tarp-covered form between us. We looked at each other in silence. Butch hadn't returned and likely wouldn't. I pulled on the warm cardigan I'd brought with me.

Christopher said, "I feel like we should do something."

"And we will. Help me get the tarp off. We'll check the body for signs of trauma and try to determine the cause of death."

Christopher stared at me in apparent horror. "I meant maybe we should say a prayer."

"Good idea," I said. "You pray while I check the corpse for bullet holes, entry wounds, or ligatures. Pray he doesn't have one of those cadaver spasms and give me a heart attack."

He stepped back, eyes wide as he watched me unfasten and remove the tarp. Seeing Christopher's horror had a stabilizing effect on me. I felt more capable in comparison to him, and more confident by the minute.

Franco wore the same clothes I'd seen him in Sunday night, jeans and a black T-shirt with a screen-printed tuxedo design on the front. A visual inspection of the front of the shirt and jeans revealed no signs of blood or breaks in the fabric.

I asked Christopher, "Was he like this when you found him?"

"Dead? Yes."

"No, smarty-pants. I meant his body position. See how his right leg isn't flat, how the knee is bent? And the left arm is bent as well. Was the surface of the ledge flat, or were there rocks propping up these two limbs?"

He pulled out his phone and showed me the photos they'd taken as evidence before moving the body. The surface was flat and didn't explain the body's condition.

I gently grasped the left arm and tugged it. The whole body shifted, but the arm didn't release its pose. I pulled up the T-shirt and shooed Christopher away from the light source, which was a lamp overhead.

The body had an even purple haze all along the left side of the torso. On the crime shows, they refer to this as lividity or liver mortis. The suggillation, or hypostasis, was the pooling of heavy red blood cells that happened after Franco's heart ceased beating.

I explained my findings to Christopher, who nodded mutely while I continued the examination.

Time flew, and I was glad for my warm cardigan.

Who knew spending time with a corpse could be so much fun? I did feel a little bad about enjoying Franco's company much more after he was deceased.

I was careful not to disturb the body any more than it already had been.

On his right hand, he had a sticky, yellow substance across the palm. It smelled familiar, yet not exactly like pine sap. Some small twigs were stuck to the goo.

We gently tipped him to the side so I could examine his back. There were no wounds, nor was there any blood. Even if the rains had given him a thorough rinse, there would have been residue or stains on the clothes if he'd been stabbed or shot. Other than some superficial cuts and scratches on his hands, plus a few crow nibbles on one cheek, he had no visible injuries.

"However he died, it was on his side," I said. "He was on his side for maybe six to twelve hours, then someone moved him onto his back. There's some dark purple across his shoulder blades, see, but not much. He was already quite dead when someone rolled him onto his back. Rigor mortis had already started setting in on his left arm and right leg, which is why they're still bent."

Christopher continued staring—at me and at the body, his expression equal parts awe and horror. "I'm really glad you know all this stuff, but… someone moved the body? I almost wish I didn't know. Someone could have killed him."

"He might have died of natural causes, or from alcohol poisoning. He was only drinking beer, that I saw, but we don't know what happened inside his room. He could have hit the strong stuff."

Christopher blinked. "Yes, alcohol poisoning. Let's check for that."

"I need access to his liver. Marie's got that machine for slicing pepperoni. I'm sure with some modifications, we could…"

Christopher started moving toward the cooler's door, presumably to get the pepperoni slicer.

"Come back," I said. "Get back in here. I was just kidding about the slicer. Are you always this literal? I don't have the medical training to start digging around in corpses. I shouldn't even be looking under this one's fancy tuxedo T-shirt."

Christopher opened his mouth and let out a sound that was almost a burp, but not exactly. He stepped toward the door again, shaking his head. "Nope. Can't do it."

"We're almost done here. Grab the tarp."

With his help, I covered the body with the blue plastic tarp. Christopher kept making the burp-like sound the whole time, to his chagrin.

"Let's get out of here," he said.

"Wait! Look at his boots." In my single-mindedness to examine the body, I'd missed the fact that his boots were on the wrong feet.

"We didn't touch his boots," Christopher said. "What does this mean?"

"Either he was in a hurry, or he was already dead when someone else put these boots on his feet."

Christopher made the burping sound again.

"He must have died inside the lodge," I said. "Rigor mortis peaks around twenty-four hours, give or take a bit for various factors including temperature. He's quite stiff right now, so he could have died about this time yesterday, either late morning or mid-afternoon. He wasn't in the room at dinner time, when Butch and I were in the room with Della."

"What are you saying?"

"He wasn't there… because someone had already put his boots on and hauled him outside. They tossed him over that ridge to make it look like an accident."

"Who?"

"Isn't it obvious? Your cousin, Butch. Either he or Della discovered that Franco was dead in the room and then one of them—or maybe both of them— hauled him outside. Butch had been talking to the insurance company that morning. He's worried about money, and about bad publicity. That ridge was outside of the property line, wasn't it?"

"I don't like this side of you," he said. "That's my cousin you're talking about. This isn't a game."

He grabbed my hand and pulled me with him out of the cooler. He pulled hard. I twisted my arm to get free, angled my body, and stopped just short of throwing him onto the kitchen floor. I let go of his bent arm and he stumbled back, a confused expression on his face.

I didn't say anything, except with my eyes.

He shook his arm and stayed in place. "Stormy, I didn't mean to grab you like that. I'm sorry."

"You would have been double sorry if I'd swept my leg."

"I swear I'll never grab your arm again."

We stared at each other for a tense minute. Finally, I said, "I know you mean well. You care about your cousin, and maybe you even care about me, and you're trying to protect both of us. But you need to keep your eyes open."

I glanced at the open door of the walk-in cooler, and the tarp-covered shape within.

"You're right," he said solemnly. "I need to keep my eyes open."

"We're a good team, and you're tougher than Jessica. If there's something going on up here, and we're in danger, I need to know you have my back."

He took a deep breath and nodded. "I've got your back. Say the word, and I'll do anything. Even if it means going against my family."

"Let's hope it doesn't come down to that. We're going to keep a low profile and ride this out until the roads clear and the police show up. Not a peep to anyone about what we found out, or what we're thinking."

"Not a peep." He mimed zipping his lips.

We'd stopped talking just in time. By the sound of the footfalls, someone was approaching the kitchen in a hurry.

CHAPTER 30

WHEN YOU CAN'T see the solution for a problem, start telling someone how impossible it is. Inevitably, the answer will come to you before you've finished your thought.

Christopher and I needed to secure the body in the cooler, or at least set a trap so we would know if anyone tampered with it. Someone was approaching the kitchen, and we had no time. I started telling him that a trap would be impossible, unless we had a powdery residue we could sprinkle on the floor around the gurney. My gaze fell upon a bag of flour, left out from the pancakes, and I had my solution before I could finish telling Christopher there wasn't one.

Working together, we quickly set up the trap inside the walk-in cooler. He unscrewed all but one of the interior light bulbs, and I sprinkled a light dusting of flour on the floor while we backed out. If someone entered, they'd track footprints through the white flour and not notice, because of the dim light.

We exited the cooler and nearly bumped into Marie, who looked bleak. Even her gray clothes seemed more drab than the day before, her brown ponytail less springy.

"How are you holding up?" I asked.

Marie pushed up her glasses and snapped, "I'll be better when people stop talking to me like I've turned stupid." She went to the pantry and started pulling out loaves of bread. "I don't care about what you're doing inside that cooler. I'm only here because people still need to eat, so I'm going to make lunch."

Christopher and I went to the sink and washed our hands thoroughly. We should have been wearing gloves when we handled the body, but it was too late for that. I would keep gloves in mind for my next amateur autopsy.

Marie pulled out pots and pans, making enough noise to wake the dead. She watched me out of the corner of her eye while I made a Do Not Enter sign for the door of the cooler.

Christopher and I both offered to help with lunch, but she declined, saying she'd hired Jessica for the rest of the day, then she kicked us out of the kitchen.

We met Jessica in the dining room, on her way in. She looked better than earlier, with just a little puffiness around her eyes. She'd put her red hair up in a tight bun, and looked professional in a crisp, white blouse and black skirt she sometimes wore for catering.

She glanced around the empty dining room, then asked us in a hushed tone, "Did you really put the you-know-what in the walk-in cooler?"

"There's a sign on the door," Christopher said. "You won't stumble over it by accident."

She looked only mildly relieved by the news.

"How are you feeling?" I asked.

She gave me a weak smile. "You know how Jeffrey likes to smell your mouth after you brush your teeth? I was on the bed, and I let him do that, and he sneezed right into my mouth."

"That's terrible news." I shook my head. "Right in your mouth? That's probably going to be fatal."

She wrinkled her nose. "Are you sure a cat sneezing in your mouth isn't good luck?"

"It's either instantly fatal, or good luck. One of the two. I guess we'll have to wait and see." I put my hand on her shoulder. "It was good knowing you."

She patted my hand. "We'll always have our memories."

* * *

Back in the privacy of the room, I called Officer Peggy Wiggles with my report. She was driving, and asked me to give her only the executive summary.

Without getting into details, I told her how Franco had been blackmailing Benji, and how she'd been right to suspect the body had been moved. I relayed my findings from my inspection of the body, then waited for her to yell at me for touching it in the first place.

"That's interesting," she said, to my surprise.

"We forgot to wear gloves," I confessed. "I should have known better, but I got carried away. I wasn't even grossed out by the body."

"You're a natural," she said.

I laughed. "A natural what?"

Her voice muffled as she yelled at someone, "You bonehead! When we get it back, I'm going to hit you over the head with it!"

"Is this a bad time? I can call back."

"I have to go. Would you mind getting a look at the body site? I need some pictures with a wider angle."

"I'm glad you asked. I wanted to get out there anyway."

"Stormy, be safe. You're no good to me, or anyone, unless you're safe."

I agreed to be careful, but she probably didn't hear me, because she was berating someone with her colorful language.

* * *

Christopher answered my knock with one hand over his stomach. "I think I have a touch of what Jessica had earlier."

"Did Jeffrey sneeze in your mouth, too?"

He managed a weak smile. "Strangely, I think it was the strain of watching my former fiancée perform an autopsy right in front of me."

"It was more of a preliminary report. With a real autopsy, I would have examined his stomach contents, and so many other cool things."

He held his hand over his mouth as he made a retching sound.

"Do you think you'll feel better soon?" I asked. "I need someone to show me where the body was found."

"It's easy to find. I'll draw you a map, like Benji did for us."

* * *

The dump site—assuming Franco had been dumped, already dead—wasn't more than two miles from the Lodge, but it was still a challenging walk over rough terrain. The snow had melted, and the muddy patches were both messy and slippery.

I got to the ridge above the site and peered over the edge.

To my surprise, I was looking down at a man, who was lying on his back, looking up at me.

"Butch! Once again, you've nearly scared the dickens out of me."

"What about my dickens?" he called up as he got to his feet. "Every time I find a quiet place to think, I see your face hovering over me."

"Sorry about that." I started making my way down to him, walking around to a stepped area that I could descend without equipment. I reached his level and asked, "What are dickens, anyway?"

He waved his hand over the neckline of his shirt. "They're the little white half-shirts you can wear under things."

"Those are dickeys."

He blinked at me, then shined up his smooth head with one meaty hand. "What are you doing out here?"

I shrugged. "Getting some fresh air." I looked around. "Is this where Benji found the body?"

He narrowed his eyes at me. "How would you know?"

I almost laughed at the idea of him being suspicious of me. "Benji showed all of us the photos."

"Right." He nodded slowly.

I pointed to the ridge above us. "How far would you say that drop is? Ten, fifteen feet?"

"Maybe twelve. Doesn't look like much, but I've seen guys step off a curb the wrong way and break an ankle."

We stood in silence for a minute, contemplating the distance.

Butch said, "The fall didn't kill him."

"You think he died somewhere else, like back at the lodge, and someone tossed him here to make it look like an accident?"

Butch turned to me, his forehead ridged with frown lines. "I was making a joke. The fall didn't kill him because the landing did."

"Right." I took out my phone and stepped back to take some photos. Still frowning, he circled around me to stay clear of the photos. He slipped out of his jacket and rolled his shirtsleeves up over his tattooed, muscular forearms.

In light of my suspicions, I didn't feel comfortable with him standing behind me. "Say cheese," I said as I held out my arm and snapped a picture of the two of us. "Christopher wanted me to check in," I explained as I sent the photo to Christopher.

Butch didn't react to that.

"Why are you out here?" I asked.

"I'm trying to understand what happened," he said.

"Same here. Franco was supposed to be a genius, so why was he out here without even a jacket?"

Butch shrugged. "Damned if I know."

"No theories?"

He shrugged again, but it was an exaggerated shrug. He was lying. Just like Benji, he had some theories, but he wasn't sharing them with me.

He scowled up at the ridge again, then started to walk. "Might as well go back to the lodge now. Are you staying out here, or coming with me?"

"Coming with." I skipped to catch up with him.

We'd been walking for ten minutes when Butch said, "I don't know what happened, and I'm done puzzling over it. There's no solution to this... enigma. It's impossible. The only thing that could explain this would be if Della did something to Franco."

"What makes you think it was her?"

He kept walking, his face tilted up so he could look at the blue sky between the towering treetops.

"No one else fits," he said. "The two of them were in love, and it takes a powerful love to turn into a powerful hate."

He had a good point. Della had been the last to see Franco alive, plus she had a bad temper, not to mention the fact she'd left the lodge without him—as though she'd known Franco was no more.

As my suspicion shifted to Della, I felt more and more sorry for Butch. He'd made some mistakes, sure, but his whole world was falling apart.

I knew I couldn't fix everything, but I wished I had a way to speed up the healing process, or at least get everyone to open up and share what they knew with me.

We hiked back to the lodge under the spring sunshine, both of us with our winter coats off and draped over our forearms. On the ground, tiny green shoots seemed to sprout up before my eyes—new life, in the wake of a terrible storm.

In the wake.

"Butch, we need to have a wake for Franco."

He scowled up at the sky, then at me. "I don't know if we're set up for something like that."

"Do we have a dead body, lots of food, and some whiskey?"

The wrinkles on his forehead smoothed. "Yes."

"Then we're set up. The body is optional, but we're three for three."

CHAPTER 31

IT TOOK SOME cajoling, but with Butch's help, we got everyone gathered in the recreation room for a lunch-time wake. He seemed hopeful that it could be an opportunity for him to talk to his wife.

Marie, who had changed into a dark gray dress that was nearly black, didn't look chatty. Her brown hair was drawn back into a ponytail so tightly, it made her look five years younger and slightly surprised.

She bustled about, preparing enough food to satisfy ten times as many people as we had on hand. She was grieving the loss of a friend, and possibly the end of her marriage, so I could understand why the woman wanted to throw herself into her work.

Butch attempted to break the ice by teasing her. "Marie, I think we've got enough sandwiches. Even if the wake runs straight through dinner, we couldn't possibly eat all of this."

Marie turned to Benji, who'd been following her as though lost. She said, stiffly, "Benji, would you please inform Butch that, unlike certain husbands, *cooking* has never betrayed me."

Butch blinked as though punched. His shoulders broadened as he straightened his back. One eye began to twitch. Wearing the black dress clothes he'd changed into for the wake instead of his usual light-colored shirt and khakis, Butch looked downright dangerous.

Benji's jaw moved, but he didn't repeat Marie's words. He'd also changed and wore a dark suit that fit him better than his other clothes, but not by much. The shoulders of his jacket were too wide, while the waist was too narrow.

I stood near the edge of the recreation room, rubbing the goosebumps on my forearms. The stone surface of the cave that enclosed us, forming the room's ceiling, seemed to be casting a damp chill. The ceiling also seemed lower than I remembered.

Standing beside me, Jessica leaned in and whispered, "Seems to me those two are about even. He doesn't know about his wife's plans with the honeymoon suite, does he?"

"Don't be so sure of that," I whispered back. "Look how his eye is twitching. Either he's dehydrated and it's just a muscle spasm, or he's holding back something that makes him angry."

Butch couldn't have heard me, but he glanced our way and his eye seemed to twitch even more.

Marie sighed over the sandwich trays. "Benji, would you tell my husband to find something more useful to do than stare at me while I take care of everything?"

Butch rolled the sleeves of his dark shirt up over his tattooed forearms, as though preparing for a physical altercation.

Dion, who'd been standing quietly near the room's karaoke stage, crossed over to stand between Butch and Marie. He wore the same too-small purple shirt he'd worn the first night at the lodge. The popped button had been sewn back on with black thread.

Dion looked back and forth between Butch and Marie. He said, his deep baritone voice commanding, "Are we okay here?"

Butch puffed up his chest. "I'm okay. It's my darling wife who likes to get all high and mighty in front of everyone. She thinks she's so clever, always getting one over on me, but I know all about her feelings for Franco."

Marie said, icily, "Franco and I were never more than friends."

Butch took slow steps closer to the pool table that he and I had covered with a tablecloth thirty minutes earlier. He plucked squares of crustless sandwiches from Marie's trays.

With each sandwich, Marie flinched, as though resisting the urge to slap his hand away from her food.

Everyone's attention flicked briefly to the door of the room. Christopher entered, wearing his usual wardrobe of a blazer and dark jeans. He'd swapped out his Vans sneakers for a pair of shiny black shoes borrowed from his cousin.

He nodded at the others, then walked over to join me and Jessica. Softly, he said, "And then there were seven."

The goosebumps flared up again on my forearms. We were short two people—Franco and Della. One of them was chilling in the walk-in refrigerator.

Butch and Marie returned to their standoff. A nervous-looking Dion remained between them, wiping his sweaty brow with the cuff of his purple shirt, while Benji tossed one—or maybe more than one—pill into his mouth and washed it down with a can of cola.

Butch grabbed more sandwiches.

Marie made a disgusted sound.

"Marie, don't act like you're perfect," Butch said as he piled his plate high. "You were cheating on me."

She gasped. "I did no such thing!" She picked up a pair of tongs and used them to slap the top of his hand. "Leave some sandwiches for the rest of us."

Butch shrugged and tossed three of his sandwiches back onto the tray.

Benji leaned in and took the slightly-squashed sandwiches, his movements awkward and jerky.

"You're still a cheater," Butch said calmly. "I saw it on one of those talk shows. It's called an emotional affair. People can get involved without even being in the same city. Say what you want to your friends, but I know that every time you had your phone in your hand, you were sending a message to Franco or checking to see if he'd sent one to you."

Marie's cheeks flushed. She said, "Benji, would you please inform my husband that if he had done more than yawn whenever I wanted to talk to him, I wouldn't have had to pour my heart out to a friend. And that's all Franco was. A friend."

Butch nodded slowly. "Then who did you have the top floor honeymoon suite set up for? You said the mattress hadn't shown up yet, but I checked the room on my rounds Monday morning. There was a bed in the room, all made up with our best linens. The pillow smelled of your perfume."

Everyone froze in silence. I glanced over at Jessica with an I-knew-it look.

Christopher muttered under his breath, "This is going to get ugly."

Dion squared up his chest to Butch and said, "You thought something was going on between Marie and Franco. That's what happened, right? Then you decided to even the score, using my sweet little sister."

Butch snorted. "Your little sister isn't that sweet. She threw herself at me, with Franco right next to her in the bed. If he'd woken up, he would have found himself in the middle of an unwanted threesome."

Dion's nostrils flared. His plate shook in his hand. He didn't take his eyes off Butch. "You'd better shut your mouth, baldie, or I'll shut it for you."

"Is that so?"

Butch glowered at Dion until he backed down, muttering, "Not worth it." He walked away from Butch, running his free hand through his black curls.

Butch turned to Marie. "Well? No explanation for what you had planned with the honeymoon suite?"

Benji said, "Maybe it was for the two of you." He smiled crookedly and cracked open another can of cola. He seemed to be enjoying the chaos.

Marie jerked her head toward us, her nose high in the air. Stiffly, she said, "Jessica, could I trouble you for some help with the sandwich trays?"

Jessica nodded and ran to help Marie. They set out even more trays, these ones containing chopped vegetables and miniature tarts.

I caught a whiff of the food and realized I was hungry.

Christopher and I visited the pool-table buffet to gather some food. We took our plates over to the seating by the karaoke stage. The tables were smaller than those in the dining room, meant to hold only a drink or two, but were more than big enough for our lunch-sized plates and finger food.

We watched as Butch followed his wife around. "Marie, I don't blame you for any of this. Listen, I know you don't want to be in the same room as me, but we really need to talk. I know things haven't been great between us lately, but I don't really believe you're a cheater. We should talk. In private."

She snapped, "Whatever you need to say, you can share it in front of our friends." She looked around the room, stopping on Christopher. "And in front of your family."

Butch pulled a handkerchief from his pocket and mopped his bald head as he eyed us.

I said to Christopher, "I think having you here is making things worse for your cousin."

"That's no good." Christopher got up and went to his cousin's side. He put his arm around Butch's shoulders in a supportive gesture. "Butch, you and I both know the Fairchild method of dealing with difficult emotions is to repress them, to shove them down with the help of a martini or two. But if you have something to get off your chest, I'm right here with you. I'm not judging you."

Butch kept mopping his forehead. A minute passed, then he asked, "Do you guys know if Franco had any sort of medical condition? Maybe a heart thing?"

"He did go to the doctor a lot," Dion answered. "There was his gluten issue, which made him feel sluggish. Now that I think about it, he complained about his heart racing sometimes."

"His heart?" Butch shrugged off Christopher's arm and started pacing. "This is bad," he said. "So bad."

Benji cleared his throat. "Attention, everyone." He coughed three times. "Butch, I need to put you out of your misery."

Butch raised his eyebrows. "I don't like the sound of being put out of my misery." He tucked his handkerchief away and sat on the beat-up sofa at the edge of the room. "I appreciate your concern, but I need to be forthright about a few things."

Benji said, "You don't have to tell them, Butch. I will." He pulled something from his pocket and tossed it into his mouth, followed by a swig of cola. He burped.

Dion gave his friend a sideways look. "You okay, dude? What are those pills you're popping?"

"Medicine," Benji said with a hand wave. His attention flicked briefly to me, and the corner of his mouth quirked up. Whatever he was taking, he'd had it hidden somewhere other than in his bathroom.

Benji addressed the group. "Guys, it's my fault Franco died. I brought the drugs to the resort. I'm going to tell the police everything, and I'm going to be abundantly clear it was all my fault, no matter what."

Dion said, "Really?"

Marie asked, "What drugs? Do you mean that bag of powdered sugar? Stop joking around, Benji. This isn't the time for your bizarre sense of humor."

"I'm not joking." Benji hung his head. "None of you should be friends with me. I don't even deserve to be alive.

Marie ran to Benji and wrapped her arms around him. "Don't say that. Even if you did bring drugs up here, you would never force Franco to take them. Franco never did anything that wasn't his idea."

Dion snorted. "You can say that again."

Benji peeled Marie's arms off him and pushed her away. "Don't you understand? I'm the one who brought the TDX here, to the lodge. I was going to use it to kill myself." His face reddened. "It's all my fault."

"It's not your fault," Marie said. "Why are you talking crazy? You can't kill yourself. There are only three of us left, and I can't bear to lose another dear friend."

I rose from my chair and raised my hand. "Excuse me. I have a question. Benji, you said that bag was sugar, for a joke, and now you're saying it was TDX? Isn't that the made-up drug from those sci-fi books you guys read, about Planet Toad-something?"

Benji took off his glasses and rubbed his eyes. "Planet Toadonx." He gave the glasses a quick smear with the edge of his dark brown jacket, then put them back on. "Toadanhydrotetrodotoxin, or TDX, is extracted from the venom of animals on Planet Toadonx. The Toadonians use it for rituals and vision quests, as well as for euthanizing their terminally ill."

"And you had a bag of this drug?"

Benji nodded. "The Toadonian elders said humans couldn't be trusted, and I fear they were right."

I exchanged looks with Jessica, then Christopher. Both were aghast at Benji's apparent break from reality.

Marie took Benji's hand and gently led him to a chair. "I'm going to get you some water," she said softly.

Dion took a seat near his friend and watched him warily. "Benji, are there any Toadonians in this room right now?"

Butch got up from the sofa, fuming. "This is ridiculous! Your friend has clearly lost his mind, and you're all humoring him." He went to the end of the buffet table, to the whiskey, and proceeded to pour and consume three amber shots in a row.

"Who's next?" Butch asked as he wiped his mouth with the back of his hand. "Plenty of whiskey for everyone. Let's get this wake started."

Christopher raised his hand, then looked around at the shocked faces in the room and lowered it. He rejoined me at our table near the karaoke stage.

Benji said, "I'm feeling much better now, I swear. When I woke up this morning and found I wasn't in a Toadonx hell dimension, I realized that dying was no solution. I wanted to live. I wanted to see the sunrise, the dawn of a new day."

Christopher said under his breath, "That does explain Benji running around this morning crowing like a rooster."

Marie took away Benji's empty cola can and handed him a glass of water. "Even if Franco did get some of your drugs from that planet, he wouldn't eat a whole bag of it and then fall off the side of a mountain."

Benji sipped the water. "Actually, if he'd ingested the entire bag, he would have been violently ill. His body would have rejected the chemicals before they could take effect."

Jessica, who'd been hovering near the food trays, asked Benji, "Was it TDX in the Rainforest Delight that made me think I was a squirrel?"

He looked at her as though he couldn't believe she was asking such an obvious question. "It would appear so," he said in a patronizing tone.

She caught my eye and raised her eyebrows. I nodded to let her know I was on the same page. Whatever substance was in the smoothie mix, he'd been testing it, as well as other chemicals, on himself.

Butch, who'd been pacing near the couch, stopped and pointed at Benji. "That's it! Benji, you poisoned Franco. You slipped it to him that first night. It didn't start to take effect until later, and…" He started pacing again, shaking his head. "Now you're putting on this act, about being crazy, so you can plead insanity. This is so devious. This is exactly what a genius would do."

Benji said plainly, "You're sounding paranoid, Butch."

Butch pointed at Benji and growled, "I'm going to get some rope and tie you up before you hurt anyone else."

Marie walked up behind Butch and began punching his back. She was tiny compared to him, and looked like a mouse trying to dismantle a mountain, but she kept at it, raining down blows on his broad shoulders and back.

"You leave Benji alone!"

Butch turned around and tried to catch her wrists, but she was determined. He let his arms drop to his sides and allowed himself to be used as a punching bag.

When she had tired, and the punches slowed down, he said, "Marie, I accept that you may never forgive me. But when we took our marriage vows, I swore I would protect you. If one of your friends is a crazy, pill-popping madman, I need to protect you."

Marie spat, "And who's going to protect me from you? Other than Della, you're the one who saw Franco last. You said he was drunk when you helped him back to his room at three in the morning, when you were doing your rounds. But was he? Was he drunk? Or was he already dead?"

Butch recoiled. "You think I killed Franco?" He looked around the room at the rest of us. "Is that what the rest of you think?"

Dion frowned and crossed his arms. "Butch, she does have a point. You had a motive to get rid of Franco. You were jealous of the emotional affair he was having with your wife. Maybe you should sit down. Maybe all of us should calm down and get our stories straight before the police show up."

Butch said, "Get our stories straight?" He made eye contact with me. "Are you hearing this? Franco's former business partner, the one who stands to take over the entire business now that his partner is deceased, wants us to *get our stories straight*. Does that seem suspicious to anyone?"

I kept my expression neutral and didn't answer. Butch was right, though. It did seem suspicious for Dion to be talking about getting our stories straight, and he did stand to benefit from Franco's death.

The attention of the room shifted to Dion. The rings of sweat on the armpits of his dark purple shirt seemed to be growing.

Dion pointed at Marie. "She tried to sleep with Franco! That's why she had the honeymoon suite set up. He told me on Sunday night, in the float tank room."

Butch said, "I knew it!"

Marie said, "Liar! Dion, stop trying to distract everyone! What's your insurance policy on the pub like? What do you stand to gain?"

Dion said, "We only have basic insurance on the building, not on each other. We're debt-free, because we bought it outright using the funds from the patent on that ski clasp we invented." He shook his head. "Why am I on trial? Marie, just admit that you tried to seduce Franco on our first night here."

She glared at him, her eyes piercing, her face tight and hard under the severe bun. "You don't know anything."

Dion pivoted and gave Jessica a pleading look. "You remember. You were there when Franco told me all about it in the float tank room. He was laughing about the bondage-style underwear she had on, but he did say she had a hot little body."

Marie looked as though she might faint. "He did?"

She looked to Jessica for confirmation, as did everyone else, including me.

"Tell them," Dion said.

Jessica, who looked as if she wanted to run out of the damp-smelling cave room, grasped the edge of the pool table to steady herself. She accidentally pulled the cloth and made the chafing dishes chatter.

"I didn't hear anything but muffled voices," she said. "Those tanks are made to block out sound."

Dion narrowed his eyes and scanned the room, giving everyone a withering look. "Everyone's got great hearing when they want it. Butch, Marie, if you think I killed Franco, say it to my face. I loved that man. He was like a brother to me."

"I loved him, too," Marie said. "As a friend," she quickly added. "Maybe there were a few minutes of confusion, but only because I've felt so distanced from everyone else lately. I would never hurt Franco." Her expression grew cold. "But I wouldn't hesitate to take revenge on any person who did."

"Me, too," Dion said.

Benji whimpered, "Please, just make it fast."

Dion and Marie gathered around Benji. "We know you didn't do anything," Marie said. "You loved Franco as much as we did."

Benji said, "He was my best friend."

They hugged, and their voices jumbled together while they gushed about how much they loved Franco. The three of them broke down as though they were in a contest to see who could grieve the loudest.

Butch walked up behind Marie and tried to get in on the group hug. She whipped her head back and cracked him in the face with the back of her skull. She got him right in the nose, and hard.

He spat her brown hairs out of his mouth and went down, howling, to his knees. Blood trickled from between his fingers.

"You broke my nose," he cried.

He struggled to get back up, but could put only one foot on the ground before he buckled forward, swearing about how much his face hurt.

Amid Butch's howling and swearing, and the others bawling over who loved Franco more, I could barely hear myself think.

I put my fingers in my mouth and whistled to get their attention. Everyone went quiet, except for some sniffles. The six other people in the room blinked at me expectantly.

"We need to establish a timeline," I said. "Let's assume that whatever happened to Franco was truly an accident, maybe from him taking Benji's alien drugs. There's nothing to be gained from throwing mud on each other needlessly, if there was no criminal intent."

They all stared at me. Marie spoke first. "Have you started a timeline as part of your investigation?"

Butch's head jerked. "Your investigation? Is that why you were at the body site? Why you've been following me around?"

The pressure of everyone staring at me was intense.

Benji said, "Stormy, did you tell anyone else you were investigating on my behalf?"

Marie did a double take. "You're working for Benji? I thought you were working for me."

"I am," I said. "Sort of."

Marie sputtered. "Are you billing him? That's quite the racket you've got. How do we know you didn't do something to Franco just so you could get paid?"

I held up my hands. "Guys, calm down. I haven't billed any of you, and I wasn't going to."

"Good, because you're fired," Marie said.

"Fired," Benji said. "Fired, fired, fired."

I raised my eyebrows. From the look of Benji's huge pupils, he didn't even know what planet he was on, much less why he was firing me.

Dion shot me a dirty look, then shook his head.

Even Butch seemed to have turned on me, clutching his bleeding nose and scowling at me as though I'd been the one to head-butt him.

The heat of their rage-filled glares threatened to set me on fire. I got to my feet.

A smart person knows when trying to defend herself will only make things worse. This was one of those times.

CHAPTER 32

"THAT WASN'T THE best wake I've organized," I said to Jessica and Christopher as we walked back to our rooms. "But on the bright side, it was the second-best."

"You've only thrown two," Jessica said.

"Exactly."

"I missed your other one due to excessive drug use," she said.

Christopher paused on the stairwell to give her a questioning look.

"Cold syrup," I explained. "She had a cold, and it probably didn't help that she jumped off a waterfall into freezing cold chuck the day before."

Christopher grinned. "You said *chuck* instead of water. I've missed hearing that. Chinook Jargon, right?"

I smiled, happy for a change of subject after the drama of the wake. "My great-grandmother on my mother's side was Chinook, but that's just how we locals talk. Even my father says chuck, and he's straight-up Irish."

Jessica said, "The chuck that day was skookum, too. Skookumchuck."

"Skookumchuck." Christopher chuckled as he continued down the stairs.

We got to the hallway, and Jessica held up her hand, gesturing for us to wait there a minute. She touched her toes once, stretched twice, then started running. Like a gymnast, she did two perfect flips followed by a near-perfect third, just a little wobbly on the landing. She threw her arms in the air anyway, and we both clapped.

"I guess you're feeling better," Christopher called out. "You've gone from nearly fainting, to flipping down a hallway."

"Movement is the body's natural stress relief," she answered. "But you know all about that, with your yoga practices."

"I'm very new," he said. "I've only learned enough to realize how little I know about anything."

She smiled sweetly. "That's life. I thought Dion was my future Mr. Right, but he's kind of a weirdo."

"Kind of? That whole group is nuts," I said. "No wonder they called themselves *batty*."

Christopher followed us to our door rather than go to his. "Let's just hope Marie doesn't poison us all at tonight's dinner," he joked.

Jessica wasn't laughing.

The three of us entered the room, and once the door was closed, she said in a hushed voice, "We probably shouldn't eat anything unless it's from a shared serving bowl and Marie's eating it, too."

"Good point," Christopher said.

Our conversation was interrupted by a rhythmic sound—Jeffrey's paws on the glass door. He'd had enough of being cooped up in the small room and demanded access to the patio.

We opened the door between our room and Christopher's, which distracted him for two minutes before he returned to wailing at the patio door.

We couldn't risk letting him out and having him get lost and then eaten by the local wildlife after nightfall, so the three of us collaborated on a craft project. We used the sewing kit Jessica had packed, plus an old T-shirt I'd brought for sleeping, and created a stylish body harness and leash for Jeffrey.

We put it on him while congratulating ourselves for our excellent invention skills.

Jeffrey, however, was not impressed. He lay on his side, legs straight out and ears back. He looked as happy as one of those cats whose owners dress them up as pumpkins or turtles for Halloween.

"Why's he acting like that?" Christopher asked. "The harness isn't tight. It's not even restrictive. He's acting like he's paralyzed."

"There's an antidote." I went to the patio door and opened it.

Jeffrey raised his face and sniffed the cool air coming in. His ears twitched. Beyond the door, birds chirped happily in the warm spring weather.

With a little help, he got to his feet and made his way outside, weaving like a drunk until he hit his stride. The leash wouldn't let him range very far, and we wouldn't leave him out unsupervised, but the fresh air promised to help with his cabin fever.

As we cleaned up the craft supplies, I wished it could be as easy for us humans.

My phone buzzed with a message from Peggy, requesting I talk to her using the video chat on my laptop. Since Jessica and Christopher weren't likely to be leaving the room soon, I confided in them that Peggy had asked for my help on the case.

"The police had better be paying you," Jessica said. "I know you're really good at bargain shopping, and you barely take my money for groceries because of all those coupons you use, but you deserve to get paid."

"Coupons?" Christopher gave me a funny look. "Stormy, you would never—"

I pinched the back of his arm to quiet him. I would explain later. Jessica was too proud to take charity from me, so I had to fib and pretend to get bargains all the time. She paid me rent for her bedroom, but I would have let her stay for free, so I applied the rent money to other things.

"The Misty Falls Police Department will be paying," I said. "And I wasn't really charging the others. I only let them think I was working for them, to gain their trust."

Christopher said, "Your deviousness runs much deeper than I ever imagined."

Jessica punched his shoulder. "She's clever, not devious, because she uses it for good."

I opened my laptop, and after some fussing around to download drivers and reboot to get the soundcard working again, all three of us were on a secure video call with Officer Peggy Wiggles.

Peggy had been to our shared hairdresser since I'd seen her last, and her gray-streaked pixie haircut was on the short side. She took in the addition of Jessica and Christopher without showing any surprise.

"How are things in Misty Falls?" I asked.

"Still running around like a house mouse with a backpack full of catnip." She turned to bark an order at someone off-screen, then turned back to us. For someone who was technically a rookie, she seemed to have a lot of authority.

She said to Christopher, "You're the bonehead who insisted on moving the body?"

Christopher raised his hand. "My cousin, Butch Fairchild, insisted. Is that normal?"

She told someone off-screen to bring her a coffee, large. "Yes, that's normal. It's normal for civilians to disturb the crime scene and make everything harder for us. It happens all the time. The paramedics show up and the old man's tucked in bed, wearing a pair of pajamas with no wrinkles except the fold marks from the drawer. Now, maybe he was on the throne when he met his maker, and I can't say I blame anyone for wanting to protect his dignity, but the body doesn't tell any lies. The body doesn't care, and speaks the truth. Like your fellow there. He's trying to tell us something."

At the word *body*, Jessica had stood, and now she excused herself. Once she was over on Christopher's side of the adjoining rooms, Peggy asked us how Jessica was doing. We explained she was holding up well enough, and Peggy commented, "The brave ones can be so delicate. It's why they have to be brave." She got her coffee, and asked to review my case notes.

She wasn't driving and in a hurry, so I was able to go into more details about my inspection of the body, and how the purple bruise-like markings of the pooled blood were on one side of Franco's body, while the photos of how he'd been found—plus the positioning of his limbs when rigor mortis started setting in—didn't match.

"He was definitely moved after he died," Peggy said. "Even before you knuckleheads moved him again. Please, tell me you don't have a hobby taxidermist there who has already started the embalming process."

"No, ma'am," Christopher said. "He's safe and sound in the walk-in cooler."

"Fridge or freezer? Tell me it's not the freezer. You think thawing out a big Christmas turkey takes forever!"

"Fridge," he said. "He's on a food trolley. Not like a real food trolley. I mean, it's a trolley that's used for food, but we're not going to eat him. He's not food." Christopher's cheeks reddened with embarrassment, but he couldn't stop himself from talking. "We know he isn't food. Sure, we're trapped up here for heaven knows how long, but we've got plenty of food, and even if we didn't, the Fairchilds are a respectable family, and—"

"Breathe," she barked. "Count to ten while you breathe in, twenty when you breathe out, and don't talk again until you reach three hundred."

While Christopher sat counting and breathing, Peggy and I discussed the case. I tried to find out what she knew, but she declined to comment, saying it was for my protection.

I told Peggy about my trip to the body site with Butch, and then about the disaster that was the wake. She listened with interest, leaning in until her forehead bumped her camera.

"Marie broke her husband's nose?" Peggy asked. "That woman sounds violent. Steer clear of her."

"What about the food she makes?"

"Pshaw, y'all are just fine. The mudslide is a good thing, because it's keeping the killer from being able to eliminate potential witnesses."

"The killer is on the other side of the mudslide? Are you saying Della did it?"

She waved a hand. "Just pulling your leg. I bet you didn't know I'm a real prankster."

She turned and said something to someone offscreen. Then she turned back and started pulling on her jacket. "Stormy and Christopher, I have to go do cop stuff. Keep your eyes open and keep taking notes on everything. Don't trust your memory. Write everything down." She held up her hand to wave goodbye, told Christopher it was nice to meet him, and then ended the video call.

"Two hundred ninety-nine," Christopher said calmly. "Three hundred. I do feel better."

"I feel better knowing the killer isn't up here with us."

"You mean Della? Peggy was just joking around."

"My father jokes around. Jessica jokes around. You're not the funniest guy, but you've been known to lighten the mood with a quip or two. Officer Peggy Wiggles, however, does not joke around. She doesn't pull legs and she is not a prankster."

"Then I guess we're safe."

I walked out to the patio and stared at the trees and the valley that stretched out for miles, with no other building in sight. Safe? I would feel safe when I got home.

Jeffrey, however, was a happy kitty, even in his harness. He'd found a dark-colored boulder at the edge of the patio to sun himself on.

"Move over," I said. He gave me a sleepy look, and—just like every other time I'd requested he move over—he ignored me. I found another rock that was almost as good, and draped myself forward over it.

Jessica came out and joined me, lying on her back on a smaller, flatter boulder.

"This is surprisingly good," she said. "The stone really radiates the sun's heat, so you feel like you're in the middle of a sun sandwich."

"When the resort opens for business, they should put this on the brochure. They could give it a snazzy name, like the Human Lizard Feature."

"Or how about the Solar-Powered Deep Tissue Release? People would pay good money to cuddle up to a rock!"

I rolled myself over to warm my back. "We should be writing these ideas down to…" A dark object whizzed through the sky at the periphery of my vision. "Jess, did you see that?"

"See what? I hear something, a buzzing, like a giant dragonfly."

The flying object circled back. "Look, the ranger is spying on us."

Jessica waved at the hovering drone, which was the size of a remote control helicopter, but strangely silent.

"The ranger probably does regular patrols using that thing," Jessica said. "It would make her job a lot easier."

"This might sound crazy, but what if the drone caught some evidence on its camera? I would love to get my hands on whatever footage it's accumulated over the last forty-eight hours."

"That's not crazy," Jessica said. "Not crazy at all."

"We just need a giant butterfly net."

She laughed. "Or we could ask nicely."

* * *

Jessica made the call to the ranger, who said she would look into the footage. The drone didn't capture video or audio, but it did snap aerial photographs along its programmed route.

We hadn't heard back by dinner time, but the ranger had said she would need clearance from her supervisor. There were some legal and privacy issues regarding the photographs, since the laws were often a few steps behind technology.

The lodge telephone in our room rang, and Butch informed us that dinner would be served at six o'clock.

I asked how things were going with his wife, and he told me, "Mind your own business."

* * *

Dinner on Tuesday night at the Flying Squirrel Lodge promised to have a level of tension I hadn't experienced since the night I met Christopher's parents, and showed up to the Fairchild mansion looking like—in his words—a *ragamuffin*.

Tonight, at least I wouldn't be wearing a tie-dyed dress paired with combat boots.

I chose a flattering A-line denim skirt with a floral-print tunic—both new items that the staff at Blue Enchantment had set aside for me when their first spring shipment arrived.

Jessica wore a favorite pink dress that showed off her figure, yet was also demure.

Christopher wore his usual Vans sneakers, along with dark jeans, a non-wrinkle dress shirt, and blazer.

The three of us looked like three normal people who might be going to a very normal dinner at a mountain resort. The only thing abnormal would be us signaling each other about sleeping pills in the food, or people accusing each other of murder, and juicier secrets coming out.

Dinner promised to be memorable.

CHAPTER 33

WE ALL SAT together at one communal table, in the same arrangement as the first night, minus Franco and Della.

To my relief, the food was served family style, with everyone taking helpings from larger serving dishes.

After the fallout at the wake, everyone was cautious and slow to speak. Christopher, being accustomed to tense Fairchild family events, led the conversation with ease.

Soon, we were talking like normal people at a mountain resort, making small talk about the changing seasons, how good the food was, and whether it would be possible to have a full menu using only local foods. The rest of America wasn't as interested in the slow food movement as people in Oregon, but it could be a talking point in various eco-minded publications, which would result in free publicity for the lodge.

Nobody came out and said it, but everyone knew the lodge would need positive publicity to offset reports of the lodge owners storing a corpse in the walk-in cooler.

As for the food, it was good enough, but I barely tasted anything, because I was focused on observing the others.

Butch's swollen eye transformed his whole look, making his forearm tattoos look thuggish.

Marie wouldn't look at him, but doted on Benji, asking how he liked each part of the meal.

Benji was quiet, doing little more than nod at Marie's constant questions while chewing his food slowly. Marie and Dion had been taking turns keeping him company during the day, so he didn't hurt himself. I couldn't tell if he was actually crazy, or just pretending, laying the groundwork for a future insanity defense.

Dion tried to flirt with Jessica, but when she responded coolly to his advances, he quickly gave up.

Christopher kept talking about marketing plans, and a rosy future for the lodge. He didn't seem to care that the owners weren't listening, but I appreciated the distraction, and encouraged him to keep going. I even offered some ideas of my own, based on the promotions I'd tried with the gift shop. There were ways to reach the budget-conscious consumer without devaluing the prestige to the top-end consumer by visibly discounting.

We were eating dessert—a raspberry custard served from a communal bowl—when a thunderous crack rang through the dining room.

Everyone froze. The noise was similar to the one we'd heard before, when the glass door had broken.

Benji yelled, "They're coming for me!"

Christopher threw his napkin on the table and stood. "We need to secure the building."

Butch stood next. "You might just be a Boy Scout after all." He pointed to me then Jessica. "We'll form groups. You two come with us, and we'll take the north-east end, with the guest rooms. Marie, you're on the lobby, the spa, and the mechanical, with your buddies." He frowned at Benji, who looked as if he might be wetting his pants. "Unless you'd rather take me, instead."

Marie turned to Dion, her nose high in the air. "Tell my future ex-husband that I don't need him."

Dion, who remained seated, said to Butch, "Sure, we'll take care of that end, but what are we dealing with? Is someone breaking more of the patio doors? Or was that a gun?"

All eyes went to Butch.

"A gun?" Butch crossed his arms. "Why's everyone looking at me? How did I get to be the expert on gunshots?"

Dion hiccuped over his empty wineglass. "Because you're the one who did a stint in prison." He refilled his glass, dribbling from the bottle.

Coldly, Butch said, "You don't know what you're talking about."

Dion waved his wine glass drunkenly. "Marie told us all about it after the wake. The group of us friends decided we're not going to keep any more secrets from each other."

Butch started to tremble, as though he were a volcano about to erupt. He shook his finger at Marie. "That wasn't your secret to share! Not even my family knows about that." He turned and shook his finger at Christopher. "This conversation didn't happen."

They were interrupted by Benji sputtering, "G-g-guys?" He pointed at the picture window. The sun had set, and there was nothing to see except the muddy grounds and the dark outline of the mountains against a midnight blue sky.

Marie said, "Benji, get a hold of yourself. What is it?"

"S-s-something's out-t-t there," Benji said. "With glowing eyes."

Dion hiccuped again, then held his finger in the air. "Waiter, check this man for drugs! If he has any, he has to share with the rest of us."

Marie laughed, but nobody else did.

Christopher said, with calm authority, "Folks, if something is out there, that's all the more reason for us to check that all doors and windows are locked. We won't be impenetrable, but if someone smashes in, at least we'll have some warning."

Butch growled, "There'd better not be any more smashing."

"Let's take precautions," Christopher said. "What's the Boy Scout motto? Something about being prepared?"

After some chaotic grumblings, we were on our way.

Benji got up and tottered after Marie and Dion. Marie had a master set of keys and knowledge of the building.

Butch led our group of four, grim determination on his bruised face. Christopher looked concerned and alert. Jessica looked as if she needed to either throw up or do three flips.

We took the stairs down to the smaller suites, which were at ground level and deemed more vulnerable. Butch used his master set of keys to let us into each of the six guest rooms.

All the patio doors that had been intact that morning were still intact, and the room with the wood covering the broken door looked undisturbed. So far, so good.

Next were the three deluxe suites on the upper floor.

When we reached the door to the honeymoon suite, Butch stopped and wiped his sweating forehead.

"I don't feel so good," he said. "This is how I feel before I have one of my sleeping attacks." His hand trembled, and he couldn't quite get the key into the lock.

Christopher took the keys, opened the door, and flicked on the light. His voice thick and low, he said, "Uh, that's not good."

The room was the same as when I'd seen it from the outside, from my perch in the tree, except for the bed. The mattress had been shredded, the weapon of its destruction clearly the giant meat cleaver embedded in its heart.

Dryly, I commented, "Marie has been doing some redecorating in here."

"Or getting out some pent-up aggression," Jessica added.

Christopher led the way, and the three of us checked the room and the adjoining washroom while Butch waited in the hallway.

"All clear," Christopher said when we were done. "The patio door's still locked. You'd better add a king-sized mattress to your shopping list. And a new meat cleaver, too. Looks like she nicked it when she hit the springs."

Butch nodded, but didn't comment. Christopher locked the door and we moved on.

The upper floor suites were twice the size of the lower ones, so there were only two more to check. Both were empty of furniture and quick to inspect.

We'd already secured the fire exit in the stairwell, so we returned to the dining room to reconvene with the others.

Their group had found nothing on their inspection, except for more wine. Marie, the cleaver-happy mattress murderer, plunged the corkscrew into one bottle with a zeal that did not go unnoticed by her husband.

"False alarm," Dion reported. "The bang must have been a loose boulder tumbling down onto the roof. Mountains. Go figure." He shrugged.

"Mountains," Butch agreed.

Dion grabbed the bottle of wine Marie was trying to open and finished the job, popping the cork with a flourish.

"Time to continue the wake," Dion said. "You guys are invited to stay and have a drink. Have a few. No hard feelings, right? We're all just humans, except for Benji."

* * *

With the wake back underway in the dining room, I quietly slipped away from the group, into the kitchen.

I wouldn't admit it out loud, but I'd gotten the creepy feeling the loud bang had been Franco, up from his gurney and walking around like a zombie.

I opened the door and relaxed when I saw his boots sticking out from the bottom of the blue tarp. I knelt down to inspect the dusting of flour that would let me know if anyone had been inside the cooler in the last seven hours. There were no tracks through the white powder, but there were some curious brown cubes.

I picked one up and crumbled it in my hand. It was mud, from the sole of Franco's hiking boots. As I was kneeling and leaning forward, another cube dried and fell down, dropping onto the back of my head, scaring away what little dickens I still had in me.

"Nice one," I said to the body as I caught my balance. "No, I haven't had a single drop of wine. This is just how jumpy I am now. How about you? Enjoying a little peace and quiet? Your friends are a rowdy bunch."

Franco didn't answer.

I leaned down to look at his boots. I plucked a perfect cube of dirt from between the treads.

"You were walking around out there," I said softly. "You walked through the mud, and it was after you got to the lodge. The first night, the grounds were covered in snow, but things were melting by the next morning. I know this mud wasn't from before your trip up here, because nobody with any sense at all would pack a suitcase with mud-crusted boots, and you were some sort of genius."

I patted the toe of his boot.

"You got yourself outside, on your own two feet, and you died." I took a deep breath and continued, "I don't know if the sun was shining down on you when you did, but I hope you went into the light, Franco."

He didn't answer me, which was a good thing.

An Irish blessing sprang to mind, so I said it softly as I adjusted the blue tarp, tucking it tightly around him. "May the smile of God light you to glory."

I hadn't left the cooler yet when my phone buzzed with an incoming call.

The call showed as a blocked number, but something about the buzz made me think it was Logan. I answered with a syrupy, "Well, hello there."

The line crackled, and all I caught was, "—Wiggles. I need to warn you"—the sound cut out again—"that bonehead. Whatever you do, don't—"

The sound cut off again. The call was terminated. Was Peggy trying to warn me about something? Or was I imagining those words due to stress? I had just checked a walk-in cooler to make sure a stiff corpse hadn't climbed his way off a food trolley.

I stepped out, closed the door, and tried calling Peggy from the kitchen. My call went to voicemail. I tried two more times with the same result.

My next call would have been to the police dispatcher, but I heard people in the dining room saying my name, asking where I was.

I stepped out and waved. "Sorry to wander off. I'm right here."

They all had grim looks on their faces.

Benji started rocking on his chair, chanting, "They're coming. It's them. They're coming."

Christopher said to me, "If you weren't just knocking on the lobby door, that means someone else is up here."

Somebody was knocking on the lobby door, and I heard it. The knocks were persistent but forceful, like those of someone who didn't care if they broke the glass.

Jessica, her face bright and hopeful, said, "That must be the road crew here to tell us the mudslides are cleared."

Her hope was contagious, and soon everyone was happily filing out to see who was at the door.

Christopher held back and brought up the rear with me.

I told him about the troubling phone call I'd just gotten from Peggy.

"Don't worry," he said. "We'll be out of here soon enough."

"How about that bombshell about your cousin? Did you know Butch was an ex-con?"

"Not a clue. I guess the truth always wants to come out. What's that thing you and your father say?"

"Never lose hope in your quest for the truth, because even a little hope can light the way."

"Right. Hope. Let's have hope that this is the road crew." He put his arm around my shoulders and pulled me against his side. His touch was comforting, and I rested my head against his shoulder, taking solace in an old friend.

We caught up with the others in the lobby, where Butch unlocked the glass doors.

I couldn't see any vehicles pulling into the parking lot, or lights, or signs of anyone, except for one person standing on the other side of the door.

CHAPTER 34

THE PERSON WAS small in stature, with short, dark hair, mostly covered by a brown outdoorsman hat.

"That's got to be Rory," I said to Christopher. "She's the ranger who was going to get us aerial pictures from the drone. I thought she would just email them to us."

"The more the merrier." He smiled and gave me another shoulder squeeze.

Rory came in and introduced herself. She tried to show her identification to the group, but they were too drunk, too worried about glowing-eyed forest monsters, or too excited about the roads being clear to listen.

"Calm down, people," Rory said, her voice surprisingly authoritarian for such a petite frame. "One question at a time. Please." When that didn't slow down the barrage, she yelled, "SILENCE!"

Everyone hushed.

"Where's Jessica?" Rory asked. "You? The redhead? Good. You're my official point of contact, and I'll talk to you in a minute. The rest of you, remain calm. The roads are not cleared yet, but it won't be long. Don't ask me for a time, because I'm not a wizard, and I'm not a liar. While I speak to my point of contact, the rest of you should carry on with whatever you rich folks normally do at these fancy resorts. Please be careful to ration the caviar, so there's no need to turn on each other and riot."

Marie laughed, but the others didn't seem sure if they should be amused or offended. Caviar riots? Who did the ranger think we were?

Rory took hold of Jessica's elbow and steered her over to the area that would eventually be the lounge, once the construction materials were replaced with lounge chairs.

Jessica perched on the edge of a stack of wood, resembling a ballerina between acts, in her delicate pink dress and with her shining red hair up in a bun.

Rory straddled a sawhorse as though it were an actual horse. She asked questions about which days everyone had arrived, and what their business was at the resort.

Christopher and I stood within earshot of Jessica and the ranger, while Marie, Benji, and Dion returned to the dining room.

Butch stood by the front door, staring wistfully into the darkness as though he were a dog longing to be free. After a few minutes, he did something curious. He turned around three, four, five times, as though chasing his tail, and then he curled up on the floor and went to sleep.

* * *

Ranger Rory spent a good twenty minutes telling Jessica all about her remote-operated flying device. Christopher and I crept in closer and closer, then quietly joined Jessica in sitting on the stack of wood.

Rory kept bringing up the issue of citizens' privacy, and dancing around whether or not the drone had picked up any clues about what happened to Franco. She kept her focus on Jessica the whole time, ignoring me.

I leaned over and whispered to Jessica, "Ask her for a peek at the photos. Ask nicely."

Jessica did, and Rory responded, "That's a mighty big favor." She changed her position on the sawhorse, swinging her leg over to ride it side-saddle. "But I didn't hike all the way up here just to see how the rich pretend they're camping."

Jessica smiled sweetly. "Just a little peek? We won't tell."

Rory was already pulling a computer tablet from her vest. She wouldn't let us touch the tablet, but held it facing us while she narrated, in the manner of a kindergarten teacher doing story time with a very creepy book.

"Where's Waldo? Not in this one." Rory zoomed in on an aerial shot of the lodge, the L-shaped building hugging the mountainside like a bracket fungi on the side of a tree.

She continued, "Waldo's not seen in these photos, either, but that doesn't mean he's not there in the trees." She whipped through the slideshow of photos with increasing speed. "What's the gentleman's name? I'll just keep calling him Waldo. That's my ranger humor for you. Helps to grin through tough times. Folks get lost in the woods plenty. They go for a picnic, get a few cans of beer in 'em, and decide they're going to climb a peak so they can get the perfect photo with their dumb faces blocking out half a perfectly good view. Sometimes it's the last picture they ever take, because they're not prepared for the local wildlife."

"Franco," Christopher said. "His name was Franco, and he was two miles south of the lodge when he fell off a steep bank."

"He didn't fall," she said. "Not in the photo I have, anyway. Where is that picture? Trees, trees, trees…"

I leaned in, excited to see Franco's body somewhere other than the ledge where someone or something tossed his dead body.

Jessica asked, "What time of day were these photos taken?"

"Eleven o'clock in the morning. The same time you were on your snowshoes, enjoying Flying Squirrel Peak. How'd you like that, by the way? Are you into snowshoeing? How about camping?"

Jessica, who'd been leaning in to study the photos with me, pulled back. She covered her eyes with her hands. "B-b-bod-body," she gasped.

Rory leaned over and confirmed with a nod. "There he is, stretched out on his side, resting on a patch of snow like it's a beach blanket. Even the least sensible of the weekend woodsmen wouldn't take a nap on a patch of snow, so I think we can assume he's already dead here. This photo is timestamped 11:23 a.m. For your reference, my drone flew over that morning at 8:23 a.m., and that same patch of ice was larger, and free of bodies." She jumped off the sawhorse and knelt before Jessica, who still had her hands over her face. "You feeling okay? Can I get you some chocolate? Anything sweet is good for times like this."

Jessica dropped her hands and forced a smile. "Dead you-know-whats make me squeamish."

"As they should," Rory said. "I'm awful sorry you had to see that."

With Rory distracted by Jessica, I scooped up the tablet from where she'd left it on the sawhorse. I scrolled forward and back through the photos to make sure Rory wasn't hiding anything from us—she wasn't—and then zoomed in on the image of Franco.

His position matched my prediction based on the blood pooling. The photos were bright, the sun not yet clouded by the incoming storm that caused the mudslide.

The mudslide.

"Nobody moved the body," I said.

Christopher came over to look at the screen. "Then how'd it get moved? Wild animals?"

"Didn't you ever roll down the side of a grassy hill as a kid? Don't tell me your mother was too protective to let you do that."

Christopher scoffed at my insult, then frowned at the screen. "The weather."

"Exactly," I said. "The same sunshine and rain that set off the mudslide and closed the roads also melted this snow under Franco just enough to shift his body, and then gravity did the rest. He rolled right down here, between the trees, and then over the ledge. Do you know what this means?"

Christopher stared at me, his hazel-brown eyes wide. "It means you're really good at this, Stormy."

"And it means nobody moved the body after all. I've been thinking it was Butch, moving the body off the property because he was worried about his insurance. But now I think Butch was only acting strangely because he was worried about an investigation, and having his criminal record come up."

"Too late for that," Christopher said. "I wonder what he was in for. He did disappear to Thailand for about a year, a while back. He brought me back a souvenir—a carved elephant."

"The sort of thing you can buy in any gift shop?"

"Exactly." Christopher glanced over at Butch, still sleeping as though he were a bulldog by the front door. "You think you know someone, but appearances can be deceiving."

The ranger gave me a dirty look as she took the tablet back. She pulled up photos from earlier that day. "Here's a photo of the same patch of ground taken today, at the same time. You see all that snow's melted away. I would agree with your theory that the body rolled down the hill. Yes, that's my assessment."

"Case closed," Christopher said.

I smiled. "I'll wait for the official toxicology report to find out what he ate or drank before he wandered out there, but for the sake of us all sleeping easily tonight, I'll say it. Case closed."

Jessica's cheeks had color again, and she looked relieved at the news. "Case closed," she said.

"Case closed," the ranger said. "It's customary for you to offer the ranger some refreshments after she goes the extra mile to hand-deliver you access to classified photos. Please tell me there's beer on the premises, and none of that fancy stuff."

The four of us headed toward the dining room, leaving Butch sleeping on the floor where he'd curled up.

Behind us, the lobby echoed with the sound of banging.

Someone else was at the glass doors, trying to get in.

The person was shrouded in layers of clothes, dirty, and swaying.

"I've seen a lot of crazy things, but that's a new one," Rory said. "High-heeled hiking boots. Who knew there was such a thing?"

CHAPTER 35

JESSICA RAN TOWARD the door. "Della's back! We've got to let her in. Butch, wake up, you old hound dog. At least give me your keys."

She tried to wake Butch, but to no avail. He slept like the dead. He didn't stop her from digging through his pockets for his keys.

Della stumbled weakly into the lobby, tottering on hiking boots that really did have stacked heels. "Am I actually here?" She looked at me, Christopher, Jessica, then Rory. "Who's the Boy Scout?"

Rory stuck out her chest. "Ma'am, I'm a ranger."

"How'd you get here?" I asked. "Are the roads clear?"

"Not quite." Della took off a muddy outer jacket and tossed it aside like garbage. "I had to park and hike the rest of the way through the mud, and all the trees, and there were wild animals chasing after me."

"That can't be true," Rory said. "In those boots, if the wild animals on this mountain wanted to eat you, they would have. You probably just spooked yourself."

Ignoring Rory, Della asked Jessica, "Did you know I was coming?"

"We didn't know. You could have called your brother. He's been worried about you. Did you come here to identify Franco? You didn't need to do that. We're sure it's him."

"My Franco," Della said softly, then, "I need a shower." She waited expectantly for one of us to do something about her shower needs.

Jessica jiggled the big ring of keys in her hand. "I've got these, so that makes me the innkeeper. What do you say to our most luxurious room, on the top floor? We'll get some new sheets for the bed, and you'd never guess the mattress lost a battle with a meat cleaver. Follow me."

After Jessica disappeared, the ranger lost interest in the previously mentioned refreshments and moved toward the door. "I'll be on my way out," Rory said. "No need to throw a parade. I can find the door handle."

"Thank you so much for your efforts," I said. "The police will be in contact with you directly for the photos."

"I'm sure they will." Rory pushed the door open, glanced down at Butch, then told us, "Remember to ration your caviar. The road crews will be back early morning, so lunch time tomorrow is the soonest you could be dug out, but don't quote me, and don't tell anyone I gave you an estimate."

Christopher said, "Out by lunch time? You mean the end is in sight? I could kiss you!"

"No thank you, sir." She tipped her hat, told us to stay safe, and left.

Christopher and I stood at the glass doors and watched her disappear into the forest.

He said, "She doesn't even have a flashlight."

"She might be a shapeshifter," I said. "Part coyote. Like a skinwalker."

"Don't make fun of me," he said.

"I'm making fun of the situation, not you."

"Hanging out with your father brings out your *fun* side."

I smiled, because he was right. "Speaking of fun, should we go see if there's a grape or two worth of wine left in the dining room?" I raised my eyebrows. "I'll need to speak to everyone about *rationing the caviar*."

"I guess we'll leave my cousin here, on the floor by the door."

"He's not much of a guard dog. When Della showed up, he didn't even bark once."

"But he's a good visual deterrent," he said.

I chuckled. "Like that horrible ceramic pot-bellied goblin your mother keeps by the front door."

"That's a bust of Great-Great Uncle Chester Fairchild."

"I didn't know you were descended from goblins."

* * *

One hour and two glasses of chardonnay later, everyone had been caught up on the news of the aerial photos and Della's arrival. Dion went to comfort his sister in her new room.

The group was in agreement that Franco must have wandered out on his own, possibly drunk or on drugs, and passed out before dying of exposure. The melting snow had shifted his body. Case closed.

Now was the time for grieving and healing. The wake continued, with everyone's spirits raised by the idea of being dug out by noon the next day.

Marie sipped her wine at a steady pace, and Benji seemed almost normal, keeping his comments about imaginary aliens to himself.

Christopher and Jessica laughed over my quirks as a roommate—quirks I didn't find that quirky. So what if I complained about finding human hairs on the bathroom floor half an hour after vacuuming? Were there other, better roommates who enjoyed seeing hairs on an otherwise clean floor?

We were quibbling over that very important issue when Della made her entrance.

She was dressed to kill in sparkling heels and a shimmering, ruby red dress. She must have had the change of clothes tucked in her purse, a designer bag she had over her shoulder.

"This dining room is too big and open," Della said. "I vote we move this wake to that cozy room, the recreation room."

Her brother said, "Only if you sing for us. That is, if you're feeling up to it."

Della dramatically swept her elegant long, black bangs to the side of her forehead as though in a music video. Breathily, she said, "I'll sing Franco's favorite song. In his honor."

I was tired, and wanted nothing more than to cuddle up with my cat until the road crews arrived, but Jessica gave me a look that said we couldn't refuse the wishes of someone who was basically a widow.

We gathered some refreshments and moved as a group through the lobby.

Butch woke from his nap and stretched like a dog on his hands and knees. He was surprised to see Della back at the lodge, and asked his wife if he should go to their room or come along with the group.

Marie told Dion, "You tell Butch he can attend the party, but he'd better be sitting on his hands the whole time."

We got set up in the recreation room, and Butch turned on the karaoke system.

Della took to the stage, stunning from head to toe, with her long hair falling in waves over her bare shoulders and glittering red dress.

She said, into the microphone, "Before I do something for Franco, does anyone have a request?"

Jessica answered, "Anything you want, Della."

Della nodded, then reached into her purse and pulled something out. Unfortunately, the black object was *not* her own professional-grade microphone.

She had a handgun, a model similar to my father's service revolver.

"I'm the one with the request," Della said.

The room went so quiet, I could hear the soft sound of Marie setting down her wine glass.

Dion spoke first. "This isn't the time! Della, put the gun away. I told you, it was an accident, and we need to let the police deal with everything. Put the gun down." He started to move toward the stage, but she stomped her foot and pointed the gun at him.

"Stay back," she said. "Don't make me hurt you, Dion. Sit your butt in that chair, and let me do what I need to do."

He tilted his head to the side nonchalantly. "Fine. Play out the drama. Please don't shoot anyone, okay?"

She growled, "I can't promise you that."

With her extended arm trembling, Della turned to Marie and aimed the gun at her. "I said I have a special request, and it's for you, Mrs. Fairchild, the owner of the lodge. I want you to get up here on stage and take this microphone."

"You're being crazy," Dion warned.

She stomped her foot again. "Don't make me shoot you, big brother, because I will. I know how to use this gun. I might not hit you with the first shot, because I can barely hit a tree from ten feet away, but I will do damage to something if you don't SHUT UP AND LET ME FINISH!"

The room got quiet, and Della motioned for Marie to get up on the stage, as requested.

Marie stayed in her seat and crossed her arms. "Della, you beautiful, talented idiot. It's all wasted on you, isn't it?"

"Get up here and say that to my face, you washed-up old hag."

"You pretty, gorgeous moron. The public would love you, and then they would throw you away, because you're trash."

While the two of them faced off, calling each other worse and worse names, Christopher caught my eye and whispered, "I can take her. You cause a distraction, and I'll rush the stage."

He had a look of determination on his face, and I knew him well enough to know he was going to try it, whether I caused a distraction or not. I used my knees to tip up the edge of my table, until it was angled enough to send a platter of cheese and crackers sliding toward the edge.

As the plate tilted over, time slowed down, and I heard my father's voice in my head:*Stormy, never have a plan, because plans go wrong.*

As predicted by the oh-so-helpful voice in my head, my plan went wrong.

The broken dish did cause a distraction, but only for a second. Della looked at the plate, then me, then turned toward Christopher and pulled the trigger.

The gunshot was deafening. In the stone-enclosed room, there was nowhere for the noise to go except directly into our heads.

She had her arm in the air, the gun pointed at the ceiling. Christopher hadn't been shot, but he fell to his knees with his hands in the air. He was shouting something, but I couldn't hear anything but ringing.

I scanned the room and checked that Jessica was also unharmed, and then I looked down at myself, for good measure.

Nobody had been shot, but the bullet had ricocheted off the stone ceiling and shattered a bottle of red wine. The crimson liquid wicked across the white tablecloth. Everything was too much for Jessica, and she fainted against me.

People were yelling, but I couldn't hear anything over the high-pitched tone ringing in my ears. Nobody dared to rush Della, not even her brother, lest they share the same fate as the wine bottle. I helped ease Jessica gently to the floor. She was better off down there anyway.

My hearing slowly returned, the room's voices a loud layer on top of the ringing.

Della said into the microphone, "Sorry about that technical adjustment, ladies and gentlemen. It wouldn't be a real karaoke night if we didn't have something go wrong. Please stay in your seats, because the best part of the show is just getting started. Marie is going to get up here and tell us why she killed Franco." She gave Marie a malevolent look and beckoned her with the tip of the gun.

Marie got to her feet as though she were a marionette. She moved awkwardly toward the stage. "I didn't kill anyone," she cried.

Della spat into the microphone, her words amplified, "You must have poisoned him. You were the one preparing all our meals, and I know Franco wouldn't take drugs. We made a pact to each other. And he never drank more than two or three beers, at the most."

Marie, shaking her head as though she couldn't believe what she was about to do, reached for the microphone.

"Stop," Butch yelled. "It was me."

Heads whipped around to look at Butch. His deep voice was loud enough to be heard over the ringing in my ears.

"Della, my good days are over," Butch said. "The love of my life won't even speak to me, so just go ahead and shoot me. Leave Marie out of this."

Butch unfastened the top three buttons of his shirt and exposed the left side of his chest. He had another tattoo there, a heart, with Marie's name in a banner.

Della took the microphone off its stand and held it to her mouth. Marie ducked her head and skulked back to her chair.

"Butch, I will shoot you," Della said. "But first you have to admit it. Did you kill Franco?"

"I brought him to your room, and tucked him into bed next to you. I put a dead man in your bed. I tried to forget about that, but I couldn't. I came back to move him again, and when you woke up, I said I was there for you."

"You… what?"

He undid one more button, and thrust out his exposed chest. "I am the shame of the entire Fairchild family. Shoot me now before I do any more damage to the name." He looked to his wife with sad eyes and mouthed some words. *I'm sorry.*

Della breathed heavily into the microphone. "Are you telling me I slept next to a dead guy? Butch Fairchild, you'll get what you deserve." She took a deep breath. "If only I could kill you twice."

She dropped the microphone and used both hands on the gun to take aim at his chest.

I jumped to my feet. "You've got it all wrong!"

Everyone turned to me with stunned expressions, none more stunned than Christopher. My brain kicked into overdrive, whirring with thoughts, processing everything I'd learned during my investigation.

Della trained the gun on my chest, which was a bigger target than my head. "You killed my Franco? But you barely knew him."

"Della, please lower your gun. I didn't hurt Franco, but I know who did, and I know what happened."

"You're bluffing," she said.

"I may be in way over my head, but do you really think I'd be bluffing at a time like this?"

"It was Marie," Della said. She moved the aim of the gun off me and back on Marie, who made a sound like a squeaky toy being stepped on.

Calmly, I said, "Della, you had a really good idea to bring us all together in this room, to get everything out in the open. We are so close to discovering the truth, but you need to give me a few minutes to ask everyone some questions."

"Start asking."

I looked around at the faces in the room and let go of any semblance of a plan. If this was going to work, I needed to trust my process, and my process was asking questions.

"Benji," I said.

He also let out a sound like a squeaky toy being stepped on.

"Benji, I'm not accusing you of anything. Answer me honestly. What was the white powder in the plastic bag?"

"TDX," he said.

"And how did you come by this drug?"

"I made it in the lab, based on the ideas the Toadonians gave me in a dream. They didn't give me the full formula, but it wasn't too hard to figure out, once I cross-referenced it to known toxins found here on earth."

"You had a bagful of a drug you manufactured?"

He nodded. "I was going to use it to kill myself. You can't ingest that much, or your body will reject it, so I mixed it with some cream and made a poultice." He frowned. "I guess it was a good thing it didn't work, or I wouldn't be here." He patted his chest. "Am I here?"

Marie spoke up, "Leave Benji alone. He doesn't know what he's talking about."

"But he is a chemistry genius," I said. "Whether he thinks the recipe came from little green men on Mars or some other planet, he still knows how to synthesize drugs." I turned to Benji. "When you applied the poultice, did it smell like lavender?"

His eyes widened behind his glasses. "It smelled like flowers, yes. Like lavender."

"I thought so." I cleared my throat and pointed to the bottle of whiskey. "Would someone pour me a shot? My throat's a little dry."

Nobody dared move, so I walked over to the bottle and poured two fingers into a tumbler, then took a sip.

"Della," I said. "Put the gun down. Now."

"Are you saying it was an accident?" Her arms trembled, and she wiped the sweat from her brow with her shoulder. "Am I supposed to believe Franco broke his promise to me and took some drugs nobody's ever heard of?"

"I don't expect you to believe that, because it's not true." I took another taste of the whiskey. "Now, put the gun down, because you don't want to shoot your brother. Dion is the one who killed Franco."

CHAPTER 36

DION JUMPED TO his feet, knocking his chair over. "You have no proof!"

"As sure as this is the finest whiskey I've tasted, I have all the proof I need."

Dion snorted and told the others, "She's making this all up. It's quite the story, too. Very entertaining. Except you're wrong. I loved Franco. We all did. I looked up to him my entire life. Sure, I had some reservations about him and my sister getting married, but we were going to get through it, just like we did with everything."

"Like you did with your father?" I asked. "Did you work out all your issues before he ended his life and made everything better for you? Is there any chance you were there, when he took those drugs that killed him?"

Dion fixed me with eyes as fiery as any I'd ever seen. "You'd better shut up, right now."

"Dion, you don't like people who aren't good for your family. You loved Franco, but you didn't want him marrying your sister."

Della said, "It's true. Dion was always saying I deserved someone better."

I continued, "When Benji dropped that bag of powder on the table and said it was TDX, just like the drug you all read about in your sci-fi novels, you believed him. He tried to play it off, saying it was only sugar, but you had some on your finger, and got a little taste. You knew it wasn't sugar. What happened next? Did your finger go numb? Did you have some strange feelings? Not enough to knock you out, but enough to let you know the powder was exactly what you needed?"

Dion crossed his arms and tilted his chin up in defiance, eyes still blazing.

"You let yourself into Benji's room, probably when he was returning my cat to me, and you swapped out the powder for the lodge's complimentary lavender laundry detergent. Then you went down to the float tanks with Franco and Jessica. You tried to talk some sense into Franco. You tried to get him to break up with your sister. And when he wouldn't agree, you dumped that bag of powder into his tank."

Butch blurted out, "That must have been what happened. Franco was dead already when I found him."

Everyone turned to Butch.

Marie said, "And you didn't tell anyone? You didn't call the police? Oh, Butch."

"I panicked," he said. "All I could think about was how bad it would be for the inn, that somebody died in the spa before we were even open. I figured at least if he died in bed, there wouldn't be an investigation."

I nodded. "And no investigation meant nobody finding out about your criminal record."

"But what about the video?" Marie asked. "I had a look at some of the security footage of the hallway, and I saw you and Franco walking to his room. He was not dead or in a coma yet, because he was walking."

I took another sip of my whiskey. The next part was going to be hard to explain with a straight face.

"Marie, have you seen the eighties screwball classic, Weekend at Bernie's?" She nodded, so I continued, "As the owner of the lodge, your husband knew that camera was operating in the hallway." I glanced over at Christopher. "If you'll recall, Butch fell asleep just after dinner, then woke up refreshed at three in the morning and did his rounds. He found Franco dead in one of the float tanks. He hit the drain button and hauled him out. It's possible that enough of the drug seeped into his skin to alter his choices and increase his paranoia." I glanced over at Butch. "Would you say that's a fair assessment?"

He nodded, but didn't speak.

I explained to Marie, "Butch thought he was doing the right thing when he got Franco dressed, then used waxing supplies from the spa to stick a beer to Franco's hand. He tied the two of them together at the waist and ankle. It wasn't perfect, but it was convincing enough for the security camera footage. And if you want proof of that, you'll find it on Franco's palm. That sticky leg wax is impossible to get off unless you know what you're doing."

Della wailed at her brother, "How could you?"

"She's lying," Dion said. "You're going to believe her over me? Even if I did put something in Franco's tank water, that didn't kill him. He went walking around outside, and fell."

Benji raised his hand like a shy student. "The TDX dose was diluted in the large tank. He would have been near death, with a slow rate of respiration. To a layperson, he would have seemed dead. The drugs were killing him, but in stages. He must have gained consciousness in the morning, then gone outside in his confusion, where he had another attack and fell onto the snow."

Dion said to Della, "You heard Benji. He died from exposure."

"Liar!" Della screamed. "You're a liar!"

Holding my hands up in front of me, I slowly made my way around my table and toward Della. Speaking softly, I said, "You don't want to shoot your own brother. He's made a mistake, but he thought he was doing what was best for you. That's how much he loves you."

Tears rolled down her cheeks, and her extended arm started shaking.

"Della, my job is to make sure that justice is done. That's not up to you. Now, just hand the gun to me, and I'll..."

To my relief, she placed the gun in my hand.

It was heavier than expected, and I nearly dropped it, but didn't.

Everyone started talking at once, and Butch grabbed Dion before he could hurt anyone else.

I winked at Christopher and went to tuck the gun into the back of my jeans. Unfortunately, I was actually wearing a skirt—not jeans—so that was when I *did* drop the gun.

Luckily, it didn't go off.

* * *

With Benji's help, Butch put Dion under a citizen's arrest.

Marie was quick to volunteer a pair of handcuffs —candy-apple red handcuffs that nobody questioned the origin or previous uses of.

Jessica regained consciousness shortly after Dion had been tucked away for cold storage, and reported that she'd had pleasant enough dreams. True to her sweet disposition, she apologized for not being more supportive of me, or at least witnessing my star moment. She promised to do some extra baking as my reward once we got home again.

* * *

Nobody could sleep a wink that night, not even Butch.

Some of us were playing board games in the brightly-lit dining room when the foreman of the road crew arrived at 11:47 a.m. to tell us the road was clear.

We all cheered, and kept playing our game.

Moments after the foreman left, Officer Peggy Wiggles arrived with my other favorite rookie, Kyle "Dimples" Dempsey.

I had already been in contact with Peggy by phone. We'd made the appropriate emergency calls and reported the incident. Peggy had been on her way up the mountain, checking out the mudslide for herself, when she'd called to warn me about Della's green Volkswagen, abandoned on the side of the road. She'd been in a patch with bad reception when the call to me dropped. She couldn't get through again until I reached her, two hours later.

During that call, she'd confirmed that I would be getting paid for my investigation, and—most importantly—getting full credit toward the hours I needed to take my license exam.

Now, at noon on a gorgeous spring day, overlooking a stunning Oregon valley, Officer Peggy Wiggles walked up to our table and said, "Monopoly? Are you kidding me?"

Jessica waved her hand over the plastic houses and hotels. "It was either this or a jigsaw puzzle with no edge pieces."

Peggy shuddered. "No edge pieces. Nasty." She frowned at the game board. "Monopoly was originally designed as a lesson about the immorality of capitalism."

Christopher grinned up at her. "The immorality of capitalism has always been good to me."

"That's because you're winning," she said.

"Christopher's not winning," I said. "We're only three and a half hours in. It could still be anyone's game."

Peggy asked, "Where's Dion?"

"He's cooling off," I answered.

"Did you really put him in the walk-in refrigerator with the body?"

"We gave him a warm jacket."

"Fair enough." She glanced around. "Where's his sister? I need to arrest her, too."

"Della? But she's already been through so much."

Peggy turned to Kyle and said, gruffly, "What's your call, Dimples? Do you want there to be a rumor flying around town about how a young woman got the drop on you and took your service revolver? Or do you want to press charges and make the front page of the Misty Falls Mirror?"

Kyle gave me a sheepish look. "A rumor's fine," he said.

"We need to speak with the young lady," Peggy said.

I rolled the dice for my turn and told them, "Della's in the room at the end on this level. She was up all night, and I'm guessing ten hours is too long for her to wear one fabulous outfit, so she's probably doing a costume change."

Peggy raised her eyebrows. "When this goes to court, I'm sure her testimony will be very colorful. Now, about the matter of the gun."

I reached into my purse and retrieved the revolver, which I had placed in a sealed sandwich bag, just to be thorough.

Peggy thanked me and passed it to Kyle.

"That's not an official evidence bag," I said. "But it's a fresh one, never used for sandwiches."

"Good job, Detective Day."

I smiled. I really liked the sound of that.

Peggy went off to find Della, while her partner Kyle excused himself to go check on everything we'd stored in the walk-in cooler.

Butch and Marie got up from the board game and went with him, because they had the combination for the lock we'd used on the door. Butch had one tattooed arm protectively around Marie's waist, the sight of which made me smile even wider.

In the hours following all the excitement, the group of us had done what people are supposed to do at a mountain resort. We'd shared stories, bonded, cried, laughed, and even sung a karaoke song or two.

As the sun came up, Della apologized to everyone for being suspicious of the wrong people. She even confessed to Marie that she really had thrown herself at Butch, and he'd insisted they stop.

Aside from the question of who'd kissed whom, Butch had already redeemed himself in her eyes. He'd shown his true colors by jumping in to draw Della's rage away from Marie and toward himself.

Was that love? Being willing to take a bullet for each other?

I couldn't imagine caring for someone that much, but then again, I'd never been married.

As we watched Butch and Marie walk away, Christopher reached over and patted my knee.

"We'll all be back home soon," he said.

"We will," I agreed.

CHAPTER 37

IN CRIMINAL CASES, eyewitness accounts are sometimes the weakest form of evidence. Each time we access a memory, we overwrite it just a little, degrading the truth, like a photocopy of a fax of a photocopy.

That's why Peggy had us give her our statements while we were still at the lodge.

At three o'clock in the afternoon, she finally released us, saying, "Best you drive back home now while it's daylight, because once that sun sets, you'll realize you're not in your teens anymore." She shook her head and muttered about the foolishness of us staying up all night playing board games.

Christopher had already packed his things, so Jessica and I returned to our room to get our bags and the stowaway cat.

Jessica rolled her clothes, item by item, and packed everything into her suitcase as though arranging sushi rolls.

"You and Christopher are looking romantic," she said.

"Is that so?"

I wasn't really paying attention. I ruffled the back of my hair and then tried to roll my sweaters the way she'd shown me, so they'd be *happy* sweaters. After everything we'd been through, it felt good to worry about something silly, such as getting my clothes rolled just right.

"Christopher regrets letting you leave him."

I snorted. "He didn't *let* me leave. He helped me pack."

"I can't believe you two broke up over a spider."

I raised my eyebrows and paused mid-sweater roll. "He told you? I thought he'd be too embarrassed."

"He says you trapped a huge spider under a bathroom cup on purpose, just to terrorize him, but he forgives you."

I scoffed and went back to rolling my sweater. "How generous of him to forgive me for something I didn't do on purpose."

"Honestly, it's his fault," Jessica said. "I don't know how anyone can see an upside-down cup and *not* assume there's something awful hiding underneath, but then again not everyone grew up with my brothers. If it wasn't a spider, it was fake dog droppings, or a plastic snake. One thing never changed. There was *always* something hiding under the bathroom cup." She laughed. "And they even got you a few times, too, when you stayed over."

"They did?"

Suddenly, I remembered. I'd just brushed my teeth at Jessica's house, then picked up the bathroom's plastic cup to find an enormous, hairy tarantula the size of my palm staring back at me.

"They got you with Tito, their fake tarantula," she said. "When Christopher told me about the spider incident, I didn't tell him you learned that trick from my brothers. I was already having a tough time keeping a straight face."

"Tito," I said. "I remember that stupid plastic thing, with its glow-in-the-dark eyes." I sat on the edge of the bed and rubbed my forehead. Jeffrey climbed onto my lap to tickle my face with his tail.

I stroked his soft gray fur while a terrible realization washed over me. Now that Jessica had mentioned it, I could clearly remember the Kelly brothers' plastic spider under the bathroom's opaque water cup. I could see their freckled faces, hear their boyish laughter.

My cheeks felt hot. Maybe Christopher was right, and I had left the spider under the cup on purpose to scare him.

As an eyewitness to my own life, I wasn't as reliable as I thought.

How well did I really know myself?

The night of the spider incident, we'd been fighting throughout the day. For the life of me, I couldn't remember how it had started, but I could see myself getting furious, fists clenched, like an angry woman in a movie.

I'd already gotten changed for bed, and it was late. We had a big meeting in the morning with some investors, but he was doing something on the computer and wouldn't come to bed. Each time I looked at the clock, I got more annoyed at Christopher for making my insomnia worse. I brushed my teeth furiously, making my gums bleed. And then... I saw the spider. I got the idea to scare him, to even the score for how much he'd annoyed me.

Or did I?

There was an alternate movie in my head. In this one, I could see myself from a distance, like a stranger. This woman trapped the spider and went looking for a sheet of paper, so she could escort the unwanted houseguest outside. Before she could complete the task, she got distracted and wound up in the bedroom. She didn't forget about the spider, though. When she climbed into bed, she remembered, and imagined how its discovery would alarm her fiancé. She considered returning to her search for a sheet of paper, but her pillow was so soft. And she didn't exactly *hate* the idea of her fiancé screaming.

The second version was as bad as the first.

I searched my memory for a third version, in which I legitimately forgot, but there wasn't one, because how can you have a vivid recollection of yourself being absent-minded?

We finished packing and then loaded the car.

Christopher offered to drive, saying he'd taken one of his cousin's pills and would be more than alert for the next few hours. I thanked him and climbed into the back seat with Jeffrey and my thoughts.

As I went over and over my memory of the night that ended our engagement, I only made it messier, like a bad photocopy of a fax of a photocopy.

* * *

We got home after sunset. Logan's side of the duplex was dark and his truck wasn't in the driveway. While we unpacked the car, I sent him a brief text message to let him know I was home. He replied immediately, saying he'd be back by dinner the next evening.

Jeffrey did a frantic patrol of his house, making sure everything was where it was supposed to be, then gobbled down a full bowl of stale kitty kibbles, then tossed them back up again into Christopher's shoe.

I apologized and took the shoe to the bathroom to clean it while Jessica searched through the refrigerator for dinner ingredients.

I looked up from the wet shoe to find Christopher standing in the bathroom doorway, an unreadable expression on his face. His hazel eyes locked on mine.

"You'd make a good mother," he said.

I nearly fumbled the shoe into the toilet. "Because I'm great at washing barf off things? Thanks."

"Because you're great at everything." He fidgeted with the light switches on the wall, flicking the fan on and off. "I mean it, Stormy. Is there anything you can't do? The way you handled things up at the lodge was almost surreal. I know I was there, but now it all feels like a weird dream."

"How many of Butch's pills did you take?"

He pinched the top of his nose and closed his eyes. "I guess everything will make more sense in the morning."

"Sleep will help." I gave his shoe another rinse, then started stuffing the interior with a towel.

"Is there anything I could do or say to convince you to pack your things and drive to Seattle with me tomorrow morning? Your cat can come."

I swallowed. "I don't think my cat wants to leave Misty Falls."

He held very still in the doorway. "Your cat could give it a shot, maybe for a few months."

"My cat already knows what he likes."

"The Seattle house has an incredible view, and a beautiful garden. It's in a great neighborhood, quiet and peaceful, like living in a small town, but close to everything. Jeffrey would love it."

"Christopher, I—"

"Don't say it. Don't say no. Promise you'll sleep on it and decide in the morning."

I nodded and continued stuffing the towel into his shoe.

A quiet moment passed, then Jessica called to say dinner was ready.

Christopher turned to leave, but I stopped him with my hand on his arm.

"I'm sorry about the spider," I said. "My memory might be rearranging things, but I'm pretty sure you were right, and I did leave the spider under the bathroom cup on purpose to annoy you."

"Pretty sure? Can you give me a percent?"

"Seventy percent. No. Eighty. Eighty-five."

My hand was still on his arm. He slipped his hand around mine and gave it a squeeze. "Thank you."

"I'm sorry," I said again.

"Thank you," he repeated.

* * *

Christopher slept on the couch.

He was gone before I got up in the morning.

I'd known from the way he was acting after dinner—quiet, polite, not making eye contact—that he would leave without talking to me. Christopher hated to hear the word no, and would walk away from business deals when he sensed a rejection was coming.

He'd left behind a note, written on Flying Squirrel Lodge stationery.

Dear Stormy, Jessica, and Jeffrey:

Thank you for your friendship and the memories. Remember, my door is always open for you. Seattle has many wonderful restaurants, art galleries, and concert halls. You should come visit some time.

Jeffrey, you're one lucky guy.

Kind regards,

Christopher Fairchild

CHAPTER 38

THE DAYS AFTER I returned from the lodge were hectic.

Both of my gift store employees came down with stomach flu, so I was on retail duty through the end of the week and the weekend.

News about what had happened at the lodge spread like wildfire, which resulted in a phenomenal sales week when word got out that I could be found inside Glorious Gifts. People came in to get gossip and left with cloth napkins, scented candles, and several of the new glass fruit centerpieces, which weren't cheap. I didn't reveal any more details than they could have read in the Misty Falls Mirror, but everyone seemed happy enough just to see me and talk to me.

On Sunday afternoon, Ruby stopped by with pastries. She didn't pry, but told me to come by her store when things settled down. "You can catch me up on how things are going with a certain lawyer," she said with a knowing wink.

"Who?" I asked innocently. "If you mean Logan Sanderson, it's nothing but business as usual."

Laughing, she gave me a big hug, then left, holding open the door for more curious customers.

The truth was, it had been business as usual with Logan. We'd both been busy, but even when we had crossed paths, neither of us brought up what we'd discussed on the phone when I was at the lodge. I wondered if my memory was playing tricks on me, or if something had happened on his trip.

At closing time on Sunday, he showed up as I was closing out the cash register.

My breath caught in my throat when I realized the handsome man who'd walked in the door was there to see me. He wasn't wearing his usual weekend gear of patched jeans and baggy sweaters, nor was he dressed in his other extreme, his weekday tailored suits. He wore dark, slim-fitting jeans and a stylish leather jacket. Under the jacket was a blue button-down shirt that made his bright eyes dazzle. His beard was trimmed neatly and his neck had that pink look of having just been shaved.

"Here you are," Logan said. "I should have known I'd find you in the gift shop. All the bad seeds hang out here."

"If I had known you were looking for me, I would have hidden myself better." I reached across the counter and touched the sleeve of his leather jacket. "Someone's been shopping."

He locked eyes with me and smiled. "I had to step up my game, because the woman I'm trying to date has a knack for fashion. She claims to buy her outfits straight off the mannequin in the window display, but I don't believe her. The lady has style."

I laughed, leaned forward, then looked at his mouth and pulled back. I'd nearly leaned across the counter and kissed him without realizing it. Logan had that effect on me, where he made me feel as giddy as a teenager, yet also comfortable and relaxed, as though I was with a close friend.

"Well, it's a great jacket," I said. "This woman you're trying to date will probably compliment you on it. She might even notice how the blue shirt brings out your eyes." I busied myself with the final steps of closing the cash register for the day.

"Being color blind, I'll have to take her word for it." He leaned on the counter and glanced around the store while he waited for me to finish.

I grabbed my coat from the office and jingled my keys.

"Now what?" he asked.

"We leave and lock the door."

"I mean after that. Dinner?"

I crossed my arms. "This woman you're trying to date, is that how you ask her out?"

He grinned. "Stormy Day, I know this is short notice, but will you do me the honor of accompanying me to Accio Bistro for dinner tonight?"

"Are you sure we're not banned from that place?"

"If they so much as hint at banning us, I'll sue them six ways to Sunday."

I played up a dramatic shudder. "Mr. Sanderson! When you get all litigious like that, you make me weak in the knees."

"Then this date is off to a good start."

* * *

The waiters gave us some funny looks, but we weren't turned away from Accio Bistro.

Over dinner, we discussed a few of our ongoing cases, and I caught him up on the few details he didn't already know about what had happened up at the lodge.

When I was done, he tented his fingers and said, "I bet you'd like to know what Butch Fairchild was in prison for."

I inhaled sharply and leaned in. "Tell me."

He leaned in until our foreheads were nearly touching. "Paper hanging," he said. "Otherwise known as check kiting. Butch claimed he'd written the checks while sleepwalking. The judge was sympathetic and let him off the first time, but not the second."

I laughed. "I wonder if he really was sleepwalking. I saw him circle around and then sleep on the floor like a dog."

"He needs someone to keep tabs on him."

"You should have seen the look on his face when Jessica suggested he get a babysitter."

Logan laughed and rubbed his face. "Hopefully this is the end of his trouble."

"At least he's still alive. Dion didn't confess to it, but we're guessing he figured out that Butch moved the body and then whacked him on the head and left him out in the rain."

"Maybe Dion would have hit him again, if Christopher hadn't been there."

"Maybe." I leaned back and took a sip of my wine. "How did your trip go? We've hardly talked about it."

Logan shrugged. "No murders or walking zombie corpses. Not much to discuss."

The waiter arrived with our lemon mousse. I took a bite. The dessert tasted as good as it looked.

"This is amazing," I said. "Stop watching the door. Christopher's in Seattle. He's not going to come in and hit your fist with his face."

Logan laughed. "I hate it when guys hit my fist with their faces."

"And, for the record, nothing happened between us up at the lodge. We're just friends, and whatever we had, romantically, is gone."

"Why didn't it work out with you two?"

I frowned at my lemon mousse. "Mixing business and pleasure, among other things. We were so intertwined. Even during the times we weren't dating, we were still… intertwined."

Logan cleared his throat. "That sounds familiar."

I couldn't meet his eyes. I hadn't seen the parallel, or I wouldn't have worded it that way.

He continued, "Living under the same roof, working together on cases, then trying to mix business and pleasure. That's a recipe for getting sick of each other."

I looked up, into his blue eyes, and felt myself falling—falling forever.

"Logan Sanderson, I might get sick of you one day, but it hasn't happened yet."

He blinked. "That's not the most romantic thing I've ever heard, but it's making me smile." He grinned. "And I feel the same way about you."

"We can make this work. We just need some ground rules."

"How about just one rule?"

I raised my eyebrows and nodded for him to tell me the rule.

"One rule," he said. "On any given day, our relationship is either business or pleasure. One or the other."

I took a breath. It wasn't a bad rule.

"Agreed," I said.

"Let's shake on it. We already discussed case work at the start of dinner, so today's a business day."

I shook his hand. "Yes, sir. All business today. We are in complete agreement."

"Good. Let's order another lemon mousse to make up for the one we didn't have last time."

I gave him a look of admiration. "You are just full of excellent ideas tonight."

"I am." He winked at me, then looked around for our waiter.

* * *

We discussed some more business over our second dessert, then drove home in our own vehicles.

He gave me a business-like wave goodbye as we walked to our separate doors.

I spent the remainder of the evening in a pleasant daze.

Jessica went to bed at eleven-thirty, but I stayed up to finish catching up on some of my favorite TV shows.

Someone knocked on the door at 12:01 a.m.

I ran to the door and flung it open.

Logan stood on the step with a bouquet of flowers.

"Today's a new day," I said.

He stepped inside, tossed the flowers on the table, took me in his arms, and kissed me.

THE END OF BOOK #3

TO BE CONTINUED...
IN STORMY DAY MYSTERY #4

ANGELA PEPPER

www.angelapepper.com